The Devil Drinks Monsoons

SueBird Sparrow

Bayou Wolf Press

CONTENTS

Copyrights — IX

Dedication — X

1. Chapter One — 1

2. Chapter Two — 4

3. Chapter Three — 8

4. Chapter Four — 11

5. Chapter Five — 15

6. Chapter Six — 17

7. Chapter Seven — 19

8. Chapter Eight — 23

9. Chapter Nine — 27

10. Chapter Ten — 31

11. Chapter Eleven — 33

12. Chapter Twelve — 35

13.	Chapter Thirteen	38
14.	Chapter Fourteen	42
15.	Chapter Fifteen	46
16.	Chapter Sixteen	48
17.	Chapter Seventeen	51
18.	Chapter Eighteen	56
19.	Chapter Nineteen	58
20.	Chapter Twenty	60
21.	Chapter Twenty One	63
22.	Chapter Twenty Two	65
23.	Chapter Twenty Three	69
24.	Chapter Twenty Four	70
25.	Chapter Twenty Five	73
26.	Chapter Twenty Six	75
27.	Chapter Twenty Seven	79
28.	Chapter Twenty Eight	81
29.	Chapter Twenty Nine	84
30.	Chapter Thirty	88
31.	Chapter Thirty One	91
32.	Part II	93
33.	Chapter Thirty Three	98
34.	Chapter Thirty Four	101
35.	Chapter Thirty Five	105
36.	Chapter Thirty Six	107

37.	Chapter Thirty Seven	113
38.	Chapter Thirty Eight	118
39.	Chapter Thirty Nine	124
40.	Chapter Forty	127
41.	Chapter Forty One	129
42.	Part III	136
43.	Chapter Forty Three	142
44.	Chapter Forty Four	146
45.	Chapter Forty Five	148
46.	Chapter Forty Six	150
47.	Chapter Forty Seven	153
48.	Chapter Forty Eight	160
49.	Chapter Forty Nine	162
50.	Chapter Fifty	164
51.	Chapter Fifty One	166
52.	Chapter Fifty Two	173
53.	Chapter Fifty Three	176
54.	Chapter Fifty Four	179
55.	Chapter Fifty Five	182
56.	Chapter Fifty Six	185
57.	Chapter Fifty Seven	189
58.	Chapter Fifty Eight	192
59.	Chapter Fifty Nine	195
60.	Chapter Sixty	198

61.	Chapter Sixty One	200
62.	Chapter Sixty Two	204
63.	Chapter Sixty Three	206
64.	Chapter Sixty Four	209
65.	Chapter Sixty Five	211
66.	Chapter Sixty Six	214
67.	Chapter Sixty Seven	219
68.	Chapter Sixty Eight	224
69.	Chapter Sixty Nine	227
70.	Chapter Seventy	229
71.	Chapter Seventy One	233
72.	Chapter Seventy Two	237
73.	Chapter Seventy Three	240
74.	Chapter Seventy Four	242
75.	Chapter Seventy Five	245
76.	Chapter Seventy Six	246
77.	Chapter Seventy Seven	249
78.	Chapter Seventy Eight	252
79.	Chapter Seventy Nine	255
80.	Chapter Eighty	259
81.	Chapter Eighty One	260
82.	Chapter Eighty Two	261
83.	Chapter Eighty Three	262
84.	Chapter Eighty Four	264

85. Chapter Eighty Five   265

86. Chapter Eighty Six   267

87. Chapter Eighty Seven   269

88. Chapter Eighty Eight   272

89. Chapter Eighty Nine   274

90. Chapter Ninety   277

91. Chapter Ninety One   279

92. Chapter Ninety Two   283

93. Chapter Ninety Three   285

94. Chapter Ninety Four   287

95. Chapter Ninety Five   291

96. Chapter Ninety Six   293

97. Chapter Ninety Seven   295

98. Chapter Ninety Eight   299

99. Chapter Ninety Nine   301

100. Chapter One Hundred   303

101. Chapter One Hundred One   305

102. Chapter One Hundred Two   307

103. Chapter One Hundred Three   311

104. Chapter One Hundred Four   314

105. Chapter One Hundred Five   316

106. Chapter One Hundred Six   318

Acknowledgements   322

Also by SueBird Sparrow   325

This book is dedicated to the City of New Orleans. You snaked your tenacious live oak roots deep into my heart and lassoed my soul with seductive tendrils of jasmine the very first time I visited in 1992. Don't ever let me go.

CHAPTER ONE

Wandering among the mausoleums of St. Louis Cemetery No. 1, the young couple sipped from large white go-cups emblazoned with the bar name, *Port of Call*. The sun beat down as they stumbled on the broken concrete paths between the grave sites.

"Look at this," Beth pointed. "Medelice Chanson Duvalier. What a great name, huh?" She sucked on her straw, slurping up the sticky red liquid in a futile effort to stay cool. The last of the ice had melted twenty minutes ago.

"It's kind of hot for this right now, hon, no wonder we've got the whole place to ourselves. And you're getting pretty sunburned." Paul put his arm around her waist and nuzzled her damp, very pink neck. "You want to go back to the hotel? Maybe take a nap in the air conditioning?"

Beth smiled. "Let's just check out this last row back here before we go, okay?" She handed him her go-cup, the warm dregs sloshing in the bottom.

Paul suppressed a sigh and dutifully disposed of what remained of their monsoons in a nearby trash can.

His attention snagged on a crumbling crypt. "Hey Beth, check this out." The metal door was broken and hung off its hinges at an odd angle, pieces of the rusty lock strewn across the stone steps in front of it.

"Spooky!" Beth said. "Can you see inside?"

"Not really," he squinted. "It's too dark in there."

"Hey, look at this one!" She led him further down the fragmented walkway to an elaborate marble tomb and pointed up at a statue of an inconsolably weeping angel draped over a sarcophagus. "Isn't that beautiful? How cool would it be if we got a family crypt after we're married?"

"That'd be awesome," he agreed. "But I think we'll have to take care of a few other priorities first, like maybe paying for the wedding?"

She pulled him into the sparse shade at the side of the mausoleum and kissed him. "You're so practical. That's one of the things I love about you, honey."

"Whoa! What's dis here? Cain't be having none o' dat lovey dovey stuff in da cemet'ry, you lovebirds, you." The man appeared out of nowhere. A stained, black, too-short tee shirt stretched tight across his hairy belly. Ripped black pants hung from a rope belt, the white skin of one thigh showing through, a pair of too-small flip flops on his yellow-nailed feet. His bloated, talon-tipped fingers raised a near-empty Port of Call go-cup to his lips, a small smear on the rim the exact shade of lipstick Beth was wearing. He drained it in one greedy swallow, "Ah, dat's more better. I do love me dem monsoons, for true." He swiped a dirty hand across his mouth, his red eyes gleaming. "Hey girlie, what's dat you got 'round your neck, you?"

Beth reached for Paul's hand. "It's..., it's just a locket," she said.

"Alright then, dat ain't no kinda cross, no," he muttered. The man tossed the white plastic cup on the ground at their feet. "Whoopsie!

Cain't litter here none, no. Plenty plenty rules. Hey boy, whyn't you fetch me up dat, you?"

Paul hesitated, then slowly bent to retrieve the cup.

Fast as a great blue heron spearing a crappie in the bayou, the man's arm shot out and grabbed Paul by the neck. He shook him once and flung him against the crypt, where he lay like another of the crumpled leaves fallen haphazardly on the narrow cemetery path, his head at an impossible angle. "Come 'ere, cher, you." His other arm seized Beth's wrist with superhuman strength and yanked her to him before she realized what was happening.

The marble angel carried on with her perpetual lamentations.

Chapter Two

"Does this look like a stab wound to you?" Candi's lank blonde hair fell across her face as she bent to squint at her thigh. A cheap crucifix dangled from a chain around her neck.

"Jesus H. Christ on a stick," Richard sighed. "Give me strength."

He turned down the old radio. Placido Domingo sang Puccini pianissimo while he heaved himself out of his rocking chair. He shuffled to the edge of the porch to glare down at her.

Candi hiked the left side of her short shorts up higher and threw her leg up on the third step from the bottom.

She's limber, he thought, *I gotta give her that. But Christ, I guess you gotta be limber to do all that fancy pole dancing they do these days.* He liked a good dancer as much as the next guy but why were they always asking him for free advice? You'd think he'd be able to get a little somethin' somethin' out of these situations but somehow it never worked out that way.

Can't even enjoy my morning coffee on my own goddamn porch, he thought.

He adjusted his suspenders, grasped the wrought iron handrail and descended the stairs. It was going to be another humid scorcher.

"What the hell did you do now, Candace?"

Bent over her leg like that, Candi looked like a ballerina at the barre, except this ballerina was decidedly worse for wear and gingerly prodding a crusty thigh gash oozing blood.

"Did you even clean that?"

"It really hurts. You think Imma get the tennis?"

"Christ Almighty, it's 'tetanus,' and stop that poking. Let me look." He leaned close to her emaciated thigh, patted his pocket for glasses that weren't there.

"It could be a stabbing," he grunted. "It looks pretty deep. You might need stitches. Where were you last night?"

"We worked the Quarter a bit. Not sure where we got to after that. The night done gone a little sideways." She winced as she lowered the leg.

"You think?"

"Alright baby, Imma swing by the clinic later. Maybe they take my card this time. Hope springs a kernel, you know?"

"Oh, for Christ sake, Candace! It's 'hope springs eternal.'"

"Whatever. Thanks, Dickie, you the best."

He watched her limp back cross the street to the dilapidated shotgun rental she shared with that Beuletta, wondering if those short shorts could get any shorter.

"For the hundredth time, don't call me Dickie," he called after her. "You know you've got blood in your hair too, right?"

Candi stopped at the curb, put her hand to the back of her head. It came away red. "Aww, I figured I was just hungover ."

"Go to the clinic, Candace," Richard threw over his shoulder as he made his way up the steps, one at a time. "And holy God, be more careful tonight!"

He was out of breath when he reached the top. *Goddamned whores are always getting themselves beat up. That one's getting long in the tooth for those kinds of shenanigans. That pimp of hers needs disappearing one of these days.*

Right then and there he made a decision, added a name to his List. He might have arrived at a different conclusion had she waited until after he'd had his coffee before bothering him with her latest injury.

He turned the radio back up and hummed along with Placido. A fluffy black cat jumped off the rocking chair and twined itself around his legs.

"Hey there Minnie Baby! How's daddy's little girl? Are you hungry, sweetheart?" He bent with effort and began to fill a dozen plastic bowls with cat food from a Tupperware container he kept on the porch. Felines of all sizes and colors came running at the sound of kibble being poured. Richard placed the bowls at various spots around the porch and on the steps where he knew each cat preferred to eat.

A loud ringtone suddenly filled the air. None of the cats looked up from their meal.

"Blessed Virgin, Mother of God! Who the hell is calling me now?" He fumbled in his pants pocket for his cellphone, then his shirt pocket for his glasses which still weren't there. He snapped off the radio. "Yeah, dammit, who's this?" He plopped down onto the rocking chair.

"I've got another job for Dick the dick," he heard Beau say. Beau was an attorney at a local firm Richard liked to call Dewey, Cheatum & Howe, even though they occasionally threw work his way. "You up for it?

"Just give me the details and I'll see if I've got time for your bull-shit."

Beau chuckled. "I haven't seen you at En Garde for a while. Didn't know if you were getting your pacemaker replaced or what."

"Ha. Ha. Do you hear me laughing? I'm gonna outlive your fat ass for sure. Just give me the facts."

Beau ignored him. "Miss Dina was asking for you. And Chachi. And Gator George. You know, the place isn't the same without your grumpy old ass parked at the end of the bar." He waited a beat. "It's nicer."

"They can all bite me. Except Miss Dina. Tell her I was out of town. No, don't. I'll tell her myself. I might stop by En Garde tomorrow. If I've got time."

"Yeah, see if you can work a visit into your busy schedule. But meet me on Friday at Buddy's for this one. The usual time. I don't want to discuss it in the Quarter. Too many ears. I'll give you the details then, ok?"

"Yeah, yeah," Richard pressed end on his cell. He missed the days when you could hang up on someone with a satisfactory bang. He missed a lot of things these days. A man couldn't just enjoy his beer and watch the pretty barmaids in their low-cut tops anymore without having to make small talk with every chatty yahoo tourist from Peoria. Richard conveniently forgot that he himself was originally from Wisconsin. He'd been in New Orleans for so long he considered himself a local, even if the locals didn't.

"Looking good, Papa. How you doing, young man?" he asked a big gray cat that rubbed its head against his leg. He leaned back in the rocker with a sigh, ran his hand over what was left of his hair and found his glasses.

Chapter Three

Candi felt an iron grip on her wrist a split second before she was slammed up against the pink stucco wall of Brennan's Restaurant. "Where the fuck you think you going, huh?"

"Owwww!" She knew better than to cry out, but Schwilliam had taken her by surprise. His hot breath in her face reeked of his liquid lunch.

"Answer me, bitch! Or maybe you wanna explain it to me on your knees?" He had her by both arms now, his thick fingers pressing into the meager flesh there. She'd have to wear long sleeves tomorrow. It was sure to be another scorcher, but no guy likes to look at bruises.

"Hey Schwill, baby, ease up, okay? I was just taking the long way 'round. That Miss Jeanne was standing out front of her shop with that creepy cane like she was waiting for me to pass by or whatever. Like she was expecting me even! I bet what people say about her is true."

She babbled furiously, playing for time, praying something else would catch his interest, anything to distract him from her perceived disobedience. "She gives me the heebie jeebies for sure. Just didn't wanna go nowheres near her, that's all."

"Don't you lie to me, bitch, you slacking off!" Schwilliam shook her, bouncing her head off the concrete wall before releasing her so abruptly she stumbled. "You dumb ho, when I tell you to be somewheres, I better find you there, or else," he hissed at her.

A tourist couple with a little girl passing by caught his eye. Schwilliam stood aside, giving the little girl with pigtails a long once-over and a lascivious grin, his gold incisor glinting in the sunlight. "Ain't you a pretty little thing," he purred.

The father puffed up his chest and slowed down, about to make his vehement objection known, when Schwilliam snarled, "The fuck you looking at?" grabbing his crotch and jerking it up and down.

The father quickly herded his little family away, turning to make sure they weren't being followed by the crazy pervert in the expensive-looking tennis shoes. Next vacation, he'd take them to Disney World.

Candi tried to refocus Schwilliam's attention on herself before he decided to follow the tourists. "Ain't you never been scared of Miss Jeanne at all?" she asked, rubbing the back of her head where it had connected with the wall. *She's just a little kid, that ain't right!* "Miss Jeanne done stood there looking right hard at me from across the street. Made my skin crawl, she did." Candi groped for the cross at her neck, "What should I do, Schwill?"

"Don't you never shut up?" He backhanded her in the mouth. She gasped, tasting blood. "I don't care what they say, that old bat ain't no vampire," he spat.

Schwilliam adjusted the heavy gold chain and medallion adorning his chest. "Now get your ass back to your corner and make me some green or Imma take it outta your scrawny hide. And tell Beuletta Imma make sure she where she 'posed to be, too." He pinched her ass hard.

"Wear your hair in pigtails tomorrow. And don't be giving me no more bullshit about no vampires."

Candi knew better than to push her luck when he was in a mood. The tourist family was out of sight now and she did feel lucky. This time she had gotten off easily. *That little girl done got off easy this time too.*

She fluffed her stringy blonde hair over the knot rising on the back of her head. Ignoring her swelling lip, she simpered up at Schwilliam before wobbling away down the street in her thrift store purple heels to warn her friend.

CHAPTER FOUR

The next day, the tabby had just chewed the face off a cockroach, one twitching antenna still hanging from her mouth, when she heard the white SUV turn the corner onto the one-way street. A dozen or more felines appeared out of thin air and converged on the steps of the little blue house, all facing Palmyra Street, all silently judging. If he hit the curb, he may not be in any condition to feed them right away.

"Goddammit to hell! Why am I paying taxes if they're never going to fix these potholes?" Through the tinted glass of the closed car windows, the cats could hear the old man cursing the mayor of New Orleans again.

He pulled himself out of the car, got his legs under him and stood staring at the right front tire when he noticed the new neighbor watering her courtyard garden. He generally approved of women who planted gardens. Showed a nurturing side that a female should have. It didn't hurt that she was cute as hell. Normally, he couldn't be bothered to act friendly to the neighbors. The yellow and red house two doors down played loud music at all hours of the day and night, no matter how often he called it in. The green and orange house across the street, they were just pigs, trash everywhere, all the time, while those screaming kids lived over in the pink house with the white trim.

"Well, hello there!" he called.

Most of the cats wandered off. They knew from experience it was going to be a while before the food came out.

"Hey, Richard," Molly turned off the hose. "Been over at En Garde, have you?"

He shuffled over and leaned on her fence. Getting out of the car had winded him. The beers weren't helping with his balance either, truth be told. He couldn't drink like he used to.

Richard had on his uniform of baggy jeans and a blue tee shirt. Some woman told him once that blue was his color and he remembered things like that. He always wore a long-sleeved shirt unbuttoned and loose over the tee. The shirt sleeves hid the age spots on his forearms so he never rolled them up, even in August in New Orleans. He felt that wearing the shirt untucked probably hid his gun and possibly his belly, which he had sucked in the minute he spotted Molly.

"Have to make an appearance every so often or they all go into withdrawal." He ran his thumbs up and down under his suspenders but the effect was spoiled when his big silver pinky ring caught on a button.

Smiling, Molly pushed a strand of dark hair off her forehead with the back of one hand. "Got any more interesting jobs lined up?" As a former journalist, Molly was fascinated by the details of his private investigator work and he enjoyed having someone listen to his stories. "I've got a nice single malt if you're not done drinking for the day."

The remainder of the cats leaped off Richard's porch and stalked away. It was clear they wouldn't be seeing more food until tomorrow.

"Don't mind if I do," said Richard. Molly held open the squeaky gate for him.

"Hey Miss Molly! Hey Dickie! How y'all doing?" Candi tottered across the street wearing a white bra top, green plaid miniskirt and white knee socks with scuffed black high heels. Straggly pigtails swung on either side of her head.

"Holy Virgin Mary, Candace! What are you supposed to be?" Richard turned to Molly. "Good thing you can't see this."

"Schwilliam got me doing a school girl look or whatever."

Molly said, "We were about to have a cocktail and Richard's going to tell me about his latest job. You want to join us, Candi?"

Richard rolled his eyes, let out a low groan.

"Is a frog's ass watertight? Thank you so much, Miss Molly, ain't you the nicest! But if I don't get on to work, I'll get a heap o' mess o' ugly from Shwilliam. I just wanted to say hi. Y'all enjoy!" She waved at them vigorously and teetered off on her stilettos in the direction of the streetcar stop.

"Sweet Jesus and all his cousins," Richard said.

"Come on, she's got a good heart. I can tell. Anyway, make yourself at home," Molly waved her hand in the direction of a small bistro set practically hidden in her plant-filled courtyard. "I'll get us set up."

Molly coiled up the hose and hung it on the hook on the side of the house. *Can't be too careful of tripping hazards.* She went in the side door, grabbed the square bottle from the second shelf of her bar and two glasses from the upper cabinet.

The white cane stayed on its hook near the door as she returned to her neighbor.

Molly had moved to New Orleans the previous year. She loved her little house in MidCity and often offered to help people on the block plant more trees. She understood why they would feel uncomfortable accepting her help, but she kept trying. This close to South Broad, things got a little sketchy on their street, but she felt that if her neighbors would just plant some pretty flowers outside, maybe that would lead to folks touching up their house paint, then picking up the trash, and before you knew it another whole New Orleans neighborhood would be turned around. She handed out rooted cuttings like Mardi Gras throws. Some of her neighbors even planted them.

A murder of crows alighted onto the overhead telephone wire, screaming insults as the humans below settled into their chairs in the courtyard.

"God, I hate birds," Richard said, looking up. "No redeeming qualities whatsoever. Those bastards are gonna crap all over my car." He detached a long stem studded with small pink roses that had snagged on his sleeve when he sat down. "I think what you need is more goddam plants."

"There's always room for more," Molly said. "These guys are like pets to me." She nudged away an overhanging palm frond that was tickling her ear. Pouring the scotch, she listened carefully as the liquid rose in each glass. "So, tell me a story." She leaned back into the seat cushion.

Richard smiled inwardly. *Oh, the stories I could tell!* He searched his memory for one he could safely share with her.

CHAPTER FIVE

Driving the back roads at night was getting more difficult. *Hell, everything is more difficult when you're this old,* Richard thought. *Whoever said old age ain't for sissies knew what they were talking about.* He hit stop and cut Pavarotti off in the middle of his Turandot aria. He needed to concentrate. When he saw the live oak with the twisted limb, he swung into the narrow lane.

Richard slowed, peering through the windshield, his grip tight on the wheel. Branches swept against the sides of the SUV as he inched down the bumpy lane. He hadn't used this spot in a while but he remembered there'd be room to turn around once he was clear of the underbrush about half a mile in.

He backed down to the waterline and climbed out, leaving the motor running to keep the air conditioning going. It was still sweltering even at this late hour. He had turned off the overhead interior light by habit, but there were no human eyes out here to see it anyway. He eased the door shut, the less noise the better, even this far from the city.

The cicadas in the cypress trees shrilled their electronic hum. He pulled on a pair of latex gloves. As a private investigator who dealt with evidence, he could easily justify having a box of disposable gloves in his car, if it came to that.

He had reasons on top of explanations on top of rationales, everything well-thought out. He was covered.

He pulled a flashlight from his pocket and swung it in an arc at the waterline. The rotting dankness of the swamp hung in the humid air. No red eyes glowed back at him. Nothing was there. Yet.

Ok, it's showtime.

He had it down to a science. This wasn't his first rodeo. No, far from it. *It's not about the muscle, it's about the leverage.* In a matter of minutes another scumbag was doing something useful for once, feeding the wildlife of southern Louisiana.

He stretched his back. He was going to pay for tonight's work in the morning, for sure. He dug down in his pocket and fingered the gold tooth he'd chosen as his souvenir this time. He'd have to remember to ask that crackhead Candace how her pimp was doing.

Though Richard knew no language other than English, he enjoyed pretending he understood the words as he and Luciano sang "Nessun Dorma" together driving back up the rutted track towards New Orleans and his bed.

CHAPTER SIX

olly was finally getting used to the voice-over feature on her
phone. She half-listened to the posts on the Next Door app
as she folded her laundry. She had learned to be careful when taking
her clothes off at night to keep them right-side out before washing
them. Before relocating to the South, she had learned to secure her
socks together with a big safety pin before throwing them in the wash.
Not only did it keep them from getting separated, but there'd be no
color sorting necessary. Now she mostly wore flip-flops every day. A
few little hacks could make blind life easier, for sure.

On her NextDoor app, nearby residents were complaining about
the usual: porch pirates, stolen cars and bikes, abandoned dog poop.
Some expressed gratitude for local musicians, others had complaints
about the volume of the same musicians' practice sessions.

She switched to local news. A suspicious house fire in Treme. A
double shooting in the Central Business District. Another carjacking
in Faubourg St. John. The garbage collectors were threatening a city-
wide strike. The mayor was assumed to be a shoo-in for re-election
even though crime and corruption were off the charts.

She froze in the middle of folding a fitted sheet, her mind's eye focus narrowing. The voice-over app was reporting another missing man. Last seen in the Ninth Ward, this one white, twenties, no further information available.

Molly had been in New Orleans long enough to read between the lines. Another missing bad guy, probably a drug dealer and/or pimp. This was the sixth she had heard about since November. There was never a follow up article, never any further information, and most interesting to her, never any mention of a link between the missing men. Her curiosity had been piqued since Missing Guy Number Three.

The journalist in Molly smelled a story. Except for small blurbs for her gardening club, she hadn't written anything since the accident, and she certainly hadn't investigated anything, but she felt that old itch coming alive. She had questions. With all his police contacts, she wondered if her private investigator neighbor, Richard, might be a good place to start. They grabbed a meal together occasionally. She made a mental note to bring it up the next time they went out.

Chapter Seven

"Hello? Are you Molly?"

The unfamiliar voice floated over the orange Mexican Flame vine covering the driveway gate to where Molly had her finger stuck deep into the soil of a potted persimmon tree. She had found that was the easiest way to tell if her plants needed water. Every so often, her bare hands came into contact with one of the four types of venomous caterpillars endemic to New Orleans, but fortunately that was an uncommon occurrence. She rinsed her hand under the hose she held in her other hand and turned it off. "Sorry, who is it?"

The husky voice came closer. "Oh, yeah. Right. I'm Richard's daughter. I'm Parker." Molly heard the heavy boots. She was already envisaging a motorcycle chick.

"Oh, hi! Sorry, I don't remember Richard mentioning he had a daughter."

"Yeah, well, it wouldn't be the first time he pretended he doesn't have one." Parker rested a boot on the lower railing of the wrought iron fence like she was bellied up to a bar, squashing a few blooms in the process. "Do you know where he's at?"

Molly checked her watch with one finger. "It's nine thirty so he'd still be over at the Bean Gallery having coffee. He's usually back by ten."

Parker sighed. "Never around when I need him. That's Richard." Molly heard her slap her thigh in exasperation.

"Something I can help you with?"

"I gotta get something out his house but I don't have a key," Parker said.

Molly heard the metallic rattle of a lightweight chain, imagined a wallet and some keys at the end of it, maybe black-painted, chipped fingernails, torn jeans, probably a stained wife beater. She liked to play a game in her head whenever she met someone new. Would her mental depiction of their physical appearance prove accurate? She had found her first impressions were usually spot on, uncomplicated as they were by visual distractions.

"Do you want to come sit and have some coffee with me until he gets back? I'm overdue for a second cup."

"That sounds good. I didn't stop for coffee this morning." Parker pushed the squeaky gate open.

"Have a seat," Molly gestured to the bistro table. "I just put on a fresh pot. Be right back."

In the kitchen she carefully poured two mugs and arranged them on a tray with a small pitcher of milk, a few sugar packets, and some spoons.

Back in the courtyard, Molly placed the tray on the table. "Didn't know how you take it," she said, holding out a mug and an old oyster shell she kept under the table.

"Oh, you smelled it," Parker said, tapping her cigarette into the empty shell. "Thanks. Black is good." She took the mug emblazoned with *Surely not everybody was kung fu fighting*. "Richard said a blind girl moved in next door. You seem to get around pretty good." She studied Molly, dragging hard on her cigarette.

Molly sipped her coffee as she made a decision. What was the point of paying her therapist if she never implemented his suggestions? "I was in a car accident a few years ago. Severed my optic nerves."

"Damn. That sucks."

"Oh, it gets better. My fiancé left me while I was in the hospital. He couldn't deal with the idea of being married to a blind woman."

"Holy shit, no kidding!"

"Truth. I lost my sight, my fiancé and my job all because some random jerk decided to drive home from a bar hammered one night." Molly blew on her coffee. "I was able to buy this house with some of the settlement money though, so there's that. And I dodged a bullet with the fiancé, as he obviously turned out to be an asshole. I do miss my career though. I was a journalist in New York."

"And here I thought I had bad luck." Parker ground out her cigarette in the oyster shell. Molly heard the clink of an old Zippo lighter as she lit another. "I do okay now. I'm a bookkeeper for an auto parts store, but Richard left my mom and me when I was a baby. She was like, 'good riddance,' but I tracked him down when I made eighteen. Guess the apple didn't fall far from the private investigator's tree, God help me." She exhaled. "We don't talk much. He doesn't approve of my 'lifestyle' as he calls it. Or my girlfriend, Lucy." She blew a lungful of smoke into the overhanging greenery.

"Well, well, well. Look what the cat dragged in. How much do you need this time, or did you come to return the .38 you 'borrowed?'"

Neither of them had heard Richard's car pull up.

"I told you I didn't take that," Parker said in a voice that made it clear she was used to fielding accusations. "I'm only here to pick up the check for Mom."

"Uh huh, right. We've been divorced for twenty years and she still can't find a job? Crispy Christ on a cracker, come on then, let's get this over with. Thanks for babysitting her, Molly."

Molly heard Parker's chair scrape on the bricks as she stood up. "Thanks for the coffee. I'll see you later. I mean, see you around. I mean, Jesus, sorry."

Molly laughed. "Don't worry about it. If you removed all the words relating to vision from your vocabulary just because I can't see, things would get awkward really fast. Nice talking with you, Parker. Stop by anytime."

"You'll regret that," Richard threw over his shoulder as he stalked off to his house with Parker trailing behind.

CHAPTER EIGHT

God, he hated this shit. Usually he got out of Dodge well before Mardi Gras, but he had an opportunity, and goddamn it, he was going to take it.

Richard inched along Bourbon Street, the raucous crowd packed in tight around him. Next year he'd damn sure go to Gulf Shores for this week. He patted his pocket for the umpteenth time. *This is some bullshit. I'm gonna need a stiff one after this. Goddamn tourists!* He didn't stop to note that the tourists were integral to his plan.

Immediately in front of Richard, a bare-chested guy wearing a Native American headdress and leather chaps over a tan speedo screamed out his version of a war whoop every thirty seconds, waving a plastic feathered tomahawk over his head. A lit joint dangled from his lips. To Richard's right, a six-foot-tall purple dinosaur lurched alongside, a beer bottle at the end of one tiny arm. To his left, a middle-aged woman in a sparkly green wig hoovered red liquid up from a giant plastic hand grenade hanging between her breasts. A unicorn horn protruded from her forehead and purple glitter sparkled on her Raggedy Ann-rouged cheeks.

The crowd was shoulder-locked tight, he couldn't turn to see who, or what, was behind him. He heard retching, smelled vomit and stale sweat. *Christ Almighty, just add it to the party gravy.*

A brass band blasted funk tunes, the blaring of the horns ricocheting off the old brick buildings lining the street. Elbows and knees jostled him from all directions as everyone gyrated to the music while inching forward in a zombie shuffle so as not to roll an ankle on the bottles, trash and beads underfoot.

Richard wriggled an arm free of the crowd to adjust the eyeholes on his skull face mask. He took a moment to enjoy the irony of his costume. *Hidden in plain sight. I'm probably the only sober person within a five-mile radius.* His black tee shirt with a skeleton printed front and back was perfect for this job. No one would think twice about his black gloves either, there were so many more interesting things to see.

Pressed up against his bopping target, he shambled along with the crowd down Bourbon and waited.

As his section of the horde approached a slightly less crowded side street, he reached up and plucked a souvenir red feather from the Indian's headdress and slipped it into his pocket. *Enough of this crap already, I'm done.* He stifled a chuckle, *And so is he.*

When they were nearest to Toulouse, the Indian raised both arms over his head, clapping to a beat only he could hear.

For Richard, the cacophony deadened to a dull background roar as he focused to make his move. He slid his hand from his pocket. No one heard the Indian's gasp of surprise and pain. *In, up and out. Easy peasy. This jackass won't be following Miss Dina home after closing time again. Jesus in a jumpsuit, no telling what he had planned for her next time.*

He took the knife with him when he inched over to the slightly less congested corner. He looked back towards Bourbon and saw the now-drooping Indian head dress borne slowly away with the packed crowd.

The knife safely back in his pocket, he kept the face mask on until he exited the French Quarter, away from any police cameras that might actually be working. He had a satisfying, if somewhat elaborate, routine planned for the knife, but he threw the mask on top of an overflowing trash can, one glove into a garbage-strewn lot, the other onto the streetcar tracks. *Let 'em figure that one out.*

Feeling energized, he sauntered to his car humming 'Ingemisco Tamquam Reus' from Verdi's Requiem.

***

Beuletta pushed the guy away. "Hold up there, Sparky."

A brass band on the street below belted out "When the Saints Go Marching In" for the umpteenth time, the blaring sound barely muted by the cracked glass of the room's curtainless window. In the distance, fireworks, or maybe gunshots, popped, even though it was probably only about noon.

Beuletta peered around his thick Midwestern body as he stood with his back to the window and his pants around his ankles.

She had better than 20/20 eyesight and what she was looking at on the street below seemed highly questionable.

From her vantage point on the third floor of the Canal Street motel, she stared down at her grumpy-ass neighbor man as he trudged lakeside out the Quarter. As she watched, he wrenched off a plastic skeleton-face mask and threw it on a pile of trash, then peeled off his black gloves and threw one on the neutral ground tracks.

"Jus' hang on a second," she told the guy. She stepped around him to the window, standing with her hands on her ample hips. Midwestern Guy was apparently used to being ordered around because he didn't protest even though he was paying for her time. A quick glance back at him told her he had actually enjoyed her authoritarian command.

Outside, the old man continued plodding up Canal, as determined as a tortoise. As he passed the place where the sneaker store used to be, he tossed the other black glove into the empty lot.

"What that mean old man up to?" she wondered aloud, scratching around her intricate braids with one long nail. *Imma hafta remember to tell Candi about this shady business.*

"Am I supposed to know the answer to that?" the client asked eagerly. "Because I don't." His delight in their new game was evident.

Beauletta turned from the window, once again focusing her attention on him. "Well, you a bad boy, then, ain't you?"

Chapter Nine

The hoisin sauce ran down her arm and dripped off her elbow. This time Molly felt it on her skin and swiped at it with her napkin before Richard could point it out.

"I don't know what I was thinking. This isn't the easiest thing for me to eat."

"The same thing you always think. You like it," Richard said, forking up another mouthful of Chicken with Black Mushrooms and Broccoli, his go-to meal at Six Golden Joy.

"I don't know how you stand it. Eating with me when I order this has to be a spectacle." She laid the Moo Shu Shrimp wrap she had fabricated on her plate and carefully wiped her mouth, then each of her fingers. "Can you get me more napkins, please?"

"Way ahead of you," said Richard, passing her a stack. "We've got our usual surly waiter, not that nice Chink lady we had last time. He saw you and brought extras."

She let his latest racist remark pass, for now. She needed information and didn't want to alienate him by suggesting tolerance and inclusion yet again. "I don't know whether to be grateful or embarrassed, so I'm gonna go with grateful. It's less embarrassing," she said.

"Don't worry about it. It's kind of charming, actually." Richard couldn't let that stand. "I'll bring a plastic poncho for you next time so we can just hose you off." He didn't get out to dinner much, certainly never with a pretty girl he didn't have to pay or one not looking for free legal advice or a place to crash.

"Deal. Hell, I'll wear a garbage bag and rubber gloves as long as I get to eat this every once in a while." Molly took a sip of her plum wine, emptying her glass.

Richard motioned at the peevish waiter, who dragged himself over to bring them another round. "You've got another plum wine at nine o'clock."

"Thanks." Her hands patted the table on both sides of her plate. "That would be my three o'clock, but good try. So, Spot was in my driveway this morning looking for a second breakfast. At least it sounded like Spot's meow. He let me rub his belly today."

"He's a sweet boy, especially for a feral. I've got to trap him next week for his trip to the vet. Christ on a broomstick, these cats are costing me an arm and a leg."

"Come on, you love them and besides, what else are you going to do with all your millions?"

Richard snorted.

"Hey, have you been hearing anything about all these missing guys?" Molly continued.

Richard watched her rub her arms as if she'd felt the energy shift within their corner booth. He wondered if there was any truth to the adage that other senses became more sensitive when one was damaged. "What missing guys?" he asked.

"Come on! I know you know something. I can tell. I'm like a witch that way. Yeah, I'm a witch with the hearing of a bat. You better watch yourself. I know stuff."

He gave a short bark and sat back in the red leatherette booth, folding his arms across his sunken chest. He considered her from across the table. He liked having the advantage of being able to study her for as long as he liked. She was easy to look at.

Molly's dark hair was pulled back in a high ponytail. She had a small streak of hoisin sauce on one cheek, but it was her pale blue eyes he heard people comment on whenever he was with her. You almost couldn't tell. He took a long pull from his beer.

"What? I didn't get it all?" She wiped her mouth with the napkin again, missing the cheek smear. She leaned forward, unwittingly resting one forearm in a small puddle of sauce.

Richard remained silent about it.

"Come on, tell me what your cop friends are saying about all the missing guys I've been hearing about. Why isn't this more of a big deal? I've counted six so far. They're pimps, right? Or drug dealers? Gangbangers? Come on, spill. There might be a writing assignment in it for me."

He hadn't anticipated this particular scenario with her. He chose his next utterance carefully. "Word is, yeah, they all seem to be pretty bad guys."

"Do the cops know what's happening to them? Are there any leads? Any bodies turn up yet?"

"Nope, nope and nope. But trust me, no one's sorry to see these guys go."

Molly sat back, deflated. Then she brightened. "Maybe we've got a vigilante in New Orleans! What do you think?"

"I think your imagination is running away with you, young lady."

"You're gonna have to spring for my Moo Shu Shrimp and plum wine if it turns out I'm right." Sensing Richard had finished eating, she fished in her purse and held out her credit card to add to his own. She always insisted they split the bill.

Richard paused, the last of his beer halfway to his lips as a rare moment of doubt washed over him. He hoped he'd be alive and un-incarcerated long enough to buy her dinner if it came out later that she was correct. He downed his beer and snapped his fingers at the reluctant server for the check.

CHAPTER TEN

The steak knife from Heming's was a thing of beauty. One solid piece of stainless steel ran from the point of the generously-sized cutting edge through to the butt of the tang. The grip appeared to be mother of pearl but was probably a good resin imitation. Three rivets in the shaft secured the grip to the stainless shank. The serrations were always razor sharp on every one of the Heming's knives he had ever borrowed. Richard always appreciated the balance, the solid weight, the workmanship. *They don't make them like that anymore.*

He wondered how a middling-priced steakhouse chain could afford to use such beautifully crafted knives. He imagined diners stole them all the time. He'd never do that, but he did love his little traditions, his rituals, even if this one was a bit of an overkill. He chuckled before finishing his lobster bisque, placing the soup spoon next to the empty bowl. *Overkill! Good one.*

Using his napkin to retrieve a previously-borrowed knife from the side pocket of his baggy cargo pants, he placed it on the table with the napkin over it. He had been craving a nice, juicy steak but couldn't chance being given another steak knife in the set up. Two on a table for one might call attention. He paid the bill in cash and left the restaurant.

When the server cleared the table, all the cutlery went into the kitchen, into the commercial dishwasher, "his" knife indistinguishable from the hundreds of other knives being washed and sterilized in the hot soapy water that evening.

CHAPTER ELEVEN

Richard's police radio squawked. As a private investigator in Louisiana, he technically shouldn't have access to one, but after digging up some dirt on an ex for one of the boys on the force, Richard got what he needed. He had to stay in touch. Every day some new situation pointed up the fact that he was old and only getting older. *A man needs to stay engaged to be relevant, useful, necessary, even.* Society told him someone his age didn't have much to offer. *Screw society!* He had certain proven, effective skills along with the motivation and the guts to employ them. He could still make a difference, in his own way.

He folded the newspaper and slid his glasses up onto his forehead. The cat who was trying to fill Dr. Zeus's place on Richard's lap jumped to the floor when he pushed himself out of the rocking chair with a groan. He already missed old Zeus something fierce, but the diabetes shots had stopped working. *Just didn't want the poor little guy to suffer.* The early morning drive to the veterinarian hospital and a ride home with an empty cat carrier had done nothing to improve Richard's glum mood.

He was dabbing at his eyes with the handkerchief from his rear pocket when he heard the alert tones. He shuffled across the room in his slippers to the radio on his work desk. His hearing wasn't getting any better these days, not that he'd admit it. He turned up the volume.

"St. Louis Cemetery No. 1. Two unidentified victims. Unresponsive. Coroner en route."

Richard shook his head. *Two more murders of innocent people. Christ on skis, the bad guys are running amok.* "This city is going to hell in a handbasket despite my best efforts," he told the cat. He made a mental note to ask Dan for the details of this tragedy over coffee in the morning. *I also gotta ask him if the boys in blue have any leads on the completely justified killing of that fool stalker dressed like an Indian for Mardi Gras.* He returned to his rocker and continued grumbling about the state of his city as he read the rest of the newspaper. The cat jumped up again and resettled itself back onto his lap with no hard feelings.

CHAPTER TWELVE

The next morning Dan's hands shook slightly as he stirred a heaping spoonful of sugar into his coffee at their outside table at The Bean Gallery. If Dan's black lace-up shoes didn't give him away as a cop, then the fact that he sat with his back to the wall, perpetually scanning Carrollton Avenue, did.

"Where you been, man? Didn't see you yesterday and you didn't answer your phone neither."

"Had to take Dr. Zeus on a one-way trip to the vet. That old bastard was with me for fifteen years." Richard swiped at his nose, looked away. "So, what's this I hear about two tourists in St. Louis No. 1?"

Dan stirred his coffee harder, the spoon clanking against the thick white porcelain mug. "I'm just saying, Dick..." He shook his head. "You know how long I've been on the force, but I swear I've never seen anything like it. They were just..." his voice faded away. He grasped the mug with both hands, staring into the black liquid. Three puffy beignets under a mound of powdered sugar sat cooling on a plate in front of him.

Richard leaned back in his chair, absorbing the unfamiliar situation. He'd never before seen anything affect Dan's appetite, as evidenced by his companion's expansive waistline. "Well, come on, man, they were what?" Richard reached across the table and pulled the beignets towards himself. "No point letting these go to waste." He bit into one, expertly leaning over the plate to avoid looking like an inexperienced tourist with telltale powdered sugar all over his pants.

Dan looked away, his brow furrowed. "I'm thinking we got ourselves one helluva big problem with this one."

"Why do you say that?" Richard swiped at his lips with a napkin. "This stuff is so good, but Christ on a crocodile, so messy."

"You had to see the scene, man. This wasn't done by some crackhead or even a gangbanger. Both of their heads were just torn off. Like really torn right off. As in ripped off. We found the girl's cradled in the arms of this weeping angel statue."

"I know that statue," Richard mumbled around another bite.

"Yeah, everybody knows that statue. We found the guy's head stuck on a fence post."

"Hmmm," Richard said, momentarily at a loss for words. "Glad I wasn't there for that one."

"Wish I hadn't been. And get this," Dan dragged it out, "stuffed in the guy's mouth was a go-cup from Port of Call."

"Seriously?"

"I shit you not." Dan lumbered to his feet. "I gotta go. All hell's breaking loose on this one. A bunch of school kids called it in and posted pictures all over the internet. The mayor's already screaming we've gotta find whoever did it fast. Bad for business, you know?" He started down the walkway to his car but turned back. "Hey, man, sorry about Dr. Zeus."

Richard looked down at his pants. He'd gotten powdered sugar on them despite his best efforts. It was going to be one of those days. "Yeah, well, it's not like there's a shortage of stray cats around here. Catch you later."

Chapter Thirteen

Molly stepped off the streetcar onto Carondelet Street at 10:20. The voice-over app on her phone told her she was twenty feet from the Times Picayune office. She tapped along the sidewalk until she found the door, switched her white cane to her left hand, and pulled it open.

She heard a perky man's voice say, "I've gotta go, someone just walked in. No, no sweetcheeks, I'll call you back." Then louder, "Do y'all need help, baby?"

"Yes, I've got an appointment with Ivy DeLongue at 10:30. Could you show me to her office, please."

"Sure thing, my love," the voice came closer. "Um, how do you want to do this?"

"If I could take your left elbow, that would be great," Molly explained.

"Okay. Here you go."

Molly reached out and placed her hand lightly on his thin arm. She briefly reflected on all the information a person could get from just an elbow and a voice. "Thanks. I'm Molly."

"Hello, darling, I'm Robbie. And, we're off!" He led her across the room and down a short hallway. Phones rang and heavy equipment made a rhythmic thumping noise in the rear of the building. "Honey, I've got to tell you, you're the first blind person I've ever met in real life. Is that okay to say?"

"Sure, I feel very special right now," Molly laughed. They stopped in front of an office doorway. The faint smells of baby powder and cigarettes wafted from inside. "You did great, by the way. For some reason, a lot of people feel they need to grab me and kind of drag me along with them. You did exactly the right thing by just walking naturally."

"Honey, my natural walk is a strut!" Robbie snapped his fingers. "But are you telling me I'd make a good guide dog, 'cause I've already got the collar!"

"What the hell is going on out there?" A gravelly woman's voice called out.

"Miss Molly is here for her appointment," Robbie said, guiding her inside the small office. "There's a chair directly in front of you, sweetheart. And *this* is Ivy, may God help you and keep you safe." Molly heard him return to the front desk.

"Jesus, you're blind. You didn't mention that on the phone," Ivy rasped.

Molly sat down and folded her cane. "Yes, well, you didn't mention that you smoke, you're short, and have a lot of tattoos, so we're even." That last was a shot in the dark that hit its mark. Down the hallway, she heard Robbie pretend to muffle his giggles.

"Did he tell you all that?"

"No, I just did my homework."

Molly heard a rolling chair squeak as Ivy leaned back.

"Okay, the pissing contest is over. What do you want? I'm crazy busy today. I got one reporter out for his wife's third uncle twice-removed's funeral and the other's out because she's got cramps again, the poor little princess." Ivy reached for a half-empty pack of Camels on her desk then crumpled it up and tossed it in the direction of the overflowing trashcan. "I'm trying to quit, but these pussies are trying my last nerve."

Molly leaned forward. "I won't waste your time then. I'd like to know if anyone's reporting on the missing guys around town. Six so far, and I haven't seen a single news article linking them all together yet."

"You wouldn't *see* any news articles, would you?"

"I've got voice-over on my phone. Technology, you know?"

The chair squeaked again.

Molly said, "How does that not drive you crazy?"

"What, this?" Ivy rocked in her chair, setting off a cacophony of creaks and screeches. "I keep forgetting to bring in some WD-40. HEY, ROVER, PICK ME UP SOME LUBE AT LUNCHTIME," Ivy shouted.

"Ewww! Girl, you don't pay me enough!" Robbie yelled back.

"For the chair, you homo!" Then to Molly, "Why're you asking about missing guys? What's it to you?"

"I was a journalist in New York before my accident," she said, gesturing to her eyes. "I'll be honest, I haven't written anything since, but I can send you my resume. I smell a big, overlooked story here. How about I do a little digging, write something up, and if you like it, you consider me for a spot on your crime desk?"

"You're crazy. How the hell are you gonna investigate anything?" Ivy leaned over, picked the crumpled pack of cigs off the floor and looked at it sadly.

Molly stood up and shook out her cane. "You let me worry about that," she said as she tapped her way to the door. "And by the way, a little of that baby powder you put in your shoes would probably stop the squeaky noise from your chair too."

"Well, fuck me sideways," Ivy mused, fingering a broken cigarette.

"Not even with a borrowed dick!" Robbie yelled from the reception desk.

CHAPTER FOURTEEN

Side by side, Candi and Beuletta folded the first batch of clothes from the dryer in the steamy laundromat. Candi held up a threadbare gray tee shirt with a picture of a panda on the front. "This here one's my favorite but it sure is getting worn through."

"I know that's your favorite. Girl, that thing so old I can read through it. Let's you and me go to the Goodwill today. Pick us out some new clothes." Beuletta swiped at her forehead with the back of her hand. "Lawd, it's pure hell in here, let's hurry this up."

Sitting on plastic chairs set along one wall, a scruffy young man in a stained white tee shirt and a woman of indeterminate age in slippers and a shapeless housedress lounged, an empty chair between them. He clutched a fifth of Fireball. She held a paper bag in a gnarled grasp with careful concentration. Separately, they had each found themselves a place where they wouldn't be hassled for sitting, at least for a little while.

The woman nodded at the guy's bottle. "I drink that too."

"Sheriff give me twenty bucks when he let me out. I got me some Fireball and some sandwiches. You wanna sandwich?"

"No, thanks." She smiled dreamily, showing gaps where teeth used to live. "I love Fireball in my morning coffee or over ice. It's a pure treat."

"You a drinker too?" he asked, certainty tingeing the question.

"Yup, you ain't alone. That's why I love this town. You ain't never drinking alone. I'm actually drinking this here to slacker off." She waved the paper bag.

"Yeah, you gotta do that every so often, uh huh."

"My daughter, she don't like me when I'm drinking. Leastways I ain't smoking crack or hurting nobody. I did some last week but I'm fine now. I did some meth to sober up, by the way."

"I do that from time to time. But I like to drink."

"I like to drink too." They both stared at their feet while the clothes dryers hummed and the washers churned.

The woman said, "I been on the street a year now. I woke up once and there was a young boy sniffing my feet. I gotta say that ain't acceptable."

The guy nodded his agreement of her boundaries and they drank in unison.

On the other side of the noisy, humid room, Candi opened the washer she and Beuletta shared that held the last of their meager wardrobes. She patted her pockets. "I ain't got no more change. You got any?"

"I got plenty change. This guy, yesterday? He done give me quarters to pay, can you believe that! Not the whole thing, but he left me quarters for some of it. Some folks just be like that, you know?"

"Yeah, but now we can dry our clothes, so it's all good. Not like last time when we had to lug 'em home wet and hang 'em up all over and whatever."

Beuletta fed coins into the dryer while Candi moved their things over from the washer. "Hey, I done seen that cranky ass Richard walking down Canal on Mardi Gras day."

"Yeah?" Candi's voice echoed up from the bottom of the washing machine where she struggled to reach a pair of panties spun flat against the side.

"Yeah. He was lookin' all kinds of shady throwing his mask and some black gloves away all up and down the street. He was looking like he up to no good."

"Huh? Why'd he do that?"

"I don't know, girl! How would I know anything that nasty old man does? I can't figure why you like him."

"Aw, he ain't so bad. I kind of feel sorry for him, you know? He's all crabby and such, but all o' those cats sure like him."

"That's 'cause he feedin' them! Hell, I'd probably like him better if he fed me once in a while too."

"And I think Miss Molly likes him." Candi thought hard. "For all intensive purposes or whatever."

"Huh? I don't know nothing about that."

Candi was still thinking. "I wonder why he'd be throwing away his stuff on the street."

"Girl, I don't know." Beuletta moved to stand under the struggling air conditioner. "Hey, you seen Schwilliam anywheres? He ain't been around to collect for a bit."

"Nah, I was gonna ask you. I bet he'll be by tonight, probably just biting his time or whatever somewheres outta the heat for now."

"Fine by me if I ain't seeing his ass no time soon. He been nothing but angry lately. It still hurts when I breathe deep."

"Yeah, he cracked my head on the wall outside Brennan's for no good reason."

"Well, at least we know what Schwilliam's deal is. I don't know nuthin' about that grumpy ass neighbor man and Imma keep it that way. Something ain't right there."

"You're too suspicious and whatever, Beuletta, he's just an old man who likes cats."

"Ol' man, my big beautiful ass. Mark my words, girl, he ain't right."

CHAPTER FIFTEEN

S omething scurried into a corner as Richard felt his way around inside the unlit toolshed. "Christ on the crucifix, am I the only one working around here? Cats sure as hell aren't doing their job," Richard said under his breath.

He bumped into something that clanked, put out a hand to quiet it. His index finger brushed against something sharp. Even in the dark he knew he had cut himself. He stuck his finger in his mouth before it dripped on anything. Even though this was his shed, he didn't want to leave fresh blood around. Just in case. No need to create problems for himself.

He reached behind a moldy cardboard box of screws on a high shelf and pulled out his mother's rusty Uneeda biscuit tin. He pried it open, rummaged in his shirt pocket, then dropped in a red feather. A little something to remember that Indian asshole by.

He had read that serial killers often saved souvenirs from their victims to relive the kills, but he just did it for laughs. He certainly wasn't one of those screwed up freaks. He held the tin up to his ear and shook it. His other mementos rattled satisfyingly. *If it ever comes to it, I could have this shed in flames in under five minutes.* He gathered the items he needed without incident, without any more bloodshed. Yet.

Chapter Sixteen

Molly kicked off her flip flops and placed them at the foot of her lounge chair before stretching out. An app on her phone told her the moon was directly over her back deck. She imagined she could feel the moonlight beaming peace and serenity down upon her.

Moonbathing, she called it, this practice of laying quietly outside under the full moon. It was similar to the Japanese *shinrinyoku*, or forest bathing, but adapted by Molly for her own unique needs. In addition to gardening, this form of meditation had helped her get through many difficult times after everything that had happened.

A muffled clank echoed from Richard's toolshed on the other side of the fence. Molly sat up. An ambulance raced down Banks Street, the siren blanketed by the humid air.

Despite how much fun the city could be, Molly was quite aware of the rampant crime in New Orleans. Yesterday she had heard about two more carjackings in Faubourg St. John and an armed robbery in broad daylight just a few blocks away. She did feel safer living next to Richard since he volunteered to run the MidCity Neighborhood Watch. As ludicrous as it seemed with Richard being so elderly, she hoped it was enough of a deterrent to keep the bad guys off their block, at least.

In the yard next door, the shed door squeaked. A car alarm blared rhythmically on South White Street before falling silent. Molly heard shuffled steps, then Richard muttering. She breathed a sigh of relief and lay back. She had no idea why Richard was so often in his toolshed at this hour, but good neighbors respected each other's privacy. Besides, elderly people could be odd.

Look who's odd, she thought. *Laying outside under a moon you can't see.* She remained quiet on her deck so as not to startle him.

Molly reviewed her possible first story for the Times Picayune. *What do I know so far? Not much, just that six men have gone missing. Where can I go to get more information? Police reports, interviews with officers and locals, off the record or on, maybe check back with Richard.*

Molly was happy her grumpy neighbor seemed to like her since they lived so closely side by side. And she liked that he shared his interesting private investigator stories. It was important to her that he didn't seem to feel sorry for her, as she could tell many did. She enjoyed the companionship of an occasional shared meal or cocktails if she and Richard both happened to be free, but she did miss having a romantic interest in her life, too. So far, she hadn't met anyone who piqued her interest enough to date in New Orleans. She had to admit, she did get lonely sometimes. She wasn't really looking yet, though. Her new girlfriends in town kept trying to hook her up, but Molly wasn't ready. She knew she still had some stuff to work through, mostly trust issues, some grief, some anger, and a lot of sadness, before she'd be ready for another relationship. The therapy sessions were really helping her feel alive again though, as was her garden and her nightly meditations under the moon.

She heard a soft click as Richard closed and locked his back door. *It's true,* she thought. *I've got the hearing of a bat now.* Images of the accident flashed through her mind. *Stop it,* she chided herself. *Look ahead, not behind.* She recalled her therapist's words only about ten times a day now.

Molly lay back in the lounge chair again. Another deep breath told her the flower buds on the night-blooming cereus had finally opened. Ten more minutes in her moon bath then she'd try to type up a description of that bewitching fragrance for her garden club, and maybe get in a little online research about the missing guys before heading to bed. She'd sleep well tonight.

CHAPTER SEVENTEEN

"Push that goddamn chicken off, will you?" Richard stood beside the only table not already occupied by bar patrons. This particular high top however, definitely did have an occupant. A chicken.

Miss Henrietta preened on the table in front of a mirrored wall etched with the word *Buddy's,* as she softly clucked to her reflection and fluffed her shiny greenish-black feathers.

"I'm not pushing her off. It's her table. You can do it, but prepare yourself for a fight from Maurice." Beau nodded to the bouncer glowering at them from his chair by the door.

"I'm not touching that filthy thing," Richard said, looking around. "Holy hell, there's nowhere else to sit."

"Still not over that bird thing, huh? You know they have desensitization therapy for all kinds of phobias now. I hear they get good results." Beau set their whiskeys on the table's edge.

Miss Henrietta chose that moment to hop down onto one of the stools, then flutter to the floor where she strutted off through the crowd, a mix of neighborhood hipsters and locals who made way for her as if she were the reigning Mardi Gras Queen.

"Thank God for small favors. And you know what you can do with your therapy talk." Richard hitched his jeans and heaved himself onto the barstool. "Gimme the details on the new job."

"I know the window of your life is closing rapidly, old timer, but can we slow it down a bit here? I don't get to enjoy a cocktail out very often since the twins were born." Beau sipped his bourbon and loosened his tie. He glanced up at a painting of a magnificently bare-chested brunette high on one wall. "You know, I think about that painting whenever we get a hurricane in the Gulf. Always hope she'll be okay."

"Who, Tits? Yeah, that's a pair worth bronzing. Life wouldn't be worth the trouble of living without her in the world." They clinked glasses in a silent toast to Tits the Magnificent.

"So, I've got this dude who needs a summons served." Beau played with his bar napkin. "Guy's a real-life badass, though. I mean, we're talking time in Angola for murder one, rape, all kinds of fun stuff. You name it, he's done it. This guy's the real deal. I don't know how the hell a guy like that made parole, but he's back on the street now."

Richard snorted his opinion of the city's revolving door justice system and swirled the whiskey in his glass.

Beau nodded his agreement. "Yeah, and get this - we're handling his divorce. She waits until he gets out to divorce him. Smart as bait, that one."

"I'll do it." Richard caught Roxanne's eye and motioned for a backup round. More hipsters had come in and the crowd was getting louder.

Roxanne shouted over the hubbub, "Hey, baby, how you doing?"

"I feel so good it should be illegal," Richard deadpanned.

She blew him a kiss and set to work pouring their drinks ahead of her other orders.

With one finger in the moisture from their glasses, Beau drew an aimless pattern around the chicken footprints. "I'll be honest with you, Dickie, two other guys haven't been able to serve him so far. Or maybe they changed their minds about getting the job done once they got a look at him, I don't know. But don't you want to think it over? I would."

"Lucky for both of us, you're not me. Consider me duly advised. Jesus, don't touch that." Richard swiped the prints away with his bar napkin. "You're gonna catch some kind of avian Ebola from that goddamn bird."

"Good news is he's local. Lives and works in the Quarter. Bad news is, well I already described his charming personality, plus he's going to be decidedly unhappy to receive this particular summons. Word is he's possessive as hell over his wife. Acts like he owns her or something. I guess she's got other ideas. Sounds like she's turned her attentions elsewhere."

"Where's he work?"

"She says he's a line cook at BooBoo's."

" 'Course he is. If it wasn't for felons, you wouldn't be able to get a bite of food in this town."

Roxanne sashayed out from behind the bar and placed their drinks, complete with fresh napkins, on the thickly polyurethaned tabletop. She leaned over Richard, affording him a freckled view down the front of her tight shirt and gave him a quick hug as she whispered in his ear, "I did exactly what you told me and that DUI disappeared like magic! Thank you, baby!"

She gave Beau a toothy smile, waggled her fingertips at him, "Hey, how you doin'?" before sauntering back to the hipsters clamoring for specialty cocktails at the bar.

"I don't know how you do it, Dick," Beau shook his head in amazement.

"It's easy. Big tips, my connections, and free legal advice. Otherwise, I'd get about as much sugar as one of those fleas on that disgusting bird."

"Do birds get fleas?"

"Don't know, don't care." They sipped in companionable silence. Beau observed the crowd. Richard pretended nonchalance as he scanned the room for the proximity of Miss Henrietta.

When Beau's phone began vibrating to the strains of Joe Cocker's *Darling Be Home Soon,* he sighed, then stood up and dropped some bills on the table. He pulled his tie off, rolled it up and stuck it in his suit jacket pocket. "Fun's over. Time for me to get home to the little woman and my boys." He produced a manila envelope and slid it across the table. "Here's the paperwork, his photos and your exorbitant fee."

"Exorbitant? Jesus Christ and Mary Magdalene! I should charge you double. I work harder than an ugly stripper for my money."

"Uh huh. I had Judge Boudreaux appoint you as the process server. The creep's details are in there too." He kept his hand on the envelope. "If you're sure you want this one?"

Richard pulled it towards himself. "You're apparently sure I do. That paperwork's already got my name on it. Is his photo recent?"

"As recent as we could get."

"Yeah, I know what that means. What is it, his kindergarten picture? Never mind. What's his name?"

"Wardell Shruggs."

"Ok, I'll look at it tomorrow. You'll see, Mr. Shruggs and I will get along just fine."

CHAPTER EIGHTEEN

Wardell's hands flew in hard, jerky movements. He stabbed the knife into the oyster's hinge like it owed him money, pried the shells apart and flipped the top into a garbage can, all in one motion. Next, he swooped the knife under the oyster and sliced through the muscle so it sat disconnected in its own liquor. He then slammed it onto the crushed ice of the white platter with *Tierney's* scrawled along one edge in red script. He did this over and over and over as the crash of the busboys' dirty cutlery and dishes reverberated off the black and white tiled walls, clashing with the shouted orders of the waitstaff in the steamy kitchen.

A bead of sweat dripped off the end of his greasy nose and landed on the oyster in his hand. Stains discolored his frayed wifebeater. A rhinestone gleamed dully from one earlobe. Illegible jailhouse tats crawled up both sinewy arms. His long dreadlocks were gathered back with an old brown hair tie.

Wardell's friend at the courthouse had given him a heads-up when the paperwork for the summons came across his desk. Ralaysia's plan to serve him with divorce papers just earned her a beating and that's if he was in a good mood when he delivered it, otherwise, who knew? Maybe he'd just stomp her pretty face into the ground for good this time.

Wardell's friend also told him the name of the process server. That creepy old private investigator was well known around the Quarter. Hell, Wardell could easily avoid him. Or not. Maybe he'd take care of him too for sticking his nose where it don't belong. Shit, that old fucker had served plenty of Wardell's buddies. He was overdue for a beating or worse.

Thoughts ping-ponged around in his head, always returning to his original conviction. *That cunt! Who the fuck she think she is? She ain't gonna get the chance to serve me with no divorce papers!*

He had picked up the extra shift at Tierney's when one of their regular shuckers broke his hand in an unfortunate accident Wardell may or may not have had something to do with. If it wasn't for the mandatory meeting with his parole officer after work and his need for the money the extra shift would bring, he'd have paid Ralaysia a visit already. Unaccustomed as he was to controlling his impulses, he had learned a few things about waiting from his time on the inside. He was so much smarter now.

Chapter Nineteen

Candi limped across the street. It was past time to have those stitches removed from her thigh. "Hey, Dickie!" Under the streetlight she waved her arms to catch his attention, as if he hadn't seen her coming the moment she stepped out her front door. "Whatcha doin' baby?"

Richard straightened from pouring the cats' dinner kibble into a dozen bowls, one hand supporting his lower back. "I'm inventing a cure for stupidity, Candace." He sighed. "And don't call me 'Dickie.'"

She slow-blinked at him, then bent to give the cats some love. "Pretty kitties! How y'all doing? Hey, you think we oughta report Shwilliam missing or whatever? Beuletta and me, we ain't been seeing him for a week now."

Richard put down the bag of cat food, stretched his back. "Well, I don't know, Candace. Let's think this through together."

The neighborhood possum sauntered among the cats to his bowl, which he tilted delicately with one pink, clawed paw.

"Careful, Otto, you're going to spill that," he said to the raggedy grey animal. "Now pay attention, Candace. You listening? Wasn't Shwilliam using again and beating you gals up worse than usual?"

Candi nodded. "Uh huh, yeah, whatever."

"Didn't he put Beuletta in the hospital last month with four cracked ribs?

She nodded again, tucked her stringy blonde hair behind one ear. She picked up Papa and hugged him to her scrawny chest. He purred loudly and kneaded her sternum through her faded ABBA tee shirt.

"And didn't you say that he was talking about getting in some real young girls, like little kids, to expand his business?"

She buried her nose in Papa's willing fur. "Yeah, he done said that, true 'nuff."

"So why do you care if he's missing?"

She put Papa down, brushed some loose gray fur off the flat front of her shirt. "Well, a person gets used to things one kinda way, Dickie, you know? He'd be good to Beuletta and me sometimes." She looked away. "Once in a while."

"Jesus, Mary and Joseph in a canoe." Richard smacked his forehead. "What a waste of time. I don't know why I even... Hell, never mind.."

"What? Hey, don't be making me no escape goat," Candi said. "I was just thinking maybe you could call it in or whatever. You know I can't have nothing to do with no police. "

"It's *scapegoat*, Candace," Richard sighed. "And no, I'm not going to report Shwilliam missing. Why don't you just enjoy the fact that he's no longer around."

"I guess." Candi sounded unconvinced. "Whatever."

CHAPTER TWENTY

"**A**nd she wanted her jackass pimp reported missing! That girl's a few floats short of a parade." Richard shook his head.

Miss Dina folded her arms under her generously proportioned bosom and leaned against her side of the bar, "Everyone's been hearing those rumors about Schwilliam hurting his girls and getting in real young kids." Her faded green eyes zeroed in on something over his shoulder. "Hold on just a minute, baby."

Leaning over the bar, her straight-outta-Chalmette voice cut through the conversations in the room like a hot knife through Crisco. "Excuse me! You there, sweetheart! Yes, you. You gotta buy a drink before you can use the restroom, ok baby?"

The newbie put his hands up in surrender and slunk back out the door. The regulars chanted, "Another one bites the dust, hey! Another one bites the dust!"

Dina resumed her position. "Shwilliam musta got himself into trouble and had to leave town for a while." She checked her manicure. "I honestly hope the good Lord gave that boy a big dick, 'cause he surely did short him on brains." Always on alert, she scanned the room for people needing fresh drinks. Everyone was good for now. "Anyway, I'd a thought Candi'd get down on her knees and thank God he's gone."

"That one spends too much time on her knees as it is," Richard said.

On the stool next to him, Molly snorted her beer. Her white cane clattered to the floor.

"Easy, honey." Miss Dina patted Molly's hand, chuckling. "She still ain't used to you, huh, Dick?"

"I'm thinking there may not be any getting used to him," said Molly, from under the bar. She located the cane and slid back onto her seat.

"By the way, Dina, is that asshole claiming to be some kind of Indian, excuuuuse me, *Native American*, still giving you trouble?" Richard looked out over the room, doing his best to sound casual.

"No, praise Jesus. I haven't seen his sorry ass in here for about a month now."

Richard smiled into his glass, took another swig.

"Miss Dina, do you think we could order some oysters to go with this beer?" Molly asked.

"I'm so sorry, baby, the kitchen closed early tonight. Darryl's little girl just made sixteen and he's making her a party." She waved at a regular walking in off Royal. "Hey my baby, how you doing? The usual?" Out of the corner of her mouth, Dina muttered, "When that one walks in, the bottles of Tito's all start quiverin'."

Molly turned to Richard. "To Darryl's little girl, then," she said, holding up her glass. "Hey, let's go over to Tierney's for a dozen, ok? I'm dying for oysters."

"You ate your first one ever last week and now you can't get enough? Fine by me." Richard stood up with difficulty, stretching his back.

"Good thing you can't see them, though, 'cause they are not pretty to look at."

He motioned to Dina in a sign language borne of many years' familiarity that conveyed they'd be back, to hold their tab open. From the other end of the bar, she nodded them away while expertly pouring four margaritas at once.

Molly retrieved her collapsible cane and took Richard's elbow. In the crowded Quarter, it was easier to use his arm for guidance.

Richard maneuvered her around the corner, past the tottering drunks, gawking tourists and window shoppers. He paused to kick at four pigeons pecking at some spilled garbage around a trash can. "Goddamn birds," he muttered, before guiding her into Tierney's Oyster Bar. They scored two open stools and placed an order for a dozen each and a pitcher.

Richard couldn't say he ever minded being seen with the pretty blind girl. He felt her presence at his side added to his street creds, even if they were obviously just drinking buddies. Still, part of him wanted to believe that some might imagine their relationship as more. And the more he drank, the easier that was to imagine.

CHAPTER TWENTY ONE

Wardell pulled the sticky bathroom door closed behind him and dug the little envelope out of the pocket of his baggy kitchen whites. A little lagniappe he took off the shucker whose hand he may or may not have broken. He tapped the white powder into a line on the edge of the filthy porcelain sink and snorted it through his last rolled up single.

He fell back onto the toilet, not noticing or caring that the seat was up and the wet, brown splatters all over the rim were now all over the back of his pants. His pupils dilated as the rush hit his brain. He could feel the blood pumping hard and fast through his veins. He felt strong, energized, bulletproof. "Shiiiiit, yeah!" he yelled to no one.

The other shucker working that night banged on the door, "Wardell, come on, man, get your useless ass back out here! You know we shorthanded tonight, man."

"Fuck you, muthafuckin' asshole!" he screamed, his spit landing on the graffitied wall and sliding over 'Philip Never Died' scratched into the chipped paint.

His rat's nest of illogical, tangled thoughts turned again to Ralaysia's betrayal. *That stupid ho don't know how good she got it! I love her so much, how could she do me like this? Somebody musta put the idea in her head.* His rotted brain cast about for a target other than Ralaysia and landed on the name his friend at the courthouse had read to him from the paperwork. *I bet that fucking old dude with the summons, Richard Some-muthafuckin-thing, did this. He prob'ly done give her the idea. Imma kill him for messing in my business!*

Wardell kicked the flimsy bathroom door open with a sneakered foot. The door banged against the wall and swung back to hit him in the face as he charged out of the bathroom, enraging him further. He kicked at the door behind him, breaking his pinky toe. With both hands cupped over his throbbing nose, he was hopping up and down on one foot in the dim hallway, cursing, when something caught his eye towards the front of the restaurant.

Peeking around the corner, Wardell saw, as if delivered from heaven, the object of his wrath at the bar sitting next to a beautiful girl with long black hair and ice-blue eyes, a couple of shots lined up in front of them.

The moment was magical. The throbbing in his nose and his toe ceased. He felt the stars align. He reached down and adjusted himself in his pants. Here was his lucky break, finally.

His thoughts congealed in an unfamiliar yet orderly fashion that astonished him with its clarity. He would make that old dude pay for turning Ralaysia against him. He would fuck up the old dude's woman. *You mess with mine, Imma mess with yours.* And from the looks of her, he'd have a real good time doing it.

Chapter Twenty Two

"So, you come here often, sweet thang?"

Richard shot daggers at the blond guy with the long, scraggly beard on the barstool on the other side of Molly. The guy ignored him. "You are soooo purdy, that's what Imma call you, Sweet Thang."

"Thanks, but no thanks," Molly said. "I'm just here to have a drink with my friend."

"That's cool, that's cool. But you can have one with me too, right? What you drinkin', Sweet Thang?"

"She said 'no thanks,' in case you didn't hear, buddy." Richard was in no hurry to get in a fight with the thirty-ish hipster sporting a ZZ Top beard, but the guy looked pretty drunk, so Richard assessed the odds to probably be in his favor. He conveniently dismissed the beer and shots he had himself already downed that afternoon, plus the forty year advantage the younger guy had on him.

Turning her back to the blond guy, Molly asked Richard, "So, I've got an idea for a piece for The Times Picayune on those six missing guys."

Richard twitched. He picked up his drink with a slightly trembling hand. "Why are you looking to get involved in all that writing stuff again? If I was you, I'd stay home in that jungle, excuse me, garden of yours all day with my cats if I didn't have to work."

"I love my plants, and your cats when they come over to visit, but they don't exactly stimulate me mentally. I think I might be ready to go back to work. I need to do something with my time or I'll go crazy. I already pitched my idea for this story to Ivy DeLongue. Do you know her?"

"Of course I know her. Crazy as a squirrel on crack that one, but who isn't around here? Trust me, you wouldn't want to work for her."

"This story could be a way for me to get back on the horse, so to speak. To see if I can still do it, you know? I really miss the newsroom sometimes."

Molly looked so sad right then, Richard was almost tempted to encourage her back into the profession she loved. Then he remembered how all those guys had gone missing in the first place.

"You'd be better off learning how to knit," he said. At her disbelieving look, he rushed on, "You could knit blankets for the babies at the hospital or socks for homeless people or something..." He trailed off.

"Nah, I'm hopeless with stuff like that but thanks for the suggestion."

"You could get yourself into some real trouble poking around in New Orleans. It's nothing like up north. I just don't want to end up reading about you in a police report."

"Aw, thanks, I'll be fine." She reached for her cane. "Hey, how bad are the bathrooms here?" She slid off the barstool, wobbling a little as she did so. "Wow, that last shot just kicked in hard."

Richard snorted, "You're in for a real treat. Good food, nasty bathrooms. So, about standard for the Quarter. Turn around and head straight to the wall. You've got a clear path there. Then make a right and go down the hallway. Women's is on the left. Want me to take you?"

"I'll take you, Sweet Thang," the blond guy made another half-hearted attempt, but seeing the look on Richard's face, decided it wasn't worth it.

Molly ignored the interruption. "Nope, I got this. I should have gone at En Garde, at least I know where everything is there. I'll find it, but if I'm not back in fifteen, send out a posse."

Richard gave a wave she couldn't see. Molly swept her cane in front of her as she easily crossed the room. When she felt it hit the wall, she turned right. She could tell by the change in acoustics when she entered a narrow hallway.

At the bar, the guy with the beard threw down some bills and stood up. "No hard feelings, right, Gramps?" he said as he staggered past Richard to the door. "Can't blame a guy for tryin'," he muttered.

Richard didn't acknowledge him aloud, but he made a mental addition to his List.

Wardell waited in the hall outside the kitchen. He couldn't believe his good luck. *That old fucker's chick is blind and she headin' straight for me!* This would be too easy. He slipped a long carving knife off the stainless steel kitchen workstation and held it at his side.

"Ah, 'scuse me, pretty lady, you looking for the bat'room?"

"Yes, thanks. It's on the left, right?" Molly giggled, "I mean, isn't it?"

"That one ain't working, but we got another one back a here. Lemme show you." Wardell seized her upper arm in an iron grip.

Molly was used to having strangers force unwanted assistance upon her. If she so much as paused near a crosswalk with her white cane, someone was sure to grab her elbow and start dragging her across the street, all the while telling her about their grandma or third cousin twice-removed who was blind too, and so brave about it. If she wasn't vigilant about the do-gooders, she could easily end up somewhere she hadn't intended. Her guard was down, however, after a couple of beers and two shots, so when Wardell took her arm, it didn't immediately set off any mental distress signals. But when she felt his sweaty palm slap over her mouth, her internal alarm bell went off like an air raid siren.

She felt something sharp pressed to her throat as he whispered in her ear, "Not even one lil' squeak, bitch." He pulled her off her feet towards the propped-open back door and out into the dank alley.

Molly's cane clattered to the grimy hallway floor and rolled to a stop against the scuffed baseboard.

Chapter Twenty Three

Richard had a good buzz going. It didn't take much these days. He hadn't done tequila shots in years, but this was okay, this was fun. He blinked at the salt residue on the wrinkled skin between his thumb and forefinger, the chewed slices of lime discarded on his napkin. He'd even do it again if Molly suggested it. He considered ordering another dozen oysters for them to share.

He had lost track of time, sitting at the bar, people watching and listening to the music. Where was that girl? He thought about checking on her but he knew she'd hate that. Molly valued her independence. He ordered them another round and settled back to enjoy his buzz.

CHAPTER TWENTY FOUR

The streetlights came on as Candi window shopped along Bourbon in her frayed hotpants and scuffed white patent leather go-go boots. The orange purse she picked up at the Goodwill store over on Jeff Davis Boulevard swung from one shoulder. Business was slow and with Shwilliam still missing, she didn't have to answer to anyone. She chewed her bubblegum and cruised along the street like a vacant taxi with the "For Hire" light turned off.

At the corner of Bourbon and St. Louis she put some change in a can in front of three boys with bottle caps glued to the bottoms of their sneakers. *When the Saints Go Marching In* blared from an ancient boombox wrapped in gray duct tape while the boys tap danced, competing with the cacophony of music from the bars up and down the street.

On the next corner, Violin Girl seduced a Bach concerto from her instrument for an appreciative, if mostly drunk, audience. Candi felt bad she had no more money to contribute. She loved the violin, even wished her mama had gotten her lessons when she was little, but that was probably last on a long list of things she and her eight siblings had needed growing up.

She decided to cut over to Royal. Candi liked peeking in the art galleries. She'd never dream of actually going inside any of them, of course. Her favorite paintings were the bright primary colors of the Blue Dog series.

She tripped along the sidewalk, dodging tourists and doorway bums with their dogs, lethargic in the heat. She slowed, but did not fully stop, to admire the one-of-a-kind gems in the window of Miss Jeanne's antique store. Candi crossed herself out of habit and kissed the tarnished crucifix around her neck.

Miss Jeanne was so old everyone said she'd been selling treasures out of that same shop since the 1700s. They said that she and her assistant, David, must both be vampires or something. People spoke in hushed tones about the real bad things that supposedly happened on the regular in the upstairs rooms there. Things nobody wanted to think about for too long.

Miss Jeanne had an iron gray helmet of hair, a sweater set that she wore with a string of perfect, ancient pearls and a mid-calf length skirt with sensible shoes, as befitting a Southern woman of her advanced age and station. When not behind the display cases in her shop, she occasionally employed an ornate ruby-eyed, ram's headed cane with which to steady herself.

No one ever noticed David, except to note he was a Black man of indeterminate age, whom Miss Jeanne still openly referred to as her "boy," as if she were unaware that this was no longer acceptable. No one ever dared correct her.

Candi didn't want to think about vampires, but she sure did enjoy looking at all the pretty rings on their pink velvet displays in the window. Vampire talk always made her nervous. In her line of work, she was overly familiar with New Orleans' nightlife and knew a lot of the talk wasn't true, but enough of it was. In Candi's experience, there wasn't much difference between a real vampire and some freak convinced they're a vampire. That party would go down the same either way and she was of a mind to steer clear if she had the choice. She picked up her pace again, turned riverside on Toulouse.

She passed the lonesome alley that ran behind Tierney's Oyster Bar. She took customers in there once in a while late at night. This evening though, she was enjoying her free time since Shwilliam wasn't bossing her around. Candi didn't want to spoil her stroll with thoughts of work, so she pointed her nose the other way as she traipsed past the darkened alley.

Chapter Twenty Five

Molly thrashed and kicked at her attacker. She could feel warm rivulets running down her neck from where he held the knife pinned to her throat. She couldn't hear anything over her own pulse pounding in her ears. She fought harder, twisting in his grasp. She hadn't lived through the car wreck and all that rehab to die in a filthy alley behind a bar in New Orleans.

Wardell tightened his grip. *For such a skinny bitch, this one fights like a fuckin' rougarou.* He wasn't real big himself, but he had good upper body strength from the pushups and weight lifting he did in prison where he fought off the other prisoners in his block on the daily. *Fucking faggots!* He pushed that memory aside.

He dragged the struggling girl into the back alleyway behind a wobbly, three-wheeled dumpster, and threw her face up onto the broken concrete there, slimy with rotting kitchen refuse.

Wardell heard the sound of bone on stone as Molly's head hit the cement. She stilled, her head lolled to one side.

"Things just got a whole lot easier," he said aloud, barely registering the faint sounds of music and patrons laughing at the front of the restaurant.

Using the sliver of light from the open kitchen door, Wardell knelt, straddling her unconscious body. He ran the narrow blade down the middle of her chest and stomach, drawing a thin red line on her skin as he sliced open her shirt, then her bra, then her jeans. Neither the welling blood from Molly's wound nor her immobility deterred him in the least in his lust to avenge Ralaysia's treachery and Richard's supposed meddling.

Wardell lightly carved his initials into the skin of her chest, his tongue clenched between his teeth. A ropey string of saliva dripped onto Molly's bare stomach. Crimson droplets trickled from the slashes and rolled down her sides, soaking into her ruined blouse. He was happy with the way the "W" came out, but the curves of the "S" were harder. He was considering going over them again when Molly groaned.

"You ain't dead? Yeah, thass right. I want you awake for this, bitch," he muttered, fumbling for the drawstring on his now blood-stained white pants.

Chapter Twenty Six

Candi thought she heard something as she passed by the alley. *Maybe Beuletta got her a trick in there. Nah, she probably still stove up from Shwilliam beating on her.* She slowed her walk. Her orange purse stopped mid-swing, hanging limply off her arm.

But something didn't feel right down that narrow passageway and so far Candi had stayed alive in her line of work by paying attention to her feelings, mostly because her occasional fully coherent thought didn't always make it to the front of her brain. *Maybe somebody's needing help.* Candi retraced her steps to the dark mouth of the alley.

"Beuletta?" she called. This time she was sure she heard rustling and a whimper. *Uh oh, something ain't right.* She looked both ways down Toulouse, seeing no one on this stretch of street.

From Bourbon, she heard the strains of 'Brown Sugar' through the open doors of Funky 544 competing with 'Wobble Baby Wobble' from Tropical Isle. Candi took a deep breath and stepped into the dark alley.

***

Molly tried to roll over. She hurt everywhere. The last thing she remembered was the reek of perspiration and fish and a sticky hand on her face. Her eyes snapped open by reflex but they were of no help.

The skin on her chest was on fire, her head was pounding and there was something heavy holding her down.

The overpowering stench of his sweat brought her fully around. She screamed as she realized the guy from Tierney's was on top of her, trying to force her knees apart. Wardell leaned his face into hers and bit her bottom lip, hard.

"I already done tol' you, bitch. Shut. The fuck. Up," he panted in her ear, his mouth shiny red with her blood.

Candi crept into the alley and picked up a piece of two by four discarded in the dirt. One peek around the dumpster was all she needed. Candi was all skin and bones but she was wiry and she was motivated to help another hard-working girl. In the pale light from the open screen door of Tierney's kitchen, she swung at the back of the creep's head like she was Barry Bonds swinging for the cheap seats at CandlestickPark. She connected with a resounding thunk. He rolled off the woman and into the dirt without a sound, his fingers still tangled in the drawstring of his blood-splattered kitchen worker pants.

The two by four slid from Candi's hands. *Oh Lawd! Them police are gonna be after me now for more'n just turning tricks and whatever!*

She bent over the woman. "Hey, honey? You ok?" Candi gawped at all the blood concealing the woman's identity, but then something clicked. "Oh, Lawd Gawd, no! Molly? Miss Molly, is that you?"

There was no answer from the woman splayed on the ground but the guy twitched where he lay nearby. Candi rolled him over with the toe of her go-go boot. She recognized that face from around the

Quarter. "Awww, no! Not that badass Wardell dude! I gone and done it this time!" she whispered aloud, twisting her fingers together.

Candi heard footsteps coming slowly down the dark alleyway. She scrabbled for the two by four. Clutching it to her chest, she backed into the shadows with her eyes squeezed shut until she felt the metal bulk of the dumpster at her back.

Her heart pounded in her chest like a bass drum as she prepared to defend herself against whoever was coming into the alley. The footsteps came even with the corner of the dumpster and her eyes popped open. She understood at once that resistance was futile. Desperation rode the sharp intake of breath into her lungs, flooding her body with adrenaline.

Candi recognized the vampire lady, Miss Jeanne, and her boy, David, in the thin light streaming from Tierney's back door.

The piece of wood slipped unnoticed from her grasp as she clutched the cheap crucifix at her neck with both hands and began to pray. *Hail Mary, Mother of God pray for our sins now and at the hour of our death...*

Miss Jeanne strode past Candi standing rigid with fear in the shadows and right up to where Wardell lay in the dirt, his dreadlocks splayed out around him. She nudged him with the tip of her ram's headed cane. He produced a low moan.

Without looking around she stated, "This one's no longer your concern, girl."

Candi's knees almost gave out as she stood shaking against the reeking dumpster.

"And if you know what's good for you, I was never here tonight." Miss Jeanne turned towards Candi, the light streaming from the back of the bar glinting in her inhuman eyes. She moved aside and motioned to David, who effortlessly hefted the groaning body over his shoulder like a sack of crawfish. Wardell's long dreads streamed down David's back.

Candi's bladder let go and she felt the hot gush of pee streaming down her bare legs, splattering her go-go boots.

Without a word, David followed Miss Jeanne's sensible shoes out of the shadowed alley in the direction of her shop. The echo of their footsteps faded into the black stillness of the side street. The faint music from the corner bars on Bourbon played on. From inside Tierney's, Candi heard an angry voice yelling for someone named Wardell to get his ass in gear.

Her attention swung back to Molly lying on her back, beaten and bleeding into the dirt of the alley. Candi's mouth hung open. She closed it with a snap. Then she opened it again and shrieked, "HELP!" at the top of her scrawny lungs.

Chapter Twenty Seven

Wardell blinked.

His eyes focused on thick ropes of cobwebs, heavy with the dust of time, hanging from blackened rafters overhead. An odd, dry odor, both musty and sulfurous filled his nostrils. His head pulsed with pain. *Ah, man, feels like someone hit me with a fucking bat!* Memory flooded in…

"Shit!" he tried to sit up before realizing he was strapped down. He struggled to no avail to free his spreadeagled limbs. A rustling noise behind him drew his attention and he froze, listening. "What the muthafuckin' hell is this? Get me outta here!" he yelled, his voice echoing around the empty attic room.

Scritch, scritch, scritch. He could hear something dragging across the floor but his restraints didn't allow him to see what it was. "Hey! What the fuck? You hearing me, muthafucka?" His head pounded harder with the effort of shouting.

Out of the corner of his eye, he thought he saw movement. He swung his head to the left. "What kinda fucked up shit is this?" he yelled just before a hooked claw wrenched his head the other way.

A creature with red eyes, about the height of a man, considered him. Wardell stared in disbelief at the fiend's face as it morphed from leathery wrinkles surrounding a slobbering gash of needle-sharp teeth, to that of a white man in a ripped, too small black tee shirt, his greasy hair askew.

Wardell blinked hard. "What the fuck!"

The creature mutated back, its too-high, pointed ears twitching. "Com'ere cher, you," it croaked around a mouthful of dripping fangs.

Wardell's shrieks echoed off the rafters as the red-eyed fiend bent down close to scoop out first the left eyeball, then the right with a long, yellowed talon.

The fiend spat a gob of gristle onto the dusty floor as Wardell howled and writhed and bucked against his restraints. There was a flapping of wings and much hissing as the others scuttled after it.

When he could scream no longer, the garret was quiet except for the sucking and slurping of the red-eyed fiend and a scritch, scritch, scritching sound as the others dragged their scaly wings across the dry-rotted cypress planks to beg for scraps.

Chapter Twenty Eight

Richard had to do something. The goddamn cops were useless, they had zero leads on Molly's attacker. He was on his own with this one, as usual. *If you want something done right, you have to do it yourself.* Revenge was an idea Richard could get behind.

He had called in all his favors, asked around, questioned everyone he knew. He put pressure on acquaintances around town who lived in the shadows, on the fringe of society. *And that accounts for 90% of the population of New Orleans,* he thought sourly, his elbows on the dinged-up bar at the Cart Horse.

He was taking a well-deserved break today. *Jesus and Aunt Jemima, I'm getting too old for this crap.* He'd been feeling his age lately, the worry over Molly taking its toll. Doc Leo said she'd be alright, but, Christ! He felt guilty as hell for not protecting her. His hip was acting up, too, and he noticed he couldn't stay asleep at night anymore. *What the hell is that about?* he wondered. Richard didn't believe in doctors. *Probably'd just write me a prescription for something to get me hooked. Nooo, thank you!*

He stared into his glass and mentally reviewed the facts. *Molly's in the hospital. She can't describe the freak who attacked a blind girl. There were no witnesses, just that brain dead Candace whispering some crap about vampires in my ear. Vampires! Christ in a crosswalk, I can't stand stupid people! Don't they know there are enough real bad humans walking around without inventing monsters?*

A car crept by on Chartres Street, rap music blaring. Richard threw back his drink. *The real kicker is that Molly got attacked while I sat up front at Tierney's drinking beer, doing shots and slurping oysters.* He shook his head, motioned for Christopher to bring him another.

A tourist couple pulled up barstools uncomfortably close to him. *Haven't these goddamn people ever heard of personal space?*

The man had hardly sat down when he turned to the local on the other side of him. "You'll never guess what we just saw! We thought it was a horse coming down the street, right, Helen?"

"Oh, yah! Sounded just like a horse! So we didn't pay too much attention, right? Ya know they've got horses pulling those buggies here in the Voo Carry, right?"

The regular sipped his drink, caught eyes in the mirror with Chris, who stifled a smile.

"And then we did look, right, Helen? We turned and looked up the street and what did we see?"

"A guy walking on the street with one of those, what do you call it, Phil?"

"A fake leg!"

"That's right! A fake leg with a real horse's hoof at the bottom making that clip-clop noise. Ya know that noise, right? Just walking along like natural, one real leg, one horse hoof leg!"

The regular gulped his beer and stood up. "That's crazy! Y'all be careful and enjoy the rest of your time here, okay?" he smiled, before heading down the street to Turtle Bay, where he could enjoy a quiet drink in peace.

The tourists turned towards Richard. "So crazy! Didja ever hear of anything so crazy?"

Ahhh hell, no. He couldn't take this crap today. Everyone knew Horsehoof Man, he's good people. The bartender plunked a Jameson's on the rocks in front of Richard, kept his hand on the glass until he looked up.

"All the saints in heaven, Chris. You're a man among men."

"This one's on the house if you play nice, okay, Dick?" the bartender whispered, letting go. He slung a damp towel over one shoulder, turned towards the tourists. "Hey, have you two seen our jukebox? It's got some good tunes." He pointed to the opposite end of the bar.

"A jukebox!" Helen exclaimed. "I do love the oldies. Come on, Phil, let's see what songs they've got in there. Ya got any change in your pocket?"

Richard sighed in relief before returning to his dilemma. He needed to redeem himself somehow. How was he going to find Molly's attacker?

Then he remembered the pushy blond guy with the ZZ Top beard. That piece of crap had been overly interested in Molly. He was at Tierney's that night and he had rubbed Richard the wrong way. *I believe I have my man.* The blond guy moved to the top of Richard's mental List.

He threw back his drink and signaled to Chris for the check.

CHAPTER TWENTY NINE

At the end of the hottest day in August, the two thousand Red Dress runners were exhausted, the sun and copious amounts of beer having leached every bit of energy from their bodies and their souls.

Every year both men and women donned their reddest and most outrageous costumes to raise money for local charities. Although it was technically called a run, everyone signed up knowing you can't run without spilling your beer. Besides, no one runs in August in New Orleans. Even born and bred natives can barely manage a saunter or an amble. Certainly no one sashays out of doors in August. Many entrants never run a single step, preferring to do their part for charity with their entry fee and outlandish costumes.

Richard hadn't crossed paths with Candi yet to have her confirm the attacker's description, but he was confident his conclusion was correct. A little research had informed him that his target was a participating local this year. A charity run didn't seem like something a murderous would-be rapist would do, but hey, Richard understood everyone has their eccentricities. This guy had a motive, in that his overtures at Tierney's had been spurned that night, and he could be placed close to the scene of the attack. Most importantly, he had pissed Richard off with his smart aleck talk and, worst of all, by calling him, "Gramps."

There was no way Richard was going to wear a skimpy red costume, but he blended into the crowd easily enough by wearing a red tee shirt. It had been easy to pick out his target by standing near the registration desk and waiting for the guy to pick up his identifying numbered paper square (406) and the safety pins to attach it.

The long blond beard lay on the bare chest of Richard's target today. He watched from afar as the guy, wearing only a red tutu with a matching Speedo and red fishnet stockings with matching Keds, pinned his identifying number through the mesh on one thigh.

Richard trailed Tutu Guy for most of the day, sipping only water from a plastic cup. *Gotta keep my wits about me.* As expected, the guy didn't run, instead opting to hang in the shade near Crescent Park and consume mass quantities of beer with many of the other "runners."

Now the event was over. The sun had gone down but it wasn't much cooler, the humidity still oppressive. Most everyone had dispersed back into the air-conditioned comfort of their homes or a favorite watering hole.

Richard followed behind as the pale, bare chested guy weaved his way home in the enervating heat, tripping over everything and nothing in his path. Crows cawed at him from the overhead telephone wires in the rapidly deepening dusk.

I wonder where he's got his house keys, Richard mused, right before thinking *Ah, Jesus, no! I did not need that visual.* His disgust fueled his craving for revenge for Molly and redemption for himself.

The blond guy in front of him stumbled, going down on one knee, ripping his fishnets before staggering to his feet yet again and taking a right onto the Lafitte Greenway. He never once turned to see if anyone was walking behind him.

This will be a piece of cake, Richard thought, his mood lightening immediately. *A literal walk in the park.* Now he had a plan. He was just a man out for an evening walk on the Greenway. A very hot man, though. The temperature was still in the high eighties. Sweat rolled down his back and into the waistband of his jeans. For a second, he wished he were the kind of man who wore shorts, but that would never happen.

With the moon rising in the sky, he sauntered along behind Tutu Guy, who seemed to be concentrating solely on getting his feet to work in unison. Other strollers were few and far between along the Greenway at this hour. Richard gave silent thanks to the Parks Department, who were behind in their maintenance schedule yet again, ensuring that many of the overhead lights were either burned out, shot out or never worked to begin with. The traffic noise from Broad Street got fainter the farther along the Greenway they walked.

Suddenly, Tutu Guy lurched off the path and into the grass. *Christ eating Cheerios, this guy's so drunk he probably wouldn't have made it home anyway. This should be effortless.*

Tutu Guy tottered to the edge of the large, open, concrete-lined waterway that ran alongside the path. After the recent heavy rain, it was six feet deep with runoff from the city's drainage system. He appeared to be fumbling with the front of his red speedo and having great difficulty. The evening sounds of insects in the bushes along the Greenway stilled.

Richard crept up behind him, shaking out his telescoping police baton, another gift from a friend on the force. With a quick rip, he tore the paper ID from Tutu Guy's thigh while the drunken man concentrated on peeing.

One well-placed thunk, a big splash, and it was done. If a bloom of crimson appeared, it was undetectable in the turbid water. The floating long blond beard was the last thing to disappear as the body sank.

The insects in the bushes resumed their night songs.

Richard collapsed the baton and put it back in the pocket of his baggy jeans. He scanned the surface of the water in the light of the newly-risen moon until the ripples disappeared. He stayed only long enough to make sure no bubbles arose from the murky depths.

He felt unsatisfied somehow. He wasn't into torture, but it didn't feel fair that this pervert was just, Boom, gone after all he had put Molly through. Still, it was over. This freak wouldn't hurt Molly or anyone else again.

Richard was home in time to feed the cats and be in bed before ten o'clock. He slept through the night for the first time in weeks.

Chapter Thirty

"I done tried to tell you a million times, Dickie." Candi fidgeted with the crucifix at her neck. "It was that nasty Wardell Shruggs guy from around the Quarter."

She downed a hefty portion of the cold water Richard had given her. Recapping the bottle, she rolled it across the back of her neck. Outside, the temperature was fast approaching one hundred degrees, but it was a comfortable seventy-two in the front room of Richard's house, his home office. And it was definitely much cooler than in Candi's tiny house across the street where her sole air conditioner had recently started making dying noises.

"For the hundredth time, Candace, don't call me Dickie. Wait, did you say Wardell Shruggs? Why does that name sound familiar?" Richard opened a desk drawer, pulled out the manila envelope Beau had given him. He shuffled through the papers contained within and pulled out a photo. "What color was the guy you saw?"

"Huh?"

Richard sighed, slid a photo across his desk. "Is that him?"

Candi jerked back in her seat. The calico on her lap leaped to the floor and stalked away. "Yeah, that's him. He's a real bad guy. Was a bad guy, whatever. Why you got his picture?"

"I was supposed to serve him with a summons before all this happened. Didn't get around to it." Richard leaned back in his creaky wooden desk chair with the well-worn cushion and absentmindedly scratched behind the ears of the tabby on his lap.

Horrified, he stared at the photo as he processed this new information. *Holy Jesus! Did I take out an innocent guy? That Tutu Guy definitely isn't the one in this picture. Which also means Wardell is still out there...*

Candi shifted in her chair, bringing his focus back to her.

"Jesus's joystick, why didn't you tell me this before?"

Candi picked up one of the new kittens that had been batting a catnip-filled felt mouse around the floor. She nuzzled its soft white fur. "I been trying to tell you something else, too, Dickie." She lowered her voice although they were alone in the house.

Taking a deep breath, she made up her mind. "This here's real important. You gotta listen to me. That Miss Jeanne you met in Molly's hospital room? She...she and that David..."

"What, Candace, what?" Richard couldn't contain his frustration. "Christ on skiis, spit it out!"

"Don't be yelling at me, Dickie. Anyway, you ain't been listening to me all before this, but now you wanna hear everything all sudden-like?"

"Mother of all that is holy, give me strength!" he pleaded to the ceiling. "Are you going to feed me more of that horse crap about vampires, because I don't have time for that. Just tell me if you're sure it was this exact guy you saw attack Miss Molly."

"I'm trying to be real pacific here, Dickie, but you still ain't listening to me."

He bit his tongue, silently petitioning the heavens for patience, then he counted to ten.

She furtively glanced around the office as if someone might be hidden in one of the bookcases or file cabinets. "Can I trust you with a secret that nobody knows?

"Yes, Candace. And, by the way, that's pretty much the definition of a secret."

"Huh? Anyway, I think God done encrusted me with a gift to tell what people are about or whatever."

"Here we go," Richard looked at his watch. He raked his hand through his sparse gray hair and stood up. "We're done here. Thanks for the information about this Wardell guy."

"He ain't coming back neither. The vampire lady, Miss Jeanne and David done took him away and ..."

Richard held up his hand. "Enough with this crap!"

Candi put the kitten on the floor. It arched its back in mock bravado before skittering sideways under Richard's desk. "Alright, but you just be real careful when you're by Miss Jeanne, okay Dickie?"

"Yup, I'll do that. See you around."

"And please don't be telling her I snitched on her and David or tomorrow I could wake up dead or whatever."

"Sure, Candace, don't worry about it."

But Candi was worried. She took her unfinished bottle of water with her as she crossed the street to the dilapidated rental she shared with Beuletta. The orchid plant Molly had given her sat wilting in the blistering sun at the top of the steps. Candi moved it into the shade and poured the last of her cold water over it before pulling open the unpainted screen door.

CHAPTER THIRTY ONE

Chamonix, France, Year 1091

"Maman, s'il te plait!" Bazile's voice became fainter the farther Jeanne staggered into the woods of the estate, her heart stuttering in her sunken chest. He'd made no effort to come after her when she fled the manor house and somehow that terrified her even more.

Jeanne stumbled blindly through the underbrush. An oak branch swept her nightcap from her head, causing her long grey braid to slither free halfway down her back. Her flapping nightgown caught on a deadfall, momentarily halting her flight. She frantically tugged it free as the stark shadows cast by the full moon played over her flailing form. Wheezing with each breath, she forced her arthritic legs onward.

The gamekeeper's cottage appeared ahead in a small clearing. Jeanne staggered to the wooden door and banged on it feebly. "Hasten!" she cried. "My own son has become afflicted with a malady the likes of which I dare not describe!"

A tousled young man wrenched the door open, a small dagger in one hand. "What is the meaning of this disturbance?" Recognition and shock flashed over his sleep-addled face. "Madame! What has happened to bring you here this night in such a state?"

Their heads jerked upwards as one upon hearing a dull thud on the thatch of the roof. Jeanne gasped, her hand to her racing heart. Behind the woodsman in the darkened room, Bazile appeared, backlit by the meagre glow of the dying fire in the hearth. He reached out, snapping the young man's neck with one hand and kicking the body aside when it hit the floor. "Maman, do not discomfit yourself. Henceforth we shall be together forever." He pleaded with her, "You know I cannot be without you. Why will you not trust me in this, as you have trusted me to husband our estates these many years since Father's passing?"

"Do not dare to call me 'mother,' you fiend! You are not my issue!" Jeanne hissed. Trembling violently, she squinted around the dimly lit hovel, searching for something, anything, a miracle to turn back time, to before she awoke to find this creature standing over her, beseeching her to join him in his depraved damnation. Her eyes skittered over the gamekeeper's twisted body on the earthen floor, the most recent atrocity in a night full of horrors.

"You are a devil in the image of my son!" she shrieked.

Jeanne's will left her suddenly as she realized the truth of it, the hopelessness. She summoned the last of her strength and raised her eyes to his, so familiar yet so unrecognizably incandescent in the flickering firelight. "I am old," she spat. "Kill me if you must, but end this nightmare."

"All will be made clear, maman. This is no nightmare," he murmured, grasping her withered arm and pulling her gently inside the cottage. "This is eternity."

PART II

Chapter Thirty Two

David stood in the kitchen of the apartment he shared with Jeanne over her antique store. He stared at the long dreadlocks splayed out over the black and white checkered floor tiles as if trying to escape the blue tarp concealing the dead body. David fingered them lightly. *What a waste,* he thought. This one was destined for the vat of chemicals at the uptown furniture stripping business David used frequently, but he was loath to consign those cool dreads to being dissolved into nothingness. David had never been able to grow his hair that long, but he had always admired the look.

His mind flashed back to a clearing in an Amazonian jungle. Small brown men dancing around a fire. Gourds of chicha passed reverently hand to hand. Rhythmic pounding on forest deerhide drums. Tsantsas! *Maybe a little experiment today? I've got nothing better to do.*

He twisted the head off the neck easily and tucked the tarp around the rest of the drained body. That part could go into the furniture stripper's vat. The fiend's leftovers were of no interest to Jeanne or to him.

He studied the head in his hands. The mouth hung open slightly, the brown eyelids were closed as if Wardell were lightly dozing. The dreadlocks cascading through his hands were easily two feet long. He placed the head on the kitchen counter and pulled the sharpest knife from the drawer. Carefully parting the hair up the back, he tried to remember how that Shuar chief had done it.

Admittedly, the guy had been a bit agitated when David dropped from the sumaumeira tree that night into the middle of their spirit ceremony. The whole tribe had thought he was a devil. *And they weren't wrong!* He chuckled, remembering how the chief's hands had shaken so hard, he almost ruined the shrunken head David had forced him to prepare as a demonstration.

And David did recognize the artistry of it. The centuries of his existence had given him an appreciation of good craftsmanship in all its many forms. He remembered most of the intricate procedure; he had visited specifically to attain that rather esoteric knowledge. Those sorts of pursuits helped to alleviate the boredom of his lengthy presence in the world. *Why not put that knowledge to use today?* he thought.

He slit the scalp up the back of the skull with the knife and carefully peeled it and the face from the bone. He trimmed the torn skin at the neck with the kitchen scissors. *Not culturally correct, but the right tool for the right job and all that.* It was difficult keeping the long hair out of the way, but he did his best.

David thought about making a goblet for Jeanne from the skull, but he had enough work in front of him and she probably wouldn't appreciate it in her current state anyway. He placed it on the floor next to the body for the trip to the furniture stripper's vat. *Those corrosive chemicals really do a great job,* he remembered. *I should use that place more often.*

Next, he turned the face inside out like a rubber mask and scraped out the bits of flesh, muscle and the little bit of eyeball still attached on the inside. That fiend always went for the eyes first, he knew. He rummaged around in the cutlery drawer until he found some twine and stainless steel pins normally used for sewing a turkey shut after stuffing. Righting the skin again, he pierced the lips with three of the pins, then secured them by entwining the string around them in a figure eight pattern. *Again, not culturally authentic, but easier than sharpening three sticks and trying to shove them through these puffy lips.* Just for fun, he also sewed the eyelids shut, as the chief had told him was customary in the Shuar tribe. They believed sewing the eyes and mouth closed ensured the spirit of the dead person would remain trapped inside the skull. Wardell's eyelashes poked through the stitches unevenly. *My needlework isn't great, maybe I should have practiced on the body first.* But he knew he could be a bit of a perfectionist. He adjusted a few of the stitches. *That's better.*

David put on some smooth jazz while he puttered around the kitchen. The problem of what to do about Jeanne retreated from his mind. He felt peaceful, his mind at rest while his hands were busy. *I should try to schedule more 'me' time in the future. Self care is important.* David found he quite liked doing crafts. Maybe he'd try scrapbooking next.

Taking a short break, he peeked in on Jeanne. She was slumped on the couch, covered in gore, watching her soap operas. He made a mental note to pick up more stain remover. He closed the kitchen door quietly and headed out back to the garden.

Firing up the gas grill, David put their two largest crab pots on the burners, one filled with sand and a few smooth rocks, the other with water. He did a little weeding while he waited for the water to boil, fortuitously finding a small ball from the dog next door under the canna lilies. *Perfect!* He set it aside for later.

Next he carefully gathered the head's long hair and found a rubber band to secure it. He dropped the head, now really just a face and scalp with hair, in the boiling water along with some cypress fronds for the tannin. He wasn't exactly sure of the amount of tannin in cypress, so he dumped in a box of tea bags he found in the kitchen cupboard for good measure.

He remembered the Shuar chief being adamant that this was the tricky part. Boil a head too long and all the hair would fall out, defeating David's purpose. Boil it too short a time, and you're stuck with a mushy, gelatinous head, which would also defeat David's purpose of being able to admire the long dreadlocks forever. He set a timer for half an hour and stirred the sand and rocks in the second crab pot with a big wooden spoon so they'd be uniformly hot. He was able to replant the sago palm in the corner of the garden before the timer went off.

Pulling the head from the boiling water by its hair, he could see immediately that it was much smaller than it had been by about two-thirds. There were some brown strands floating in the greasy water, but most remained attached to the scalp. He admired his work as it dripped on the grass, marveling at the little ears. Misshapen as they now were, they were still recognizable as very small ears on a very small head.

He dried it off with paper towels as best he could, then placed it in the other crab pot and covered it with the hot sand. The chief had been reluctant to explain this important step, but after David had torn apart three of his tribespeople, he'd been much more open-minded about sharing. He'd shown David exactly how his tribe dried and hardened the heads from the inside out, getting the hot sand into all those little nooks and crannies. *Like an English muffin!* The hard-to-reach places like the eye sockets and inside the nasal cavity took some finesse. David couldn't for the life of him though, remember how long to leave the head in the sand, so he checked it every ten minutes until it seemed completely dry.

Back at the kitchen table, he brushed the grass off the dog's ball he'd found, draped the face and scalp over it to hold the shape, and set to work smoothing the skin with one of the hot flat rocks. Wardell's skin had darkened throughout the boiling process, and this necessary step darkened it even further, but that didn't matter a bit, the skin color wasn't David's concern. At this point the face was barely recognizable as human, and whether it was male or female was difficult to tell. David thought about where to display his creation. Anyone who knew Wardell could conceivably recognize him if they looked closely enough. *Maybe I'll hang it in the shop window just for fun,* he thought.

When the hot rock began to cool, David removed the rubber band and shook the dreads into place. To his delight, once the hair was completely dry, it remained satisfyingly realistic-looking. Using the last of the twine, he sewed a loop to the middle top of the scalp and hung it on the back yard fence to finish curing in the sun.

Feeling pleased with his afternoon's endeavors, David decided to treat himself. He felt the need to stretch his legs. *An invigorating hunt under the moon at the old golf course near City Park would be the perfect end to a lovely day.* He jingled the change in his pocket and headed for the streetcar.

An hour later, David was slurping coyote blood in an abandoned and overgrown field, wondering if there was a market for shrunken heads in New Orleans.

Chapter Thirty Three

Candi side-eyed the display window as she approached. The last thing she wanted was to run into Miss Jeanne or that creepy David, but if you're walking in August in New Orleans, your path is determined by which side of the street has the shade. At this time of day, Miss Jeanne's antique shop was on the shadowed side of Royal Street. Plus, Miss Jeanne always had pretty shiny things in her window and Candi couldn't resist a peek. Her steps slowed in spite of herself.

A silver necklace studded with blue stones caught her eye first. Candi didn't know the names of the colorful gems she was looking at, but she didn't need to know them to enjoy looking at them. She came to a full stop and stared into the window. Brilliant yellow stones encircled a bracelet nestled on a crush of satin. A tastefully calligraphied sign explained the ornate black and gold ring that next caught her attention was a "poison ring," previously owned by Lucrezia Borgia. Candi frowned into the plate glass window. "Who'd wanna wear a ring that's gonna poison you?" she wondered aloud, scratching her head. Candi often felt she was missing something, but she never let the feeling bother her for long.

The spell of the pretty shiny things broken, she began to walk on when her attention was yet again diverted. Towards the back of the window, off to one side, almost as an afterthought, hanging from its long dreadlocks, was what appeared to be a shrunken human head.

Candi stepped closer, squinting into the window. What was it about that little face? She tilted her head, the better to picture that face the way she had seen it last. It kind of looked like... She bent over to one side, tilting her head more. A memory from a terror-filled night bloomed in her mind. "Oh Lawd!"

Candi stumbled back, away from the window and collided with a girl in a school uniform passing on the sidewalk. "Do you see that?" she asked the girl loudly, pointing one trembling arm at the glass.

The girl cupped her hands around her eyes, peering into the window. "Cool! You think that's real? Looks like one of those shrunken heads from South America." She turned towards Candi. "I read a book about headhunters last semester. There's this tribe... Hey, you okay?"

Candi said, "I gotta go, but you have a nice day, sweetie, okay?" She started off back the way she had come, then stopped. "You study hard in school now, ya hear?" she said before breaking into a run.

***

"Dickie, I tell you, it's him! But it's just his head, that Wardell guy that hurt Miss Molly?" Candi hopped up and down in her distress. "He's hanging there plain as day in Miss Jeanne's window! But his face is tiny and all shmooshed up like this," Candi wrinkled her nose and pushed her cheeks together with her hands. "He's got them nasty old long dreads just like always, 'cept now he's plain dead, I guess!" She took a deep breath. "And he ain't got no body neither."

Richard didn't even look up from his cluttered desk. He was trying to finish filing an insurance claim report for a client so he could relax in his lounger and catch the Saints game. *Holy hell, I hate doing crap like this. Goddamn paperwork is gonna kill me,* he thought. "Uh huh, thanks, Candace. I'll be sure to ask Jeanne about that."

"No, Dickie! You ain't listening! You can't just walk up all reg'lar-like and ask her! I done told you before, Miss Jeanne and her guy, David, they took that Wardell from behind Tierney's that night and they, they musta…"

Richard slammed down his pen. "They must have what, Candace? Cut off his head and shrunk it? I thought they were supposed to be vampires. I'm no expert, but Jesus Christmas, I think you're getting your monsters mixed up." He picked up his pen again. "Now go on, I've got to finish this paperwork or I'm gonna miss the start of the game and Christ in a cab, you don't want to be the cause of that."

Candi slunk to the door, defeated. "No one never listens to me," she muttered.

"Make sure the new kitten doesn't scoot by you on the way out. And Candace, don't call me Dickie!"

CHAPTER THIRTY FOUR

1519, Florence, Italy

"The air in here is quite noxious!" Bazile unlatched the villa's casement window and pushed it open. "Do you never allow in the fresh air, Nardo?"

"Of course not! The pestilence arrives with the night air and the morning breezes hasten the drying of my oils. Even a few second's difference can throw off my technique." Leonardo waggled his bushy gray eyebrows, "And my intent, if my model is a comely lad."

"You should not be permitted such unnatural thoughts, my friend," Bazile teased, flipping idly through some canvases leaning against the plastered wall. "You are an old man now."

"And you are not!" Leonardo crossed the room to caress the side of Bazile's face. "How are the planes of your cheeks yet smooth? How are your eyes yet bright, your hair dark, your legs strong? Would that you would make me as you are!"

"Do not interrogate me, my friend, we have talked of these dark matters before," Bazile said not unkindly. "You know me as few others do. But let us not speak of these things now. I have brought another for your dissections. A young girl, in the last stall of the stable, under the hay. It would be best to begin your work very soon with this one, as I had to bring it a fair distance."

"I am eternally in your debt, my beautiful friend! I had hoped to continue my studies of the human body before this time, but alas, there are no robbers of graves to be readily found."

"Say no more of this. Will you show me what you now work upon?"

Leonardo cast his eyes about the room, his reluctance obvious. "It's a shame you could not be here to attend your mother's sessions. Madame LeClerge sat for hours with nary a blink nor a flinch. I have never seen a woman of such innate stillness. She was the perfect model." He turned to face Bazile. "But on this she did not elaborate and I dare not ask: why did she wish me to paint her? Her likeness will not change with the passage of time, truly?"

"My mother's reasons are her own. Maman is unhappy with me still. It is better we do not subject you to the tension of our meeting. Was she pleased with your work?"

"She paid me handsomely. She also seemed quite taken with another portrait I had just completed, that of a lesser Duc and his lady, persons of no great renown but striking in their way, I suppose. He is a man of immense height, red-headed, well-proportioned and said to be schooled in the art of warfare. A fine specimen of a man! It was difficult to keep my mind on my art! The duchess is famous for her raven hair and eyes of the oddest color, that of palest blue. I had the devil's own time capturing their aspect. My first few attempts had her appearing as if quite sightless, can you imagine? Your mother insisted I sell her that portrait as well, and as you know, Madame can be quite persuasive. Now I shall have to stall the Duc while I paint a copy for him."

"You complain? Did you not say she compensated you well, my friend?"

"Of course, of course! You and Madame have both been exceedingly kind to me 'lo these many years."

"We like to nurture masters where we find them."

A dragonfly flew in on the breeze and landed on the back of a wooden chair positioned near the window. Leonardo bent close to it, squinting. "Look, Bazile! Behold this jeweled wonder, this gift of nature! Do you see how the four wings rotate separately? I could make a flying machine for a man based on wings such as these. Where is my sketchbook?"

Bazile's hand came down hard, smashing the dragonfly. Its broken body fluttered to the wooden floor. "Focus your attention, now Nardo, please. Show me your current painting."

Leonardo sighed and limped to his easel. The November rains in Florence were hard on his joints and he was still recovering from a fall on those wretched stone stairs.

He ripped a cloth from the easel. "Feast your eyes," he muttered. "I labor fruitlessly. Perhaps your visit will provide me the inspiration I need to complete this monstrosity."

A small, dark canvas leaned on the rough wood of the paint-splattered stand. A brown-haired, brown-eyed young woman wearing a brown gown stared languidly back at Bazile, her face perfectly oval, her bosom perfectly pristine. She appeared perfectly content to sit and gaze into eternity.

"This commission has me pulling what hair I have left out from my head. What can be done with such a dim-witted dullard? I am not God! I cannot create a spark, an intelligence where there is none! This creature has no mental capacities at all. Giacondo has married himself a young idiot and it is there on her face for all the world to see."

"Hush, Nardo," Bazile cautioned. "You know the servants will carry your words back to him as on the wind. You cannot afford to lose another wealthy patron to your mercurial tempers." He could't resist adding, "Or to the upstart, Michelangelo."

"Bah!" Leonardo bristled at the name. "Only you may bait me so, my dearest friend."

Bazile studied the lackluster portrait. "Why not infuse the painting with some interest in the background? You are more than capable of this. Perhaps enhance her doltish look to appear a contented smile? Giacondo will like that. He prefers his wives to have a happy look about them."

"You are right, I cannot rely on your generous gifts alone, I must tend to my legacy and my commissions. This one will pay well if it pleases him. Thank you, dear Bazile, I will do as you suggest." Leonardo replaced the cloth. "Now please close the window lest other winged creatures enter and misdirect my attention. Let us go out and feast and drink one last time before you leave. I fear I will not be yet among the living when you next return. For mortals such as I, and even the vulgar pretender Buonaroti, time is a harsh master."

Once again, Bazile wished he had met Leonardo as a young man. *What a shame to have a talent and mind such as his leave this earth simply because his body grew old!* He pulled the window shut. *I learned my lesson with Maman, though. Never again will I turn one of so many years, for they grow to consider my mercy a curse.* He smiled. *But never say never!* "Let us go out, then, my friend. Let us enjoy the life you have left to live and experience all this night may yet bring!"

CHAPTER THIRTY FIVE

One hundred years later, the murky water of the Grand Canal lapped against the walls of Jeanne's villa as the sun set behind the newly built Accademia Bridge. She held the canvas near the window, angling it this way and that to best capture the waning light. A glass of Syrah glowed red on the table, competing for her attention. The passing of a century had done nothing to diminish the intensity of her scrutiny whenever she was alone in her Venetian palazzo, and she rarely had visitors. The premonition was still as strong as it had been when she first saw the oil painting in Leonardo's studio and promptly dismissed her own finished portrait, masterpiece though it was.

Jeanne hadn't seen her likeness in centuries, not since she was turned, for her kind reflect in neither still water nor glass. The portrait didn't please her, but only because Leonardo had captured her perfectly. The woman on the canvas appeared handsome in her way, intelligent and wealthy, albeit rigid and bored. The glint in her eye could be taken for determination or something more malignant, Nardo had cleverly left the interpretation up to the viewer. She had hung that painting in her dressing room and rarely considered it.

The likeness of the Duc and Duchess, though, was another matter entirely. Staring intently, Jeanne absorbed every detail of the two figures. Leonardo had presented her with a lens he made specifically for the purpose of examining small things. Holding it carefully by the handle, she polished it on the fabric of her gown and peered at the painting yet again. *One can almost see the pores of the skin!* She marveled at Nardo's genius every time.

Lodged deep within her was the knowledge that these two humans would somehow become important to her. Or to be exact, their progeny would become of importance in the future, Jeanne couldn't tell. All she knew was that she needed to memorize every detail of their faces, hoping Leonardo had captured them faithfully, so that she'd recognize them wherever she met them across time.

It might be tomorrow or it might not be for seven hundred years, but this red-haired man and the woman with the pale blue eyes would somehow factor into Jeanne's existence.

Or her ending.

Chapter Thirty Six

Beuletta hung up the phone. "The 11 o'clock class done gone an' filled up too!" She stuck her pen into her elaborate braids, her long, silver fingernails flashing. She waved the scheduling sheet in the air. "Miss Molly's gonna be real happy!"

Candi stuck her head out from the back room where she had been folding towels. "She's gonna have to get her another instructor for all of them classes besides that hunk-a-hunka burning love she call 'Dwayne!'"

They were still giggling when the object of their mirth pulled open the glass door etched in irreverent New Orleans fashion with "Blind & Crippled Martial Arts Dojo."

In spite of his great height, Dwayne moved like a panther, all sinew and grace. The girls loved to watch him as he trained his students on the mats in front of the big mirrors. Hell, they'd watch him shell peas and be happy for the opportunity. "Mornin', ladies!" He balanced a cardboard tray holding six coffees while he held the door open. Molly tapped her way into the dojo under his arm with her new cane.

The preceding year had nearly broken Molly, both physically and mentally. She still had a flashback once in a while, still woke up trembling in a sweat sometimes, but not as often now. The assault and attempted rape had left her with three broken ribs, a fractured cheekbone, lacerations on her torso, and a concussion. The skin grafts on her chest had healed so well the physical scars were barely noticeable. Her emotional scars would take a bit more time to completely heal.

She had thought long and hard during her recuperation, eventually deciding that she didn't want to live the rest of her life in fear. Working with a mental health therapist, she made the decision to never think of herself as a victim. She found a physical trainer and worked hard to get her strength back. Going to the gym five days a week, Molly found enjoyment in the workouts and the camaraderie with the other people there, everyone sharing similar goals. Next, she found a martial arts instructor who taught her the basics of self-defense. The stronger she grew in her body and mind, the more her fear ebbed along with the flashbacks and nightmares. She would always be small, blind and a woman, but there were a lot of defense techniques she could learn to take back her life and her peace of mind.

As she grew stronger and more secure again mentally, Molly began to think about others with physical challenges who probably also felt vulnerable. She realized she had found her mission and a use for the rest of the settlement money from the earlier car wreck that had stolen her vision. She wasn't quite ready to go back to the world of investigative reporting, but she could reinvent herself as a business owner and help others at the same time.

She talked with her martial arts instructor about going in together on a training studio, a dojo, for disabled people. He'd been enthusiastic, but was in the process of moving to another state, so Molly decided to find another instructor and move forward with her plans on her own. The project gave her a purpose and saved her mind and her soul from dissolving into bitterness.

Dwayne had captured her heart from the day he walked in to apply for the instructor's position. His quiet gentleness and kind, patient character had renewed her spirit in ways she hadn't thought would ever be possible in the weeks immediately afterwards, especially since the police still hadn't found her attacker. But she felt safe with Dwayne in all the right ways.

"Cafe au lait! Thank you, Mr. Dwayne!" Candi reached for one. "Wait, you didn't bring us none a' that decapitated coffee or whatever, didja?"

"No, ma'am, I surely did not," said Dwayne, straight-faced. "I told them to leave the heads on."

Candi stared quizzically into her coffee.

Beuletta couldn't hold in her news another minute. "Miss Molly! Look! All the classes for the whole week done filled up for the first time ever!"

"That's fabulous, Beuletta!" Molly held out the bag of warm croissants for someone to take, then clapped her hands in delight. "And just in time for our first anniversary. We have to celebrate. A party is in order. Let's make it our First Anniversary Bash!"

She smiled in Dwayne's direction. He grinned back at her, knowing she couldn't see him, but he couldn't help it, she made him happy. He was used to her throwing parties at the drop of a hat. Her exuberant hospitality in the wake of all that had happened to her was one more thing he adored about her, a testament to her resilience. With the studio doing well now, he hoped she'd be able to relax a bit, focus more on the writing she enjoyed, the occasional piece for the Times Picayune or another scene in her latest novel.

The front door opened and Richard shuffled in. "Jesus, Mary and Joseph on a bike, where's the coffee?" He adjusted his cap with the word *Security* on it. "How am I supposed to patrol this place without caffeine?"

"Here ya go, Dickie." Candi handed him one of the coffees. "Don't worry, it ain't decapitated."

Richard looked heavenward. "Sweet Jesus on the cross, give me strength. And don't call me 'Dickie,' goddammit, Candace."

"Whatever, baby."

"We were just planning a celebration," Molly said. "We booked our first full week of lessons and we're coming up on our first year in business! Why don't you bring Miss Jeanne to the party? Rumors aside, it was really sweet of her to visit me all those nights in the hospital just because it happened near her shop."

Molly had no way of knowing that Jeanne had only visited her due to a strong premonition that Molly would be important to her somehow in the future. Jeanne had decided she'd need to stay in touch.

Richard and Jeanne had met and bonded during many late nights spent in Molly's darkened hospital room as she slept and healed. Richard admired Miss Jeanne's capable, no-nonsense attitude. Plus, neither one cared what other people thought of them. They discovered they had other things in common too, not the least of which was a low tolerance for the kind of disrespectful, drug-crazed punks infesting New Orleans lately. The fact that Jeanne and Richard, unbeknownst to each other, each dealt with the thugs in their own way did not affect their burgeoning friendship in the least. There's always been room for all kinds in New Orleans.

Candi blanched upon hearing Molly include Miss Jeanne in their celebration plans. She knew what she had seen. But when the cops questioned her, she didn't have a single word to say about those two vampires being in the alley that night or how they took that no-good Wardell away to do God knows what to him. She had tried to tell Dickie, but he didn't believe in any kind of supernatural stuff. She crossed herself, remembering.

"Maybe I'll bring her," Richard mumbled. "If I can get her to leave that big oaf at home."

"Who? That fine David? No sir, you be sure she bring him too!" Beuletta giggled, patting her braids.

"You know you don't have to be giving no free milk to no hungry cow no more, right?" Candi said.

Beuletta slapped both hands on her ample hips, "Girl! Do cows even drink milk?"

"I don't know. Whatever."

"Christ on a camel, you two are killing me. I've gotta get to work," said Richard, finishing his coffee. "Speaking of work, everyone keep your eyes peeled for that Wardell. A rat doesn't stray far from its hole and our brilliant police department has probably stopped looking for him by now."

Molly shivered, then busied herself collecting the empty coffee containers. She didn't want to waste time dwelling on the past. She hoped Wardell would get caught so he couldn't hurt anyone else, but even if he never did, she wasn't going to let him ruin the rest of her life by making her fearful.

Candi gulped. She imagined Wardell would never surface unless Miss Jeanne wanted what was left of him to be found. But who would believe her if she told what she had seen that night? Dickie sure didn't.

Richard had made a considerable number of additions to his List in the past year, headed up by the scumbag who attacked Molly. *Those dumbass cops were worse than useless.* He'd find him, though. Apparently he'd taken a major wrong turn with that Tutu Guy. *How could I have screwed up so badly on that one?* he wondered. He'd have to double and triple check himself next time. *So much to do, so little time left.* Everyone needed a hobby, and his sure kept him busy.

Richard's daughter, Parker, joined them all at the front counter, an unlit cigarette dangling from her lip, a stack of receipts clutched in one hand. "I'm gonna need to order a different computer program for the accounts receivable, Molly. You okay with that?"

"Looks like we can afford it because we just booked our first full week of classes! It's time to plan a party!"

"Awesome!" Parker cut her eyes at Richard. "You going to ask that Miss Jeanne to go?"

"I guess. Maybe," he hedged. "Yeah, probably so. Why?"

"Well, if you can bring a vampire, I'm gonna bring my girlfriend and you can't give me any shit. At least she's human."

Candi was the only one who didn't laugh at the idea of Miss Jeanne really being a vampire. She decided her best course of action would be to practice the time-honored Southern tradition of laissez faire. She would be cordial but she'd damn sure keep her distance from Miss Jeanne and that David, just to be on the safe side. *Live and let live.* She bit into a fresh croissant. *Or whatever.*

Chapter Thirty Seven

The two old men stared into the rear of the Crown Vic. Black and white chickens clucked and pecked in the yard grass growing up around the tires. A brown mutt barked halfheartedly from the end of a chain looped around a nearby tree. A swarm of cicadas shrilled in the heat.

"So, that's what, about a three body trunk? Maybe four?" Richard asked. He pulled a yellowed handkerchief from his back pocket and wiped the sweat off his forehead.

"How's that again?"

"Oh, come on, man. You've never measured a truck by body count?" Richard stuffed the handkerchief back into his pocket and hitched his baggy jeans.

The man looked at him with renewed interest, took a slow step back. "Couldn't rightly say."

"Christ on a pony, man, I'm just jerking you around. If the a/c works, I'll take it."

"Lemme getcha the paperwork out the house then. Be right back." The older man limped across the packed dirt yard and hauled himself up the rickety back steps.

Richard's worn-out SUV was never the best for his purposes, but this big boat of a car surely was, especially if his observation regarding the trunk was correct.

Driving back to New Orleans, Richard and Luciano Pavarotti had time to sing all the greatest hits off his last CD, the air conditioning doing its job nicely.

I'll run it through the car wash, get it waxed and pick Jeanne up for the party at Molly and Dwayne's Saturday night. He was loathe to admit it, but he was looking forward to the first anniversary celebration of The Blind and Crippled Martial Arts Studio. *Jesus, I go to parties now! What a difference a year makes.* He thought a bit more. *Who am I kidding? Before this, I hadn't been invited to a party in at least ten, no, more like fifteen years.*

He let Luciano hit the big notes alone as he cruised east on US 90 back from New Iberia in the Crown Vic and contemplated the past year.

He thought about Jeanne as the scrub trees and palmettos rolled by on both sides of the road. They had met in Molly's hospital room after the attack. Richard visited almost every evening, bringing Molly's favorite snacks, Doritos and Hostess cupcakes.

He went back and forth in his head a million times over the past year. *I should have checked on her when she didn't come back from the bathroom at Tierney's. But everyone knows she hates any special attention. Yeah, but I should have checked anyway....*

Jeanne visited Molly because, well, Richard never thought to ask. Something about the attack happening near Jeanne's antique shop? He couldn't remember exactly.

He guessed Jeanne was about his age, maybe even older. She still worked in her antique store on Royal Street every day though, so she could only see him sporadically. That was fine with Richard, as long as he had his afternoon nap and a few extra cups of coffee before they went out. He couldn't imagine where Jeanne got all her energy, though. Well, actually he could imagine, but although he had heard all the rumors, he didn't believe any of that crap. *A vampire! Right, and I'm a goddamn werewolf.*

But he liked the perfume she wore. Jeanne called it her 'signature scent' of lavender oil and cloves. And he liked the way he felt when she sat close to him. Brought back memories of good times and activities he missed. It was nice to have someone to do things with once in a while, someone his age to talk to, even if he recognized that Jeanne was much more worldly than he, a real class act. *Who speaks five languages?* She was interesting too, a full-on history buff. Sometimes he marveled at how she remembered so many facts about things that happened so far in the past. What he couldn't figure out was why she'd want to spend any time with him. He didn't give it too much thought, though. He had gotten his share of attention from women when he was young. He looked at himself in the rearview. *You still got it, you dog.*

The part time job working security at Molly's martial arts studio was supplementing his occasional private investigation work nicely. He saw his semi-estranged daughter a few times a week there now. As the bookkeeper, Parker handed out the paychecks. He wasn't sure if he could ever get used to the idea of his daughter having a girlfriend, although he knew he was supposed to make an effort. Deep down though, he knew she was only in the relationship to get under his skin, to get back at him for imagined wrongs.

He pulled up in front of his blue shotgun-style house. All the cats on his porch stayed right where they were and stared at the unfamiliar car except Big Papa. As the ambassador of their feline group, he sauntered over to the Crown Vic, tail waving.

Molly watered the roses in front of her house next door as Richard's car pulled to the curb, her long dark hair pulled off her face with a yellow headband. The car door slammed. She heard him walk over to her.

"Like my new wheels?"

"Congrats. Sounds like a big car," Molly said.

"Bought it off a retired cop. It's a Crown Vic. Pimp purple."

"Really? Never picked you for a purple kind of guy."

"Nah, I'm messing with you. It's brown. Shit brown."

"Too bad, I was enjoying the first mental image a lot more than the second. Will we see you and Miss Jeanne at the party? I invited everyone so we should have a really good crowd. Candi and Beuletta are going to decorate the place for me."

"Oh Jesus, can't wait to see what that's gonna look like. Yeah, we'll be there with bells on."

"Uh huh. With bells on, driving your shit brown car. Now there's a visual." Molly turned her hose on the hibiscus next.

With one foot, Richard nudged back a bright green sweet potato vine that was trying to crawl across the sidewalk. "What should we bring?"

"See if you can get Miss Jeanne to bring some of that awesome wine she brought last time. What was it called? Blood of My Enemies? Something like that, but French. I love her style. She really doesn't care what people say about her, she just doubles down."

"I'll ask her where she gets it. I looked in Total Wine, but they don't carry it."

Molly coiled up the hose. "I should stop playing out here and go start dinner. I still have to decide about the desserts, and I've also got to find something to wear for the party. Catch you later. Congratulations again on the new car, whatever color it is."

Chapter Thirty Eight

"Damn, Molly, you look good!" Dwayne spun her around and whistled appreciatively. "This light blue dress matches your eyes exactly."

"Yeah, I knew that," Molly laughed, swatting his hands away. "That's what the salesgirl said, anyway."

Dwayne's voice grew husky. "Come here, girl."

She melted into his arms. Her feet came out of her flip-flops as he lifted her up effortlessly and started down the hall.

"No, baby, we're pressed for time!"

"I do my best work under pressure," he murmured into her neck.

She remembered when they first met. Dwayne had called about the instructor position at Molly's new martial arts studio for physically challenged persons. His resume showed he had outstanding qualifications in various styles of self-defense. He also had a degree in physical therapy and another in nutrition, which had led to a conversation about Molly's junk food addiction. He'd even done loads of volunteer work with disabled children and adults before moving to New Orleans.

He gave her a list of references. "Please call them all. I would. It's especially important when you're working with kids. God, I'm sorry! Of course you know that. I don't mean to tell you how to run your business. I'm sure you do a thorough background check on all your employees."

Molly suppressed a snort. *What's this guy going to think when he discovers his co-workers would be a pair of former sex workers, a lesbian biker chick and an elderly, racist misogynist? Welcome to New Orleans!*

She had liked his deep voice on the phone, but she was unprepared for the instant attraction she felt when the big guy showed up for the interview. Although Molly had no idea what he looked like, she could tell he was tall and she knew he must be attractive from the way Candi and Beuletta tittered and preened when she introduced them.

"Ain't she precious!"

"What's her name?"

"Can I hold her?"

"Nah, me first!"

Molly was bewildered. "What's going on, ladies?"

"Mr. Dwayne here got hisself the cutest lil' girl dog I ever did see," Candi said. "She got long brown hair and a pearl necklace and a pink hair bow."

"An' the prettiest yellow eyes! I ain't never seen no dog with eyes that color!" Beuletta declared.

"Ladies, may I introduce Miss Mimi Esperanza de la Primavera," Dwayne said. "She's a long-haired chihuahua. You can hold her if she wants you to. I let Mimi make her own decisions."

Candi and Beuletta squealed and cooed as Miss Mimi jumped up, trying to lick both of them at once, her plumed tail wagging furiously, her tiny paws scrabbling to bring her closer to their laughing faces.

Molly reached out a hand. "Oh, she's so soft!" she said. She stroked the little round head and felt a small warm tongue lick her hand.

"The secret is in the creme rinse. She does love her bath time," Dwayne said. "I adopted her from my neighbor. When Miss Ella had to go into a nursing home, she asked if I'd take Mimi. So here we are." He looked a little sheepish. "I kept a lot of her routine the same to make the transition easier for her, right down to dressing her up every day like Miss Ella used to do. Mimi loves it, don't you girl?"

The little dog spun in a circle and barked once. "She goes everywhere with me. I hope that wouldn't be a problem. She's housebroken, loves people and is great for engaging the less outgoing students."

"Well then, welcome Miss Mimi and Dwayne. Let me show you around," said Molly, completely charmed.

For all Molly cared, he could have looked like Quasimodo and had a pet crocodile on a leash. It wouldn't have mattered a bit because she could feel the attraction. Her body responded when he was near. There was a palpable pull between them. She wanted to touch him, feel his skin, the curves of his face, his arms, his chest. She found herself inhaling deeply when they were talking, breathing in his man scent. Nothing had ever smelled so good. Her fingers tingled to reach out to this stranger. And she could feel his interest in her too, pulling them closer.

She didn't remember much about the rest of the interview. Candi and Beuletta both lay on the floor and played with Mimi, not even a pretense of work in sight. Molly had tried to keep it professional. She remembered they talked about the job, went over the scheduling and the salary. She had shown him around the studio, the tapping of her cane echoing in the empty space. The heavy floor mats were pulled to the side every evening so Candi could mop. They even found a perfect spot for Miss Mimi's bed so she could supervise while Dwayne trained students.

They were near the front door when Molly heard the entry bell tinkle. "Welcome! Can I help you?" she asked.

Molly heard the sound of a wheelchair rolling on the hardwood floor. Memories of that sound from her weeks in rehab after the car accident that stole her vision flashed through her mind.

A woman's voice said, "I'm sorry, we didn't realize you were closing. We'll come back tomorrow."

"No, no, it's fine. I'm Molly. How can I help you?"

"My son is interested in learning self-defense." There was a short pause. "He's been having a little trouble with bullies at school."

Next to Molly, Dwayne spoke up. "Hey, man, I'm Dwayne. What's your name?"

She heard an adolescent voice softly say, "Adam. I'm Adam," and then, "I can't walk. Can't do anything, really. I shouldn't be here. This is stupid."

"Yeah, I can see you can't walk, Adam. That's not a problem here, my man. There's a lot you can do from a wheelchair to protect yourself from bullies. And the best part is, they'll never see it coming."

"For real?"

"Oh yeah. First thing we do is give you an evaluation, to see where you're at, okay?" Dwayne paused. Molly imagined Adam nodding. "We'll go over your diet, make sure you're eating right, getting all the nutrients you need. Then we set you up with some exercises to maximize your upper body strength and teach you some moves you can use right away. What are you, a senior?"

The soft voice responded, "Nah, I'm just a junior."

"Well, I remember what was important when I was your age. If you're planning to go to your prom, we can help with that. You've got the looks, hell, you're a good looking guy. I bet you're smart too. Have you got a girlfriend?"

Adam glanced sideways at his mom before saying, "Yeah, right."

"If you work hard, we'll give you the muscles and the moves and the confidence to get the girls. I've got some buddies with wheels. I could probably get them to teach you some dance moves too, if you want."

The mother spoke up, her emotion spilling over her words, "Th-thank you," she choked out.

Molly came out of the trance she found herself in, pulled a business card out of her pocket and held it in the direction of Adam's voice. "Please talk it over with your mom and give us a call if you'd like to schedule some classes. We'd be happy to have you train here with us, Adam."

"Thanks," he said, taking the card, his voice sounding stronger. "Thanks a lot. Come on, Mom." The rubber wheels squeaked as he rolled across the floor, his mom holding the door open for him.

Dwayne turned to Molly. "Gosh, I'm really sorry. I should've just let you speak with them, but that kid reminded me so much of my little brother. Punk was the whole reason I went into self-defense."

"Punk?" was all Molly could manage.

"Short for 'Punkin'. His name was Oliver, but he had red hair, so…. Yeah, a skinny redheaded kid in a wheelchair attracted a lot of attention from jerks. I kind of watched out for him."

Molly didn't pursue his use of the past tense regarding his brother. She cleared her throat and simply said, "You're hired."

By the time he left, Dwayne and Miss Mimi had new jobs starting Monday and Molly had a martial arts instructor and a big crush she tried to hide. But her two employees just happened to be very experienced in that kind of thing.

"Lawd, Miss Molly!" they shouted in unison as the door shut behind Dwayne.

"What jus' happened here?"

"Hoo-eeee! They's enough sparks a-flyin' round in here to start a fire in a swamp!"

"I ain't never seen you all a-flutter like that!"

"That one fine-looking man! And he sure was appreciating on you, Miss Molly! He look like he done been walloped right between the eyes from the minute you said hello."

"Lookit, she blushing!"

"I do love that pretty little dog."

"Me too!"

"And Mr. Dwayne so nice and easy-like with that wheelchair boy!"

All that weekend, Molly's thoughts kept drifting back to the new instructor, much as she tried to concentrate on ordering supplies for the dojo and catching up on chores she had let slide at home. She finally gave up, gave in, and walked to her closet. Maybe she'd wear that new silk top on Monday.

Chapter Thirty Nine

Parker rolled in early to get a head start on the accounts payable. She liked the quiet in the studio before Candi and Beuletta arrived. They were fun co-workers but those two never shut up and Parker needed some quiet, plus she could sneak a smoke in while she worked if no one else was around. It was already warm in the studio from the morning sun slanting in through the front windows, so she adjusted the air conditioning first thing.

Parker enjoyed the unfamiliar weight of responsibility that came with opening up in the morning with her shiny new key. Especially after all that crap with her gambling debts, she felt lucky to have landed another job. She had really gone off the rails there for a while. That was all behind her, though. *Was it?* a little voice in her head taunted.

But her new boss, Molly, trusted her, a unique feeling for Parker, a good feeling, a feeling she wanted to keep going, to live up to. She knew she was a disappointment to Richard, after all, he had bailed her out more than once. But that didn't carry too much weight in their relationship overall. He'd been out of her life for so long before now. Besides, it was high time her dad evolved a little, got pulled into the

21st century, even if it was kicking and cursing. Love is love. He'd just have to get used to her and Lucy being a couple. Or not, his choice.

Parker liked to work at the front desk rather than in the back office when she was alone in the studio. She turned on the computer and scooted her chair in close. She pulled a crumpled pack of Marlboros from the rolled up sleeve of her AC/DC teeshirt and lit one up.

She glanced out the front window while she took a deep drag. A big guy with a shaved head and a little dog under one arm was greeting Molly on the sidewalk. There was something about the two of them standing there talking. She exhaled as she stared, resting her cigarette in the voodoo doll-shaped ashtray, her spreadsheets forgotten for the moment. She felt the tension between them through the glass, from twenty feet across the room. The good kind of tension. She saw the guy look at Molly intensely then look away as he spoke. She realized he wasn't sure how much Molly could see, so she knew they must have met recently.

Parker saw him shift the dog to his other side, his biceps bulging under his tee shirt. The eagle, globe & anchor of a Marines tattoo jumped when he gestured, his attention fully engaged in their conversation. He didn't set off any man-alarms in Parker's suspicious mind. He seemed like a gentle giant actually, his movements purposeful and controlled.

And Molly was smiling! A smile Parker realized she hadn't seen before because, well, Parker had never seen her show any interest in a guy before. Out on the sidewalk, the couple laughed at something Molly said.

Well, I'll be damned! She reached for her cigarette and saw it had burned down to the filter.

The big guy held the door open for Molly, then gently placed the little dog on the floor where it pranced by his side, peering up at him.

Parker quickly fanned the air around her and put the ashtray under the counter. *No time to spray the air freshener.* "Hey, Molly. You're in early."

Molly's nose told her immediately Parker had been smoking in the studio again. She chose, for now, to pretend she hadn't noticed. "Hey, Parker. Say hi to Dwayne and Miss Mimi. Dwayne is our new martial arts instructor and Miss Mimi is his assistant."

Dwayne stepped up to the counter and extended a huge hand. "Nice to meet you, Parker." He mimed smoking a cigarette with his other hand, then waved at the air and grinned.

Parker bent down to pet Mimi first, then she straightened, looked the big guy in the eye and slowly reached to grip his still outstretched hand. She smiled in spite of herself. "How you doing, Rambo?"

Chapter Forty

"Jesus Christ in chains, what the hell is that?" Richard took off his ball cap and mopped his brow. It was about time for his noon break. A quick turn around the building in the midday Louisiana heat had sapped his strength. "Are Candace and Beuletta dressing up the rats now?"

Richard stared at Miss Mimi in disbelief as she pirouetted in front of him in her pink and white tee shirt with *Princess* spelled out in rhinestones. He looked up at the big guy standing close to Molly. He noted the muscles bulging beneath the clean white tee shirt, the easy smile on his tanned face. *Oh hell no!* he thought immediately, his frown deepening.

Dwayne held out his hand. "You must be Richard. I'm Dwayne, the new instructor. That's Miss Mimi, my dog. She likes you. The twirling means she wants you to pick her up."

"Christ on horseback, that's a dog? What the hell has it got around its neck?" Richard shook hands reluctantly, trying to stare the younger man down. Maybe he tried to squeeze Dwayne's hand a bit too hard for his own arthritic fingers, but he was able to hide the wince.

Dwayne grinned. "Nice to meet you. That's quite a grip you've got. Mimi's wearing her favorite necklace. She picks out her own outfit every day so you'll probably be seeing a lot of those pearls."

Richard bent to get a closer look. Mimi danced up on her back legs and pawed at his pants leg, the pink bow in her topknot bouncing.

"Holy mother of God and all the saints and sinners. Never seen anything like it." Richard extended one finger, which Mimi licked enthusiastically. He picked her up, held her to his chest. "Every one of my cats is bigger than you," he told her as she squirmed to get her face closer to his.

Richard turned his back on Dwayne. "Hey, you guys, while I'm thinking of it, have either of you been having trouble with your keys? I noticed what looks like a lot of scratches on the metal around the back door lock this morning."

"I came in the front door today. Haven't been back there," Parker said.

"My back door key worked fine yesterday, but I obviously wouldn't have seen the scratches." Molly smiled ruefully.

"I don't like it. We need to install security cameras," Richard said, staking his turf in front of the new guy. "Couldn't hurt. God knows what these punks nowadays think they could steal from a martial arts studio, but they'll try to sell anything they can get their thieving hands on, even this poor excuse for a dog." Mimi licked his face and he hid a smile.

"Parker, can you please add security cameras to the list of things to buy when I've got some extra money laying around?" Molly asked.

"I'm on it, Boss Lady."

CHAPTER FORTY ONE

The sleek roundness of it was a surprise to Molly on their second date. She hadn't given Dwayne's hair any thought at all, but with her arms around him and his lips on hers for the first time, she ran her hands across the broad expanse of his back, the width of his shoulders, up the back of his neck, and felt...smoothness. The surprise of it was somehow more erotic than she would have imagined. Why had no one thought to mention it to her? Probably because, as she thought about it, his shaved baldness was as much a part of him as his muscled bulk, his gentleness and his powerful, efficient movements. She stopped thinking...

Three months later, lying side by side in the dark, Dwayne pressed his lips to Molly's forehead, kissed her eyes. "Baby, can you tell me what you see?" he asked softly. "I'd like to understand."

Dwayne had toppled every one of Molly's many defenses without even knowing they were there. The emotional barriers she'd erected to protect herself after the attack at Tierney's, and before that, getting dumped by her fiancé, had crumbled under the weight of his kindness. She felt completely safe with him. Her hands sought him constantly almost like a touchstone. A small flutter of her fingertips and there he was, the side of his leg, his forearm, his hand. Walking around town, he guided her better than anyone else had ever, and without a day of formal training. He knew instinctively when to tell her there was an incline, a drop off, a curb, a broken sidewalk or a low-hanging branch coming up if he couldn't lead her around it or hold it out of her way.

People were already used to seeing them together, always touching, hand in hand or her hand on his elbow. With Dwayne, Molly didn't feel different from everyone else, she felt special in a good way. She felt cherished. Her spirit expanded in his presence. Already, whenever he couldn't be with her, she felt bereft physically as well as emotionally, her fingertips instinctively seeking him and coming away empty. But never for long.

She rolled onto her back, gathered her dark hair over one shoulder. She took a moment to respond, twisting her hair around and around. A summer storm had rolled in while they explored each other, the rain pounding overhead, the sudden cracking of thunder making her startle. Lightning sporadically illuminated the room and the smell of rain rode on a gusty wind that sprinkled their naked bodies with raindrops through the gauzy curtains at the open window.

With one finger, Dwayne traced the blue and green dragonfly tattoo on the pale skin of her hip.

"It's kind of like a thick grayish fog, but not exactly. Did you ever get caught in a whiteout up north? Sort of like that. No matter how wide you open your eyes or how hard you concentrate, there's just nothing there to see." She rolled towards him. "The accident happened when I was twenty five, so I already had all those years of seeing. I remember what things look like, what colors are, for example. I'm luckier than a lot of people with vision loss." She nuzzled his neck. "Right this minute I feel especially lucky."

She felt him smile.

He was quiet for a minute, absorbing what she'd said. "Do you want to know what I look like?" he asked as lightning flashed again.

She touched his face with her fingertips. "I know what you look like," she said. "Your eyes are the color of kindness." She ran her hand over the thick ropes of muscles in his arm. "Your skin has the texture of strength." Her fingers danced up his neck. "Your hair, well, you have no hair." They laughed, then he kissed her until she was breathless.

"Silly Molly Moo Moo." He pressed a kiss into her palm, then was still for a moment. "I'm no angel, you know. When I was younger, after Punk died, I went a little crazy for a while. Before I joined the Marines I did some things I'm not proud of," he confessed into her hair. "Some buddies and I broke into a bunch of cars one night outside this bar we were too young to get into. I guess we were pissed about getting turned away at the door, or maybe we were just being stupid kids. We didn't get caught that time, but afterwards, some of those guys kept on with that kind of thing. It didn't go well for a few of them. Out of dumb luck I went down a different road and eventually enlisted."

"I don't think it was dumb luck," Molly murmured into his chest. "I think you're a good guy who did some stupid things, then realized he was headed down the wrong path and turned himself around." She tilted her face up to his, kissed him gently. "You're a good man, Dwayne."

Rain drummed harder on the roof. Molly said, "Will you tell me about your brother?" She inched closer, hiked one leg over his hip, tucked her head under his chin as thunder rolled across the sky.

He wrapped his arms around her, pulling her to him, and whispered into her hair, "I can't get close enough to you, baby."

"I'm going to be behind you if you keep squeezing me like that," she laughed, her voice muffled.

"I'm sorry, sweetheart! Too tight?"

"Never," she said, hugging him back hard.

He released her, smoothing her hair away from her face. "Punk had just made thirteen. He was in a wheelchair most of the time by then. Congenital heart defect. Our mother wasn't really able to help him much. She was waitressing all the time to pay the rent on our apartment." He scrubbed a hand over his face. "That day I went for an early morning run with my buddies instead of helping him get ready for school. I was pissed. We had a stupid fight the night before over some idiotic thing that seemed important at the time. He had tried on my varsity jacket and spilled juice on it. I was such a jerk. I flipped out and yelled at him. Anyway, I figured I'd get him up when I got back from my run, but he, uh... I couldn't wake him up."

"Oh, baby, I'm so, so sorry!" She held him tightly, pulling the quilt up around them both, tucking them in.

"Thanks, Moll. I always felt like there was more I could have done. Like maybe if I had gone in a little earlier to wake him up that day, or... I don't know...something."

"Oh, Dwayne, you were just a teenager yourself and he wasn't well. You know it wasn't your fault, right?"

"I know, but still.... It's kind of hard not to feel guilty, you know? It was my job to take care of him." He exhaled, ran a hand over his scalp. "Anyway. Are you hungry, babe? Hey, listen, the rain's letting up. Let's go get you something to eat. What are you in the mood for? I could eat a horse. Or a cow. Maybe a goat or two."

"I'm here if you ever want to talk more about it." Molly didn't want to push him for more details. She felt good about being with him, about everything they had shared already. She felt sure this was a good man. She sat up against the pillows. "Food sounds good right about now. Doritos? Cupcakes? Anything except goat. But I want to take a quick shower first."

"Nutritionally, the junk food probably isn't your best idea, but I do like the idea of a shower," he said. "Let's go, Moo Moo. I'll join you."

***

The next afternoon, Dwayne led Molly off the asphalt path, across the grass, then onto what felt like bare ground. They came to a stop and she heard him digging around in his backpack.

"Here, take this and hold it up as high as you can reach." He curled her hand around a plastic cup.

"What's this?" Shaking it gently, she felt small pieces of something light inside. Molly sniffed at it. "Smells like...cereal?"

"You'll see. Hold it up now and just wait a minute."

Dwayne dropped his backpack on the ground and stood close behind her as she lifted her arm above her head.

"I feel silly. Is anyone else around?" she asked.

"No, sweetheart. Well, kind of." He lowered his voice. "Here they come. Stand still right here." He placed his hands on her shoulders.

Molly felt the cup being moved, then something brushed her fingers. She startled. "Oh! What was that?"

"Shhhh! You'll scare them. That was the long, black tongue of a giraffe. The golf course butts up to the back of the zoo here. A couple of them are leaning over the fence of their nighttime enclosure. I heard they like Cheerios, so I brought some for you to feed them."

"Giraffes? Are you kidding me? I never got to see a live giraffe before I lost my sight." Suddenly the cup was pulled from her grasp. She heard the plastic hit the ground.

"That one ate all the Cheerios, licked the cup clean and dropped it," Dwayne laughed as he bent to pick it up.

"They're so quiet! I didn't hear them coming."

"Yeah, and they're really tall with big brown spots all over. They also look like they're wearing fake black eyelashes. They're walking away now. I wish you could see them, baby."

"Well, I felt a giraffe lick my fingers. How many people can say that? And I *can* see them. I can picture them in my mind thanks to you."

"Come on, there's something else I want to show you." Dwayne led her back onto the golf course in the twilight. They strolled along hand in hand while Dwayne shared with Molly some of the things he knew about Audubon Park.

"Uh huh, I am totally sure there really is a meteorite near the tenth hole. There's probably an alien spaceship by the clubhouse too, right?" Molly was understandably skeptical, but when they reached the six foot tall mass embedded in the fairway and Dwayne pressed her hands to it, she became a believer.

"This is amazing!" she exclaimed, her fingertips roaming over the surface. "It feels almost like lava rock with all these small holes, but smoother and harder. What color is it?"

"It's kind of a dirty brown color, sweetie, maybe bronze. Do you remember what bronze looks like?"

"Yes, like a dark metallic brown, right?"

"Exactly right. I wish I was better at describing things for you."

"You're doing great. How did it get here?"

"Well, one story is, of course, that it fell from the sky and landed right here, but there's another story that says it was brought here on a horse-drawn wagon from Alabama for the World Cotton Centennial in 1884 and they just left it."

"I like the first story better."

"Me too, Moo Moo, me too."

When Molly had finished examining the meteorite to her satisfaction, she brushed her hands off, turned to him and said, "This has been a great day, Dwayne, thank you.'

"Molly, this is only the beginning."

PART III

Chapter Forty Two

A year later, Molly retrieved the knife from the cutlery drawer, its blade facing downward like all the others. She pulled the cutting board from its place beside the cabinet, then felt around in the front of the utensil drawer until she found her slicer. Just a handle attached to six metal prongs, the simple tool was invaluable as a guide for slicing food without cutting off her fingers.

She aligned the onions, celery and green bell peppers on the counter. "Alexa. Play WWOZ. Volume up." She pushed the prongs into one of the onions, then used it to guide her knife as she sliced all the vegetables, the "holy trinity," before dropping the pieces into the big cast iron pot on the stove.

Molly wiped her hands on a towel that read, "My Kitchen is for Dancing," and swung her hips as Big Freedia sang, "Third Ward Bounce," while she munched on Doritos from the open bag on the counter. She felt equal parts irritation and amusement that she couldn't get her butt to bounce like she'd heard lots of other girls' do, but she danced just the same in her little galley kitchen.

Molly heard Mimi's tiny nails clacking on the hardwood floor. "That's right, you go, Meems!" she encouraged the dog. The nails clicked faster as Mimi twirled in excitement. She loved bounce music.

"What do you want to wear today, Miss Mimi Esperanza de la Primavera?" Molly pulled a small basket off the shelf and put it on the floor. She heard Mimi nosing through the tiny tee shirts and dresses. "Got one?" Molly felt around on the floor until she located the one the dog had pulled out. "Ah, I think Dwayne said this soft one is orange. Good choice with your pretty brown hair. Come here, sweetie." Mimi crept closer and let Molly pull the garment over her head and put her front legs through the armholes. "So pretty!" Mimi spun in circles.

Molly held out a chunk of celery. The dog took it delicately then ran to hide it under the pillow in her bed for later. "I know where you're going with that!" Molly called after her. "You're so weird." She tasted the red beans, getting some sauce on her cheek in the process. She sprinkled in a little Tony Chachere's and hummed along with Dayna Kurtz when "How Do I Stop Loving You" came on next.

The knock at the side door told Molly it was most likely a friend coming to see if she was home.

"Alexa, volume down. Who is it?" she called.

"Hey, Miss Molly! It's me. Are you home?"

Molly smiled. She wished Candi would drop the "Miss," but she understood it as a sign of respect. After all, in addition to being neighbors, Molly was Candi's boss at the martial arts studio. She opened the door and went back to the stove, stirring the beans with a wooden spoon. "Good morning! Come on in. I'm just putting this on now but if you want to come back after work tonight, you're welcome to have dinner with us. I'm making cornbread too." She paused, pushed her hair off her forehead with the back of one hand. "Wait, aren't you on the front desk this morning?"

Candi stood by the kitchen door twisting her hands. "Miss Molly, you ain't gonna like this." She sniffed the air. "That sure do smell good." She looked down at her feet. "Dwayne ain't here, right?"

Molly put down the spoon. "He's not at the dojo?"

"Nuh uh. But Dickie saw some men hustling him into a van."

Molly felt her heart drop out of her chest. "What?" She reached for Candi. "Where is Richard now?"

"He talking with the police. He done sent me to fetch you."

Time slowed down.

Molly turned off the flame under the big pot. She wiped her hands and folded the dishtowel, hung it on the stove door handle, placed the wooden spoon in the sink. She retrieved her white cane from its hook by the door, put her phone in her pocket and her purse over her shoulder. "Please stay here in case Dwayne comes home, and let Mimi out if she wants to go in the yard." She waved at the stove, "And put that in the fridge when it cools down." She didn't wait for Candi's reply.

Molly stumbled down the kitchen steps, then stopped. She took a deep breath. She'd only cause more problems if she tripped and fell. *Get yourself together and pay attention. Richard had to be mistaken. But then why wasn't Dwayne at the studio? He left the house a half hour ago.* Through the thick cypress wood of the closed kitchen door she heard the high, quavering yowl of a heartbroken chihuahua.

She walked the few blocks as quickly as she could navigate the treacherously broken New Orleans sidewalks.

Richard greeted her as she approached the studio. "Molly! Candi told you? This is Detective Dan Fontainbleu. He's a buddy. Jesus on Jupiter, we lucked out that he was on duty this morning."

Molly didn't acknowledge the detective. "What's happening? Where is Dwayne?"

"I was just telling Dan. I was coming out from around back, making my rounds of the building, when a white cargo van, maybe an '08 Ford, pulled to the curb just as Dwayne walked up. Two guys got out of the van and approached him. Then I saw him collapse."

Molly gasped, covering her mouth. Her cane clattered to the sidewalk, unnoticed.

Richard continued. "They must have injected him with something or tasered him, he went down that fast. Next thing I knew, they opened the van door, dragged him in and took off lakeside up Canal before I could make it out front here. The rear license plate was illegible, had an old yellowed plastic covering over it. Looked like every other beat-up contractor's van in the city."

Dan looked up from his notes. "Richard, I'll need a description of the two guys. Now, Miss Molly, you two lived together, right?"

She nodded.

"Honey, do you know if your boyfriend was in trouble with anybody? Did he owe anyone money? Was he into drugs?"

"No, no and definitely not! Dwayne is a martial arts and fitness instructor and is very health conscious." She would not talk about him in the past tense.

"I'll need a current photo of Dwayne. Richard already gave me his description. Wait, sorry. Do you have photos, sweetheart?" he asked, picking up her cane and pressing it into her palm.

Molly's hands shook as she pulled out her phone. "Yes, I've got photos with audio descriptions. Where do I send them?"

Dan gave her the email address and Molly quickly sent him a few photos of Dwayne before the tears overflowed and rolled down her cheeks.

Dan put a hand on her arm. "I'll get his info and the van details out there right away, darlin'. He got any family that oughta be contacted?"

"No, his brother passed away a long time ago and he hasn't spoken to his mom in years. I don't know where she lives or if she's still alive. He never knew his dad." Molly swiped at her cheeks.

Richard helped her over to sit on the ledge in front of the dojo. He patted her shoulder awkwardly as she tried to hold herself together, but the sobs kept bubbling up from someplace deep down inside. After a moment, she dashed the tears from her eyes. "What can I do?" she asked Dan.

"Well now, sweetie, it's probably best if you go on home and think real hard about who might have a problem with your man. Any ideas you can come up with a'tall will help me do my job to find him quick as lightning. You can ask Richard here to call me if you think of anything."

Molly swiped more tears off her cheeks and shoved her phone at him. "I have voice activation. Please input your number under 'Detective Dan' so I can call you directly."

Dan glanced at Richard but complied, then handed her phone back.

"Richard, could you please ask Beuletta to cancel all the lessons for today and tomorrow and put the 'closed' sign on the door? I'll send Candi over to help lock up. We'll need to cancel the First Anniversary party too. Please make sure Candi and Beuletta and Parker get home okay. I'll call them each later. I'm going back to the house now."

"Sure, Molly. Anything else I can do, you call me."

She walked the few blocks to the house she shared with Dwayne and pushed open the vine-covered gate he had left through only a short time earlier. She gave Candi what little information she had gotten from Detective Dan and sent her back to the studio.

Molly slumped at her kitchen table, her head in her hands. *What the hell is happening? Could Dwayne have gotten mixed up in something bad? No, we live together, I'd know!*

But would *I know about it?* a little voice inside her asked. *He was Special Forces. He'd know how to hide things, how to cover his tracks. I'm blind, it would be easy.*

No, I'd know, she told herself. *We don't keep secrets. This is really bad, but random violence can happen to anyone.*

Then her eyes snapped open as another thought occurred to her. *Maybe he couldn't take living with a blind girl anymore,* the voice said. *Maybe it was too much for him.* She laid her hands flat upon the table. *He would never! That's just my insecurities messing with me.*

Mimi pawed at her leg to be picked up. Molly buried her face in the soft, brown fur and wept.

In front of the *Blind & Crippled Martial Arts Studio*, Richard and Detective Dan exchanged looks.

"Call me at home tonight," Richard said out of the side of his mouth.

"Will do. Stop worrying," Dan replied.

CHAPTER FORTY THREE

"Richard," said Jeanne, "may I ask an indelicate question?" They were strolling along the lakefront seawall after a lovely dinner at the Blue Claw. Jeanne was bored, always a dangerous situation for those around her. Still, she deserved a little fun, didn't she?

The twilight breeze lightly mussed her gray chignon as the streetlights came on. "Why did you give Dwayne to those people?"

Richard startled violently. "What are you talking about, woman?"

"Come, come, my dear. I know all about your payment to those rapscallions for his abduction. What I don't know is why. They'd have done it for free, by the way. Did you know they were vampires when you hired them?"

"What the hell, Jeanne! What are you saying? Now you sound like brain-dead Candace. She's always yakking about vampires! As a matter of fact, she was hinting about you and David." Richard stopped dead in his tracks, thinking the situation through. "Mother Mary on Mars!"

Jeanne studied him as the wind picked up. She'd determined long ago that this one could be useful to her at some point. She wasn't yet sure how it would play out, but play out it would, in her experience. In the meantime, she derived some small amusement from being the cause of his agitation.

A white plastic bag skittered past them, fast as a ghost, before disappearing over the low wall and into the darkness of the water. "You honestly didn't know?" She cocked her head to one side. "Vampires, sanguinarians, whatever they call themselves, it's all just semantics and the outcome will be the same for Dwayne."

"Christ Almighty on a seesaw! I just wanted the big lug worked over, relocated and kept away from Molly. I didn't want him dead!" Richard paced a few steps. *I could have done that myself,* he thought. "Wait a minute, let's back this up." He grabbed her hand, leading her to a nearby park bench. His legs felt wobbly and he needed to sit down before he fell down.

Jeanne sat, her knees together, ankles crossed. She had left her ram's-headed, ruby-eyed cane at home. It was unnecessary when she was sated, as was the case this week. Richard had never noticed her intermittent use of it, but he was easily redirected should he ever think to mention it. She buttoned the top button on her ubiquitous sweater set as the wind picked up, adjusted her pearls, folded her hands in her lap and waited for him to catch up. This wasn't as much fun as she had imagined.

Richard pulled in a ragged breath. "How in the name of all that is holy did you know I arranged Dwayne's disappearance?"

"Don't vex yourself, my dear. This town has been my home for quite a very long time. Not much gets past me unnoticed." She smoothed her hair in the breeze. "You should know I'm also aware of your other, shall we say, extracurricular activities."

Richard stood up unsteadily. He sat down again. "Dear God in heaven. Does anyone else know?"

"No one who matters, my dear." She patted his knee. The street-lamps made discrete circles of illumination all along the levee, away into the distance in the deepening dusk. "By the way, I quite approve of you helping some of our city's more unsavory personalities to 'vacate the premises,' as it were."

Jeanne gave Richard a moment to process the new information. She gestured gracefully at Lake Pontchartrain. "I do so love to see the lights on the boats at night. So reminiscent of my childhood on Le Lac Noir." She waited a beat. "But I'm curious, dear, exactly why do you want Dwayne away from Molly?"

Richard lifted his head from his hands, his sparse hair in disarray. "I did a little digging into his background and some things didn't add up. You know I've got my private investigator clearances, but even so, there were big holes in his history. There's definitely something wrong there. I've seen this kind of thing before, usually means they're mixed up in something shady. Besides, what kind of weirdo has a prissy little dog like that? He's not good for Molly. I'd have taken care of him myself, but the situation was a little too close to home."

"You're very protective of her, darling. Is she not an adult? Is she not able to make her own decisions?"

He stared out over the dark water. "You don't understand, Jeanne. You didn't know her before the attack behind Tierney's. Christ Almighty with almonds, I was with her that night, God save my sorry ass, and I... I didn't know what was happening back there. Then I had to watch her suffer through months of healing and the rehab...." his voice trailed off. "She's still not a hundred percent. So yeah, I feel like I messed up. I feel guilty, okay? She's been through a lot."

"You've got a soft spot for her, dearest."

Richard was still remembering. "And even before she moved here... She told me about the car crash, losing her sight, and the crappy fiancé who dumped her because of it." He turned on the bench to face Jeanne. "I've gotten to know her pretty well since then, and I can tell you one thing, that Dwayne is not the guy for her. I knew he wouldn't voluntarily leave her, so..." He rubbed a hand over his face, then straightened. "But wait, why are you calling those guys 'vampires?'"

Jeanne ignored the question. "Then what will you do now? Those who have him are not your usual sort of people. He won't survive their...attention."

"Jesus's friends and family! I figured they were probably mafia or something. I didn't know they were freaks!"

"We...I'm not sure, but I believe they prefer the term 'sanguinarians,' dear."

Richard appeared not to have heard her. "Maybe I shouldn't have gotten involved this time. They were just supposed to warn him off and escort him out of town, maybe rough him up a little." Richard struggled to his feet. "Come on, I've got to get him back." *And add those weirdos to my List,* he thought to himself.

Jeanne stood, smoothing her skirt as the wind off the lake gusted around them. "Well, my dear, I may be able to assist with that."

Chapter Forty Four

Dwayne swam to just beneath the surface of his mind. He fought against the swell of the current that threatened to pull him under yet again. He knew there was a reason he was fighting to awaken. A reason... or a person. On some level he almost knew where he was. The musty smell of timeless things was familiar, yet somehow not. He felt himself growing inexplicably weaker. The urge to let go was so very seductive. His fingers quivered. Suddenly he seemed to see as if from a great distance.

High above Royal Street, peering down from gabled attic windows, capering ghouls slavered and pranced, tapping long pointed talons against the wavy glass as they made their selections from the inebriated crowd below.

"This one must be returned. Tonight." Jeanne intoned her pronouncement from the landing at the head of the narrow staircase. She turned to descend, grasping the handrail. "And make sure he's alive!" she threw over her shoulder.

"Wait! Come 'ere cher, you. Where's my replacement at?" A fiend with red eyes crouched next to the large, twitching, blood-splotched body on the floor of the garret, the wood underneath stained black with unspeakable fluids and the sorrows of time.

"I sanction the taking of another, but this," she pointed at Dwayne, "will be returned."

"Too good to be true! Too good to be blue! Must be...RED!" Ghouls hanging from the rafters sang the nonsense rhyme in unison before dissolving into dust motes, forming a tightly swirling vortex, their cackles echoing in the shuttered dimness of the musty attic. The fiend turned away in disgust as the whirlwind enveloped the body. Wrapping leathery wings around itself, it scuttled into a cobwebby corner, trailing a mucousy slime.

Dwayne fought desperately to hold on as the darkness closed in around him. All meaning dripped from his mind like sand through his fingers as he slipped into unconsciousness once more.

Chapter Forty Five

"Have you spoken to your contacts yet? What did they say?" Richard paced the wide-plank cypress boards of Jeanne's antique shop.

"All will be well, my dear. My 'contacts' have assured me Dwayne will be returned with minimal damage." Jeanne painstakingly dusted a 1789 emerald brooch with a soft cloth and replaced it in the display case. She moved on to an Italian poison ring created in the sixteenth century from the finest silver. Its provenance included a Medici, a very pompous individual whom she had relieved of the ring, and the finger, as it so happened. Jeanne regretted nothing. "Possibly this evening."

A loud thump echoed from the floor above. They both looked up as dozens of crystals on the twelve-armed chandelier swung wildly, reflecting light around the shop.

"Jesus Horatio Christ! What was that?"

"Don't fret, Richard. Why don't you go to work, dear, and I'll let you know if I receive any additional information." Jeanne held an ornate gold crucifix set with precious stones up to the light. She turned it this way and that, the sunlight from the front window glinting off gems cut during the First Crusade. Smiling, she placed it just so on its satiny display.

Chapter Forty Six

"Oh, thank God!" The phone dropped from her fingers as Molly leaned against the wall of the dojo. Mimi spun in circles near her legs, stopping to bark at the phone. Molly scrabbled to pick it up. "I'll be right there!" she said as Richard came through the front door. "They found him!" she shouted. "Can you drive me to the hospital?"

"What?! Who found him?" He steadied himself. "My car's out front. Come on." Richard took her arm, glad she couldn't see his face. "You're bringing the dog?"

"Of course! Dwayne'll want to see her." Molly already had Miss Mimi under one arm. She grabbed her white cane and purse.

Richard pulled up to the Ochsner Baptist Emergency Department doors. Molly was out and through the doors before he was able to park and haul himself out of the Crown Vic. The security guard helped her to the check-in desk then guided her to where Dwayne was being worked on in the Emergency Room. No one objected to Miss Mimi's presence, if they noticed her at all.

As the automatic ER doors closed behind him, Richard saw Detective Dan come down the hallway, a coffee in one hand. "What the bloody hell, Dan! Fill me in. Where'd you find him?"

"We didn't have the pleasure. A hospital janitor enjoying his lunchtime weed stumbled across him in an outside stairwell. Says the only thing unusual he saw was a kind of mini tornado nearby. I want some of what he's smoking, huh? Anyway, that boy is unconscious and has lost a lot of blood. Doc Leo said he has some kind of weird punctures all over him."

Dan looked around and seeing no one nearby, put a hand over his heart. Leaning towards Richard he said, "The situation seems to have gone a little sideways, Richard, and I do truly apologize for that."

"Sideways my ass, Dan! I'd say it went worse than that, wouldn't you? I thought I could trust you to use the right guys for this job."

"Well, my usual boys got hung up on an overtime detail and I was trying to help you out under a considerable time constraint, if you recall. I had to outsource the 'relocation.'"

"Are you aware of who ended up with him?" Richard looked over his shoulder before hissing, "Goddamn French Quarter vampire freaks!"

"Now, Richard, let's not be dramatic. Sure, there are some bad hombres in the Quarter, but vampires? Really? Since when do you believe in that crap?"

"Christ in the crosshairs, it doesn't matter what I believe, Dan, just what they believe!" He lowered his voice, ran a hand through his sparse hair. "Whatever. I'm gonna have to rethink our agreement if I can't even trust you to handle a simple relocation."

"Our fingerprints are all over this. We need to just let it go." Dan stared at Richard. "Mistakes have been made, but the bottom line is, you got your guy back. No harm, no foul."

"Yeah, tell that to him." Richard hitched up his pants, stalked to the elevator and stabbed the Up button. Incompetence always fried his ass, and New Orleans was rife with it. Fuming, he rode to the third floor before realizing he had no idea where he was going. An orderly directed him back down to the ER. He stared at his reflection inside the elevator and smoothed his hair. By the time he arrived at Dwayne's bedside he had somewhat composed himself.

Molly sat next to the bed, holding Dwayne's hand in both of hers. A chihuahua-sized lump wriggled under the covers at his side.

"He's unconscious," Molly whispered. "Dr. Leo said he's lost a lot of blood. They'll be taking him up to the ICU in a few minutes."

She looked exhausted, dark circles ringing her eyes, her face pale and blotchy, making Richard feel guilty all over again. "They may have to remove his spleen," she said, her voice cracking. "And I doubted him!"

"What's that?" Richard asked.

Molly continued as if to herself. "I swear I'll never doubt him again if he pulls through this."

"Ah, Jesus's denim jeans. Did he say anything?"

"No, but I think he squeezed my hand," she said hopefully. "Maybe he'll be able to tell us what happened when he wakes up." She swiped at her eyes. Mimi popped her head up from under the sheet, happy to be near Dwayne again, whatever his condition. She wagged her tail at seeing Richard.

He patted her little round head absentmindedly. "So, he didn't say anything at all?"

"No," she said again, focused on holding Dwayne's hand and wishing him awake. Mimi snuggled into her usual place under Dwayne's arm. The nurses had no official comment about the little dog with the pink hair bow and the pearl necklace when they came to take him up to the intensive care unit.

CHAPTER FORTY SEVEN

Two days later, Richard gave the cop outside room 623 a one-fingered salute. "How's it hanging, Duffosat?" Not waiting for an answer, he pushed the door open. Vases holding daisies, roses, sunflowers and lilies lined the deep windowsill. Get well cards from Dwayne's martial arts students were pinned to the corkboard opposite the bed.

"What the hell did you do to yourself, Dwayne?" Richard tried to sound hearty but it fell flat even to his ears.

Dwayne struggled to sit up but only succeeded in disturbing Mimi, who climbed onto his chest and licked his face enthusiastically.

Molly was still in the chair by the bed, having refused to leave Dwayne's side. "Richard, could you do me a huge favor and take Mimi outside? The nurses have been walking her for me but they're so busy now..."

"Only in New Orleans. Sure, no problem." He plucked Mimi off the blanket. "Don't go anywhere until I get back," he told Dwayne, who raised a finger in acknowledgment.

When Molly heard the door shut, she squeezed Dwayne's hand. "Baby, what happened? Do you remember anything?"

He cleared his throat. "Two guys...white van." He took a breath. "I woke ..."

BEEEEEP!

A nurse bustled in and reset the monitors. "Where's Miss Mimi? She didn't go home now, did she? I didn't get my goodbye kiss." The nurse studied the readout. "He should probably rest now, honey. And you should, too. You're going to exhaust yourself if you don't get some sleep. Look at that, he's out again already."

She looked Molly up and down. "It's gonna take some time. It was touch and go there for a while, we had to pressure-bag six units into him. Doc Leo said we need to keep an eye on his hemoglobin and his oxygen saturation." She leaned in conspiratorially, "Baby, I'm not supposed to say, but your big strong man right here is probably going to be fine." She patted Molly's shoulder on her way out of the room. "Go get some sleep."

***

After driving Molly and Miss Mimi home, Richard turned around and hightailed it right back to the hospital. This late at night he should have Dwayne all to himself. He had some questions that couldn't wait.

Richard stood outside room 623. He kicked the chair's leg and the officer came awake with a start, his hand automatically reaching for his gun. "Christ in a crackhouse, who do you think you are, boy? John Wayne?" Richard sneered in disgust, "Go get yourself some coffee."

"I don't know, Dickie..." the cop sputtered, rubbing his eyes.

"Go on, Miss Molly asked me to stay with him a while." Everyone who mattered knew the officer was there on a bullshit assignment, but they had to go through the motions. No one was coming for Dwayne now that the "relocation" had been called off.

Duffosat stood up and stretched. "You want anything?"

"Yeah, bring me a big bowl of get the hell out of my way," Richard pushed past him.

Dwayne lay on his back, eyes closed, monitors beeping softly in the darkened room. The daffodils in their vases on the windowsill swayed in front of the air conditioning vent. Richard dragged the visitor's chair to the bedside and slumped into it. He had a herd of hungry cats to feed at home, dammit. Hell, he should be in bed by now, but this might be his only chance to get some answers, to get things straight in his mind.

"Lord God Almighty, everyone gets to sleep tonight but me," he said aloud before shaking Dwayne. No response. He shook him harder. Still nothing. "Aw, crap," he muttered before heaving himself up and shuffling past the empty chair outside the room to the nurses' station.

"Can I help you, baby?"

"Yeah, the guy in 623 seems pretty out of it. Is he ok?"

"I just gave him his pain meds, sweetie. He might wake up some but he's gonna be a little loopy."

Praise Jesus, something's going right tonight, Richard thought as he shuffled back down the hall.

In the room again, Richard shook Dwayne's shoulder. "Dwayne! Hey buddy, wake up!" Dwayne's eyelids fluttered then stilled.

"Holy Mother of God, help me. Hey Dwayne, wake up! Molly said to ask you something."

At Molly's name, his eyes opened a crack. "Rich..," he murmured.

"In the flesh, you lucky dog. Listen up, I got a question for you, then you can finish your beauty sleep, ok?"

"Mmmm mm."

"What'd you do in the Marines?"

No response. Richard looked towards the door, then shook Dwayne harder, keeping an eye on all the tubes and wires running from the monitors. "Dwayne! The Marines. What'd you do?"

Dwayne mumbled, "Special Ops...Raiders."

Holy shit on a shingle. Richard wasn't easily impressed, but this took him by surprise.

"And after you got out?"

Dwayne's head lolled to the side. Richard shook him again. "Dwayne! Come on, man! What'd you do when you got out?"

He roused for an instant, "Same... Private...sector."

No wonder he couldn't dig up anything about Dwayne during his online searches. He had belonged to arguably the most elite and secretive unit in the United States military.

Mother Mary on a motorcycle, I screwed up again? Richard heard Dwayne's breathing become deep and regular as he slipped back into his drug-induced sleep.

Richard tapped the arm of the visitor's chair as he thought. Guilt, doubt and remorse vied for prominence in his head. In the dim light of the softly beeping monitors, he asked himself some hard questions.

What the goddam hell? I got this one wrong too? Dwayne is one of the good guys! I should have been able to figure that out. God Almighty, am I getting dementia? How would I know? Jesus, what a mess. Molly doesn't deserve this. I was just trying to look out for her. A niggling little voice in his head said, *Yeah, just like with that Tutu Guy.*

Suddenly he remembered his stepfather's voice, a voice he hadn't heard in close to sixty five years. "I'm telling you Pollyann, that boy of yours could screw up a High Mass. Mark my words, he'll never amount to nothing 'lessen I don't beat some sense into him afore he's growed."

Richard's mother had accepted that as gospel, just as she'd accepted her new husband pulling Richard out of school and moving them to a survivalist compound in Nevada. Seven year old Richard had watched his dog tied to the porch of their rented shack grow smaller and smaller through the car's rear window as they drove away that day. In Nevada he learned all about loss and religion and guns before he turned eight. He also learned how to survive a beating, dig an outhouse pit, and how to live inside his head while plotting revenge. The unfairness of the daily brutality rankled and festered in his heart.

As he entered his teenage years, friendless and surrounded by zealots, he began to understand his world in stark terms of right versus wrong. It was all black or white, no gray area. His character hardened like adobe clay under the heat of the desert sun and the crack of his stepfather's old leather belt with a silver buckle in the shape of Jesus's face.

The day after Richard turned eighteen, his stepfather went missing. Although it was his first, Richard had had plenty of time to think it through. The stepfather's body was never found. Right was right. Shortly thereafter, Richard also went missing from the compound. He never spared a thought for his mother. He had never been introduced to the concepts of compassion or forgiveness. He was alone with only the hard truths he had learned.

Now, in his later years, he didn't need or want public accolades, medals, or awards, although God knows he believed he deserved them. He only required the satisfaction of knowing he had taken care of business that needed doing when others couldn't or wouldn't step up. He had made the decision to remove Dwayne from Molly's life as he had removed other troublemakers from his city in the past. The problem was, this time he had to admit he was wrong. For a second time.

Sitting in the hospital room in the dark, Richard shook his head to clear away the old memories. *Leave the past in the past. You did what needed doing, then and now. Laws didn't always protect the innocent.* But right was right and wrong was wrong. He kept it simple, even when the courts didn't.

Richard shifted in the bedside visitors chair. Dwayne's chest rose and fell rhythmically under the sheet in front of him. Richard's fingers drummed on the arm rest. He heard a nurse's rubber soled shoes squeak down the hall on the other side of the closed door.

When Richard was younger, he had never developed the insight to realize he just liked the feeling of getting away with something, getting over on those with power over him, the feeling that he was living his own life by his own rules. A maverick. As he got older, he justified his actions by thinking of himself as a loner who marched to his own drummer and kept his own council. He was definitely not like the rest of the mindless herd. *Most people are some combination of clowns and idiots. They don't have the sense they were born with.* His experiences growing up in a cult taught him to spot the crazies early on and how to blend in, go unnoticed, use them to his advantage. His solitary, secretive nature made private investigation work a natural fit for a career. And when he first rolled into New Orleans, with its "laissez les bon temps rouler" attitude, he knew he had found his place on the earth.

In the hallway, Duffosat's ass spilled over the sides of the blue plastic visitor's chair. An extra large soda and an open bag of beignets sat on the floor between his black thick-soled shoes.

"I was never here this last time." Richard jingled his keys in the cop's face. "Got it, Sleeping Beauty?" He was exhausted and there were a dozen hangry cats waiting for him.

Officer Duffosat nodded, his mouth full. Powdered sugar dusted the front of his uniform and drifted to the linoleum around his chair as he watched the cranky old guy shuffle to the bank of elevators, one hand rubbing his lower back.

CHAPTER FORTY EIGHT

Dwayne lurched upright, sweat pouring off his body, lungs gasping for air, heart pounding.

Molly was already wide awake, standing next to their bed yet again. "It's ok, Dwayne. You're here with me. You're safe in our room. Everything's okay, sweetheart. It was just another dream."

Mimi whimpered from her bed on the floor. Molly had been concerned the little dog might get hurt by Dwayne's nocturnal thrashings if she continued sleeping with them. The first few weeks of separation had been rough on them all, but even Mimi seemed to sense Dwayne wasn't getting any better and this arrangement was for the best.

He fell back on the pillow, his heart thumping in his ribcage, his pulse roaring in his ears. Now that he was awake, he understood intellectually that he had had another nightmare, but his body, the body that still bore the scars of his unsolved abduction and near-exsanguination, that body was still locked in the grip of a horror-filled memory trapped deep within his being.

A hot, musty attic room... a sticky, creaking wooden floor...a creature with a greedy, bloody mouth.

Dwayne shivered as the sweat dried on his body. His mind skittered away from those half-formed recollections.

Molly wiped his face with a cool washcloth. When she climbed back into bed he rolled away from her.

"It's okay, baby. It was just a dream," she told him as she had every night since he was released from the hospital. She put her arm around him, snuggled up to his back and tried to make him feel her love with a hug, but as usual since the attack, he didn't respond.

She could feel him slipping away from her, away from everything they had shared. She lay awake wondering how she could help him, if she could help him, or if this was all they had left.

CHAPTER FORTY NINE

Birds were singing when Molly awoke the next morning with her mind crystal clear. It was obvious what she had to do. The doctors had tried and the psychiatrist had tried, to no avail. Anti-anxiety meds and acupuncture and talk therapy hadn't worked. Nothing had been able to free Dwayne from the terrors he experienced every night and the despondency he fell into every day. He no longer shared his thoughts with Molly, preferring to keep his worries and musings private. His joy, his laughter, his confidence, his gentle protectiveness of everyone around him, all appeared to have melted away. It seemed the will to live had been drained out of him along with much of his blood when he was abducted.

Dr. Leo said it was fine to reduce Dwayne's platelet infusions to every other month now as, physically at least, he was strong again. But so far, no medical treatment had been able to restore the man Molly loved to the way he had been before.

She could no longer deny that a distance was growing between them. All her reassurances, care, and love were met with a half-hearted smile before he'd turn away, lost in his horrific memories. She was running out of hope, her heart broken for him and the lost closeness they had shared. It was time to ask Miss Miriam for help.

Soon after moving to New Orleans, Molly had met the Voodoo Priestess in line at the outside service window of Cafe du Monde. They struck up a conversation, a small breeze off the river alleviating some of the humidity as they waited for their beignets and cafe au laits. From across the street, the bells of St. Louis Cathedral pealed the hour and then another as they chatted.

Molly wasn't a religious person, she wasn't even particularly spiritual, but she was taken with Miss Miriam's openhearted warmth and kindness. Miss Miriam was struck with the blind girl's independent nature and courage. They challenged each other's assumptions of what the other should be.

Over coffee and lunches, and then dinners together with their partners, they learned and accepted and came to admire each other.

Miriam learned that blind people, with a little assistance if necessary, can do almost anything sighted people can, if they're brave enough to try.

Molly learned that her original beliefs about the Voodoo religion were mostly misconceptions. Miss Miriam's everyday, benevolent practices were a far cry from the Hollywood movies that included everything from zombies to sticking pins in dolls for purposes of revenge. Miriam's truer version of grounded-in-nature Voodoo was based on showing love to all. She believed in the natural magic within each living creature and she often made deep connections with animals, as many people do with their pets.

As the young woman and the older woman's understanding of each other grew, Molly and Miriam became close, if unlikely, friends.

CHAPTER FIFTY

In her apartment above the Temple on Rampart Street, the Voodoo Priestess of New Orleans rubbed the sleep from her rheumy eyes. She eased her arthritic legs over the edge of the bed and pulled her bathrobe on over her long cotton nightgown.

Alain rolled over and glanced at the bedside clock. His blue eyes squinted up at her. "Where are you going, my love? It's after two in the morning."

"I got a message that man o' Molly's be needing somethin' and I gotta get it ready. Lawd, it's gonna take me a whole heap of time to fix it up too. He bad off." She straightened slowly, both hands on the small of her back.

After forty-six years of marriage, Alain knew she didn't mean she had received a text message on her phone. "All right, darling, but be careful on the stairs." He turned his pillow over and plumped it up before settling in again. "And please remember to blow out all your candles this time before you come back to bed, my love."

"Mmm mm." Miriam slid her callused feet with their painful bunions into her fuzzy pink slippers and made her way down to the kitchen where she brewed herself a cup of tea. She carried it carefully as she shuffled into the adjoining room, her sacred space where Aida lay coiled in her cage near the altar. "Dream on, my baby. I've got a long, lonesome row to hoe this night." She settled on the throne chair, sipped her tea and tried to stay awake as she awaited divine inspiration.

Molly awoke the next morning with a plan fully formed in her mind. A party is the answer to every question when you live in New Orleans. The previously-canceled First Year Anniversary Bash for the Blind & Crippled Martial Arts Studio must go on.

She called the staff together and shared her thoughts. As expected, Candi, Beuletta and Parker loved the idea. Richard grumbled about it being more work for him as Director of Security. Dwayne gave a forced smile and tried to show some enthusiasm, but Molly could tell his heart wasn't in it.

That's okay, she thought. *I have faith in the magic of this city to effect change.* She turned to Candi, "And speaking of faith and magic...please make sure Miss Miriam gets an invitation."

CHAPTER FIFTY ONE

Colored garlands of crepe paper on every wall swung in the breeze from the air conditioning. Helium balloons imprinted with "One Year!" bobbed across the ceiling and gathered in the corners, their long curled streamers tickling the shoulders of the partygoers. A rented disco ball spewed multicolored shards of light around the room.

Beuletta sashayed up to David at the food table, a rum and Coke in her hand. "Hey, good looking, whyn't ya come by and see me on Monday? I work mostly mornings and I know you don't work at Miss Jeanne's shop 'til later on." She tiptoed her fingers up his arm. "Maybe you could bring me some cafe au lait? I like it hot and sweet." She batted her lengthy false eyelashes. "Like my men."

Holding a paper plate with a spoonful of jambalaya halfway to his mouth, David contemplated her. *This one seems to be proposing something, but what, exactly? Does she know about me? Is she volunteering sex without knowing what I am? Human communication is unnecessarily complicated.* He played with the word. Complicated. Mutilated. Contaminated. Terminated. Liquidated. Desecrated. Exterminated.

A new idea occurred to him. *Maybe she's offering herself as a willing donor? That could work out quite nicely...*

Beuletta broke into his thoughts. "So whaddaya say, handsome?" He dipped his head in acknowledgment before melting into the crowd, taking the jambalaya with him.

"You gonna scare that man off, Beuletta, you keep talking him up all bold and whatever," Candi said, sidling up next to her. "B'sides, he ain't got nothing but ass and face."

"I do love me a big, quiet-kinda man," Beuletta sighed, looking after him through the crowd. "He so fine, I could just eat him up."

"More likely he gone eat you up," Candi mumbled. "Bite you, anyways."

"Huh?" Beuletta finished her drink in one long swallow. "But David been working at Miss Jeanne's antique store forever now. Why you thinking he ain't got no money?"

"It ain't rocket surgery, girl. He don't go nowhere. He don't drive no car but hers. He live upstairs of her shop." Candi ticked the reasons off on her fingers. "Why he wanna live upstairs of a vampire shop, huh? Maybe I'm judging his book by discover but I s'pect he's one paycheck from being baldheaded *and* barefooted."

Beuletta blinked at her. "Judging his what by what?" She pulled her eyes away from the place in the crowd where David had disappeared and looked at her friend. "I don't believe what people say about Miss Jeanne. She nice and there ain't no real vampires. Anyway, maybe David saving up his money for a good woman." She patted her braids.

"I hope you right, girl. You long overdue for a man to treat you like a queen." Candi sighed, *She set on him. I done everything I can to put her off him short of telling her flat out that man's a vampire and she already done told me she don't believe in none of that.* She exhaled in frustration. *Ain't nobody believing me, not even my friend!*

But it was Saturday night and they were celebrating. She threw her arm around Beuletta's shoulders. "Come on, girl. A rolling stone gathers no moths. Let's par-tay!"

Miss Mimi pranced among the guests in her new dress and matching hair bow, her twenty tiny toenails painted cherry red. Every once in a while she aimed a sharp bark at the suspiciously floating balloons.

Molly folded her white cane and wiped her palms on her dress. She addressed the guests.

"It's so good to have everyone together tonight!" She waited while the noise died down. "Thank you all for being so patient and supporting the dojo through some difficult months for us while Dwayne healed and we got back on track." Murmurs of "We gotcha, baby," and the ubiquitous, "You good, you good," were shouted out from the crowd.

She looked down for a moment. "This party is long overdue, but I know you agree it's important to celebrate every good thing we can, while we can, like we do in New Orleans!" Everyone clapped and hooted.

Her voice strengthened. "I want to say thank you to all our students for your hard work. You inspire us every single day. Thank you to my fabulous staff, Richard, Candi, Beuletta, and Parker, without whom this place literally wouldn't exist. And thank you to our sensei extraordinaire, my partner, Dwayne. I love you so much and I'll always need you by my side." She held out her hand and Dwayne reluctantly crossed the floor to take it. He had never enjoyed being the center of attention, and these days he seemed to enjoy it even less. The large room reverberated with cheers and whistles.

Richard scowled at his shoes as he stood next to Miss Jeanne. "Holy horsefeathers, can we get to the food already?"

Parker toyed with the cigarette behind her ear then stepped forward. "Hang on, everyone!" she yelled over the din. "Hey, alla y'all shut the hell up, alright?"

When she had everyone's attention she said, "I think we need to thank Miss Molly here for having the vision..."

Everyone laughed, including Molly.

"Sorry, Molly, but yeah, having the vision for this place and giving us four losers jobs..."

The crowd laughed louder.

Richard mumbled, "Speak for yourself," under his breath.

"...and helping make this MidCity neighborhood safer and our students more...more...confident, yeah. And, ...dammit, what's the word... empowered!" Everyone broke into applause.

When the noise died down, Parker continued. "It wasn't that long ago I was living kinda rough. Let's call it "camping out," with nothing but my Harley." The crowd stayed quiet. "Now, thanks to Miss Molly here giving me a job as bookkeeper, I got my own apartment *and* a girlfriend." She threw an arm around a beaming Lucy's neck as the crowd clapped.

"Aw, Christ, here we go," muttered Richard, turning to leave. "I've got cats to feed." Miss Jeanne held his arm firmly in place.

Mimi capered across the floor in her red party dress. Molly felt a plumed tail circling her ankles. She bent and picked the chihuahua up, grateful for the opportunity to compose herself. "Thanks, Parker, that was sweet, but we feel incredibly lucky to have you." A tiny wet nose nudged her. "And of course, thank you also to Miss Mimi for her unconditional love and support." The dog licked Molly's face at hearing her name, her whole body wriggling energetically.

"And we have a special guest tonight! Please welcome everyone's friend, someone who has done so much good for our city, Miss Miriam, the Voodoo Priestess of New Orleans, who will bless our space here and the work we do."

A small, dark-skinned woman stepped forward from the crowd, her head wrapped in a colorful tignon that matched her flowing caftan. Her face was unlined and smooth but the depth of life experience in her brown eyes spoke to her true age. "Thank you, my baby, thank you. Now first, please alla y'all join hands." There was some shuffling as people put their drinks down.

Miss Miriam looked up past the balloons on the ceiling and raised her arms high. "Good evening to my friends all over the planes of life. We restin' here in Mother Earth on this day. Let's pray that everyone is keeping well with the pace of time. May the beautiful light of love and joy be ever flowing in our heart to hearts. No, we can't go back, but we have strong staffs to keep us upright as we go forward. Now, my soul and spiritual forces are asking questions! Have compassion for other friends and souls for they are our mother's children that are in distress. And if they's some fools, just kick 'em where the sun don't shine!"

The crowd guffawed and several "Amen!"s rang out.

"Now, we are all in this mess together with those who came before us, so let's drink the joy of life. Yes! Great joy, hope and the abundance of divine substances to last many lifetimes. May y'all be forever blessed!"

The Sloshy Walkers cranked up their first set with "Louder" by Big Freedia. The disco ball sparkled. Many of the guests and students tossed back their drinks and rushed or rolled their wheelchairs to the open floor of what was usually the training room.

Off to one side, away from the happy commotion, Miss Miriam stood in front of a slump-shouldered, listless Dwayne. She looked up at him, took both of his hands in hers, and whispered urgently in his ear when he bent down to hear her. She stretched up one hand to touch the space between his eyes with one arthritic finger. She held it there for a moment, then stepped back, her brown eyes searching his face. Dwayne blinked, then kissed her on the cheek and smiled for the first time in months. They separated, Miriam to the food table, Dwayne to the edge of the dance floor to join the rest of the crowd.

Molly was making the rounds with Mimi under one arm when she heard the squeak of wheelchair tires approaching.

"Hey, Miss Molly. Cool party! Thanks for inviting us," she heard Adam say.

"You were one of our first students, Adam, it wouldn't be a party without you!"

"I don't know about that," he said, embarrassed. "This is my girl-friend, Francie. Miss Molly owns the dojo. And this is Mimi I told you about."

"Oh, she's adorable! I love her little dress! And it's so nice to finally meet you, Miss Molly!

"Adam is our most dedicated student," Molly said. "And it seems as if all that determination is paying off." She smiled in Francie's direction.

"I'd like to introduce Francie to Sensei Dwayne, too. Do you know where he's at?" Adam asked.

Candi passed by at that moment. "I saw him over there talking with Miss Miriam. Ain't she nice? I just love listening to her fancy speechifying and whatever. I think Mr. Dwayne went to get her a chair. Her very close veins is probably actin' up."

Francie looked as if she was going to ask a question, but instead said, "Thanks, Miss Candi, we'll catch up with him later."

Over at the crowded food table, Miss Miriam and Miss Jeanne reached for the hot sauce at the same time. Their fingers brushed and they each froze. The two queens locked eyes before Miriam jerked her hand back. Jeanne nodded in acknowledgment, then disappeared into the crowd to let Richard know they could leave now.

An hour later, Molly heard Dwayne laugh heartily for the first time in more than a year. "Jeezum pete, Molly Moo! I wish you could see this!" he said, sounding like his old self. He put his arm around her as they stood on the edge of the dance floor. Over the beat of 'BDE' he said in her ear, "Beuletta's twerking is going to cave the roof in!" Molly felt everyone stomping and clapping, urging Beuletta on.

"Oh no, she just kicked off her shoes. Now it's gonna go down!" Dwayne said. She heard the crowd going wild. Dwayne was laughing so hard he couldn't catch his breath to describe the scene for her.

And as she stood there, clapping to the music along with their students, friends and patched-together family, she thought his laughter just might be the sweetest sound she had ever heard.

CHAPTER FIFTY TWO

The driver dozed in the warm bus as his passengers in their flowered dresses, pearls, and Sunday chapeaux bobbed along the wide paths of Metairie Lakelawn Cemetery. Their non-stop, bird-like chatter in that Mississippi drawl he found so annoying had worn him out. He'd parked under the moss-hung arms of a huge live oak to take advantage of the filtered shade. It was already pushing 90 very humid degrees.

The ladies-of-a-certain-age trailed after the young docent like ducklings while he pointed out details of the more noteworthy tombs. They languidly waved cardboard fans provided by the tour company as they strolled, cooling their pale skin slightly and discouraging the occasional mosquito or fly. The low, distant hum of traffic on I10 could be heard outside the confines of the cemetery's walls. Inside, the Sunday morning was quiet and still in the growing heat of the day. One robin trilled overhead as another hopped about on stiff legs searching for worms between the grave sites.

A few unladylike stomach rumblings were heard here and there. They were politely ignored, of course. Most of the women had not eaten breakfast in anticipation of a lovely brunch at Commander's Palace after the tour. More than a few were looking forward to the Pimm's Cups that would accompany their cochon de lait, eggs Benedict, or crawfish Croque Madame.

Some of the competitive gardeners among them were more interested in the flowering shrubs and trees planted along the paths than the architecture and sculpture adorning the stone vaults. That small coterie kept lagging behind or wandering between the crypts to inspect a particularly fascinating botanical specimen.

"And over here we have Miss Anne's mausoleum." The docent pointed out a brown granite building with "Rice" carved over the door. "She joined her husband here recently, as I'm sure y'all have heard." The ladies crossed themselves in unison.

Miss Eugenie raised her hand. "Excuse me, but where would one find General P.G.T. Beauregard's tomb?"

"Oh yes, we must pay our respects at that gentleman's final resting place," Miss Lily agreed reverently. The other women all nodded. Melinda Jane crossed herself again.

"We'll be visiting him shortly, if you'll come this way." He couldn't resist adding, "Did you ladies know that after his military career ended, General Beauregard was an avid promoter of black civil rights?"

There was a collective gasp and a clutching of pearls.

Making a hasty course correction, the young man said, "But we also have the graves of many other important Southern leaders from the War of Northern Aggression. We'll head to the left up here next. Let's try to stay together, shall we?"

He smiled politely as he pointed in the direction they should proceed. Inwardly, he was pondering the futility of herding cats while looking forward to his own, blessedly solitary, lunch. He hoped he hadn't blown his opportunity for a decent tip with that civil rights remark.

He led the ladies down another wide pathway and gestured at a large white-columned mausoleum. They gathered close to hear over the raucous cawing of a crow that chose that moment to deliver an accusatory rant from atop a marble cross set high on a nearby vault.

"Now this tomb has an interesting history..."

The wrought iron doors of the crypt blew open, bits of rusty metal shrapnel flying outward. A tornadic wind arose from within, stripping the overhanging live oak limbs, mixing leaves and broken branches with the gravel from the path. In an instant, it had flayed all the skin and muscle from the little group right where they stood.

A six foot tall vortex appeared, whirling darkly on the steps of the tomb. "Come 'ere, cher, you," echoed from within before it vanished into nothingness.

When the wind abated, nothing remained but a few scattered pearls and one church-going pump, the five metatarsals inside still encased in a limp web of nude pantyhose.

The crow cawed a futile, final warning, then wheeled away over the City of the Dead, one round, opalescent sphere clutched in its beak.

CHAPTER FIFTY THREE

Dan stood in the middle of the gravel path and sweated. Even in the dappled shade of the overhanging live oaks, it was brutally hot. He scratched his head as he looked around. He'd have to hurry. He sensed the threat of a thunderstorm in the oppressively humid air. He'd left his umbrella in the car, of course. The bright afternoon sun played hide and seek behind fluffy white clouds, toying with his prediction and making him put on and take off his sunglasses in rapid succession as he studied the scene before him.

He'd had the boys cordon off the entire cemetery. The stillness of the place was unnerving. Forensics had just left, so except for the crows, some rabbits, and the rumor of a coyote or two, he had the place all to himself for now.

Well, myself and all the dead people who live here.

Not live *here, they're not alive.*

"Jesus, am I talking to myself now?" he said aloud. *You're losing your mind,* he thought.

Am not, it's just this case is freaking me out.

You're arguing with yourself, boy, you are *losing it. Get to work!*

Born and bred in New Orleans, Dan had lived his whole life in and around the city. He knew it inside and out, all the current street names and the names those streets had been called previously, where all the Confederate statues had been, and what, in some cases, had replaced them. He knew all the old-time political bigwigs, the wannabes, the up-and-comers jockeying for position, which ones were in jail and which ones ought to be. He knew where the bodies were buried. Looking around, he realized that thought hit a little too close to home considering his current location.

He studied the front of the crypt. Five shallow stone steps led up to a slab on which the marble tomb sat. One of the broken decorative grills hung open, off its rusty hinges. What was left of the other was in place, but it was now a twisted tangle of sharp, broken scrap metal. An iron vase on each side of the double-columned entry held a few fistfuls of bone-dry dirt and some struggling weeds. Both vases were upright and undisturbed.

Dan circled the windowless crypt. No scratches or graffiti marred the gray marble walls. They didn't tolerate that here. He couldn't see the roof, though. *Have to call for a ladder,* he thought. *I'm getting too fat to be climbing around up off the ground. I'll send that kid Landry up to check it out.*

At the front again, he wiped his sweating brow with a ragged, stained handkerchief. The sight of it in his hand made him pause. Sherree would never have let him out of the house without a freshly laundered handkerchief. His short sleeved shirts had always been starched and ironed within an inch of their lives. Thanks to her, he used to look sharp every day when he left for work. These days, well, he knew calling his look "presentable" would be a kindness.

With a sigh, he stuffed the rag in his back pocket and started up the steps. Just as he reached the top, a strong breeze blew up and swung the broken gate shut with a screeching clang, scratching his arm deeply just above the elbow and drawing blood. "Shiiit!" he yelped, startling the watching crows. "That's just great. Probably get tetanus now."

The gate had wedged shut tightly. No matter how hard he shook it, and he poured all the frustration of his day into it, he couldn't get it open. The crows cackled from where they had resettled in a nearby live oak. *I'll have to come back with a crowbar.* He made a mental list. *A crowbar and a ladder.* He sighed. *Nothing is ever easy.*

Might as well visit Sherree while I'm here. He put his sunglasses on as he walked the gravel path, head down. His feet knew the way. He'd been coming to this place on the regular for thirteen months, one week and four days. She wasn't far.

Dan stood in front of the modest grave with its plain headstone, holding his throbbing arm. *It's just a scratch, Sher. Yes, I swear I'll stop at the ER on the way home and get a tetanus booster just to be safe. Sorry, babe, I didn't have time to stop and get your bouquet this time.* He added flowers to his mental list.

The quiet stillness was broken again by the sound of something light and plastic bouncing down the gravel path in front of a wind gust. Dan hated to see litter in this beautiful, historic cemetery. He chased after it a few feet before he caught it.

Droplets of red slush dripped onto his shoe as he stared at the white go cup emblazoned with "Port of Call" just as the skies opened and dropped a deluge of rain on the transfixed detective and the unsuspecting city.

Chapter Fifty Four

A gibbous moon had risen low in the clear night sky, its light dripping across the grass. A whip-poor-will called from the trees at the edge of the fairway.

Molly leaned back against Dwayne's chest, his legs splayed out on both sides of her as they enjoyed the peace of the darkness together. With her face upturned towards the heavens, she mouthed a silent prayer of gratitude for Dwayne's full recovery, although she was convinced it was all Miss Miriam's doing. She was so grateful to have him back, she could cry. Her eyes glistened at the memory of all they'd gone through together.

Dwayne whispered, "Give me your arm, baby, and point your finger for me." He held her arm up into the dark and aligned it with the brightest star. "Can you feel that? There's the north star."

She tilted her head back until it rested on his shoulder. She followed the trajectory of her arm up, up, up into forever. She could visualize Polaris at the end of her forefinger, exactly where it had always been in the constellation of Ursa Minor, but unavailable to her since the accident. Until now.

She laughed in delight, "Wow! Yes, I get it! Can you show me Orion? He was always my favorite."

"I think so. It's...give me a minute...it's right...over here!" He swiveled her arm a few degrees to the left and sighted along the length of it. "Right there are the three stars in his belt..." He wiggled her arm a bit then moved it a little to the right. "And there's his bow and arrow."

"More, please! Can you find me the Pleiades?"

"That's the cluster of seven small stars, right? They're kind of faint? Yeah, I think they're just over here." He adjusted her arm's position once more.

Suddenly Molly pulled away from his grasp and buried her face in her hands.

"What's wrong, MooMoo? Oh my God, I blew it. I'm so sorry, I thought you'd like to feel where the stars are, even if you can't see them."

She snuffled through her fingers. "I do. It's perfect."

"Then what, baby?"

Molly plucked at the blanket they sat on. "I thought I'd never experience them again, but you got them back for me. Sorry, I'm just overwhelmed that you would even think of doing this. Thank you, Dwayne."

He scooted out from behind and knelt in front of her. "Sweetheart, I can't ever do enough for you. You pulled me back from a really dark place in my head after...after what happened. Thank *you*." He tilted her chin up and smoothed a strand of long, dark hair behind her ear. "But are you sure this thing with the stars isn't upsetting you? It's okay? Because if it's not, then I really screwed up."

"What do you mean?"

Dwayne leaned back, ran a hand over his smooth head and blew out a deep breath. "I stuck seven constellations on our bedroom ceiling yesterday while you were out."

"What? You mean those glow-in-the-dark stars? I love that idea!" She wiped her eyes with the backs of her hands. "But how did you even know where they all should go? I didn't think astronomy was your thing."

"Well, it really wasn't, until I met you. We were trained in celestial navigation in the service, but I had to brush up with a crash course online after you told me how much you miss seeing the stars."

Molly stood up and pulled on a corner of the blanket. "Let's go."

For such a big man he could get to his feet quickly. "Okay, sure, babe. Where do you want to go?"

"I want you to point out Cassiopeia to me," she said. "From our bed."

Dwayne's surprised laugh echoed across the moonlit field, momentarily silencing the cicadas. He smiled into the darkness as he shook out the blanket. "Now that's the reaction I was going for!"

CHAPTER FIFTY FIVE

Alain had always been a light sleeper. He rolled over to find Miriam gone. Again. The Voodoo Priestess of New Orleans sometimes got caught up in her night work and forgot to attend to the more mundane matters such as sleep requirements or making sure the Temple and their apartment above it didn't burn down if one of her consecrated candles got too close to a curtain. *I'd best go check on her*, he thought.

He slipped out of their bed, adjusting his pajama bottoms, his still-thick gray hair stuck to one side of his head. He scratched his belly and yawned. The bedside clock flashed 2:13am as he started down the stairs. The old saying that nothing good happens in the French Quarter after midnight crossed his mind.

The screws holding the worn bannister to the wall had loosened again. He'd have to remember to tighten that in the morning. Miriam leaned on it heavily when her arthritis was acting up.

Navigating the turn in the stairs, Alain was confronted with the sight of his beloved wife deep in urgent whispered conversation with another woman of a certain age, that owner of one of the antique shops on Royal Street. He remembered seeing her at the First Anniversary Bash for the martial arts dojo Miriam had blessed recently. *That was one hell of a good party,* he thought.

Both women stopped talking and turned towards him, the same strange expression on their very different faces, as if they suddenly realized where they were. "Hello, Jeanne. Nice to see you again," he said, smoothing down his bed head.

She granted him a tight-lipped smile.

Miriam recovered first. "I'm so sorry, baby, did we wake you? Jeanne here was just taking her leave. I'll be to bed directly."

Alain knew when he was being dismissed. He didn't mind. *Mine is not to question why,* he thought. *Such is the price of loving an extraordinary woman.* "Your candles, my love?"

"Yes, yes, I done put them out, every one," Miriam said distractedly.

Alain raised a hand in farewell and retreated up the stairs.

Miriam lowered her voice. "So you gonna take care of this, right? One of yours done gone all crazy-like. We can't have none of this kind of foolishness around stirring up trouble for everyday folk."

Although she was born and raised in New Orleans, the elderly priestess was well-traveled, mostly due to her ministry work in Africa, Canada and Central America. She knew the veil between everyday life and the supernatural was translucent in her hometown. All kinds had always existed in the city and probably always would. Miriam accepted that. Regular folks however, were mostly unaware of the powerful undercurrents swirling around them as they went about their lives. It fell to Miriam to keep the groups as separate as possible. Nothing but trouble came when they intersected.

She gripped the neck of her bathrobe closed with one hand. Miriam saw Jeanne smirk when she noticed the silver crucifix and a small icon of Dambalah in her other. She continued, "That poor girl and her man weren't doing nothing wrong but walking in that there graveyard. And now them ladies! Church-going women on one o' them walking tours out at Lake Lawn Cemetry. Lawd, it ain't right! It's gotta be one o' yours doing this and we both know you don't want folks talking 'bout your kind. I know I ain't nothing to you, but you the only one I know of can fix this."

Jeanne reached out to pat Miriam's arm but stopped at the other woman's expression. She adjusted her pearls instead. "I agree, it cannot continue. As you know, this does happen occasionally with those of my community who have existed too long. But you have my word. The situation will be resolved." She turned to go. "However, if we're all to live in this town together without, shall we say, undue scrutiny, I may need a favor of you in return..."

"Imma have to pray on it. This ain't 'zackly right but I don't have no other choice but to ask you to fix this. They's your kind, not mines."

Jeanne paused, her hand on the doorknob. "Yes, 'misery acquaints one with strange bedfellows,' does it not?"

"Don't know nothing about that, but let's both of us make sure ain't no more misery 'round here than is natural."

"But my dear Voodoo Priestess," said Jeanne, pausing in the doorway, "who decides what is natural?"

CHAPTER FIFTY SIX

The next afternoon, the bell above the front door of Miss Jeanne's shop tinkled. In the back room, David raised his head, a hand-forged iron nail stuck in the end of his crowbar.

"Jeanne, I've gotta talk to you," he heard the old man say.

David returned his attention to the task at hand, gently prying the last few nails from the wood of the packing crate. Finally, one side fell away. He brushed aside the straw that had been used as packing material centuries ago and exposed an ivory-inlaid oak prie-dieu. The horsehair in the cushion poked through the threadbare green velvet where Ann Boleyn had knelt and prayed in vain before her beheading. She had not gone graciously as recorded in the history books. David vividly remembered her screams as they dragged her up the creaking steps of the hastily built platform to meet the executioner's longsword.

"Jeanne, I'm a little worried. Well, maybe 'concerned' is more accurate," he heard Richard say. "Aw, Jumpin' Jesus! I'm just gonna say it. Do you think I'm losing my marbles?"

In the back room David snorted. He had nothing against Richard, in fact this one seemed to entertain Miss Jeanne in a way he had yet to understand, but he knew in time, all would be revealed. David and Jeanne had all the time in the world. He gathered up the bone-dry straw from the crate, careful to get every last bit. He shuddered at the thought of the fire it could accidentally start. Fire was no friend of theirs.

"Here, my dear, hold this please, while I attach the tag." In the front room, Jeanne handed Richard a gleaming reliquary studded with rubies that still bore a trace of the sawdust it had been packed in.

Barely looking at the irreplaceable treasure in his hands, Richard said, "I've been doing a lot of thinking since we..., ah, you, got Dwayne back. I screwed up royally there." He remembered Tutu Guy from the Red Dress Run and hesitated before confessing, "And, uh, there may have been a time before that." He took a deep breath. "Anyway, now I'm kind of...questioning myself."

Jeanne took the priceless antique from him and placed it in the shop window where it once again reflected the late afternoon sun as it had when she first saw it shortly after that Jesus from Judaea was crucified. Talk about unintended consequences! *That Roman governor I turned, what was his name? I'm becoming so forgetful lately. Something with a P.... My memory certainly isn't what it once was. But what a debacle that became! I wonder where he is now?*

"Darling, you're perfectly fine." She dusted the cup delicately with a wand made of the softest down feathers from the breasts of young egrets. She waved her hand dismissively. "But there is a small matter I'd like to discuss with you as well." Working as she spoke, she next unwrapped a flat rectangular package and uncovered a heretofore unknown portrait of Henry the VIII by Hans Holbein the Younger. "I could use your assistance in the elimination of a rogue miscreant."

Richard's anxiety over his possibly-deteriorating mental competence evaporated in a rush of pleasure. *She's asking for my help! She respects me!* He felt closer to her already. "What'd this guy do? And how are you involved? Why not let the cops handle him?"

"It's not that type of a situation, dearest. This would be more in line with one of your previous, shall we say, "extracurricular activities?" Jeanne held the painting up to a bare spot on the shop's wall, closed one eye to imagine it hanging there. The fat king stared back at her imperiously. "This is a most unsavory character I'm discussing. I know you'd agree there needs to be a 'disappearance' if only I were able to provide you his details, but it's better I don't at this time." She put the painting down. "I was thinking fire."

"Wait, what?"

"A fire is necessary, dear. This fiend can only be...well, there needs to be a fire. And luckily for us, New Orleans has a long, tragic history of inexplicable fires. Another wouldn't be unusual."

Richard switched to problem-solving mode. This was his wheelhouse, much more so than introspection, and Jeanne was actually asking for his help! "So you need the body to be unrecognizable? What about his dental records?" he asked in his most professional manner.

Jeanne smiled inwardly. She could practically see the buttons on his shirt straining, his ego was so inflated at her supposed reliance on him. "Trust me, darling. This particular 'person' has never seen a dentist's chair."

"Has he had any bone fractures repaired? Sometimes metal rods, plates or screws survive a fire and can be identified. Does he have anything like that?

"No, I'm quite sure a fire would work perfectly for this individual."

"So this isn't some hypothetical situation we're talking about here? You really want me to help you torch some guy?"

"Darling, I didn't imagine you'd get squeamish on me. It's not as if you haven't taken matters into your own hands before."

He flinched. The subtle reminder of her knowledge of at least a few of his crimes hit its mark. *Dammit, I'd kill to know how she found out, but I'll deal with that later. Here's my chance to make some extra points, maybe get a little sugar down the road.*

He stood tall and hitched up his baggy jeans. "Squeamish? Me? Christ in a wheelbarrow, you know me better than that. If you say he needs to go, then that's good enough for me, I'm your man for the job. This city's got too many criminals, freaks and weirdos as it is."

"Oh, my dear," she purred. "You don't know the half of it."

CHAPTER FIFTY SEVEN

Molly smoothed the blanket under her skirt and reached into the picnic basket. She held another tiny piece of hotdog out at chihuahua height. Miss Mimi took it delicately and ran to the edge of the blanket where she nibbled on it.

"Do you remember the first time you brought me here, Dwayne?" Molly wiped her fingers on a blue cloth napkin, then produced two pairs of chopsticks. She held one out to him.

Above them, a dozen wind chimes swung gently on the long arms of the live oak, filling the humid air with a sound she associated with prayer. Towards Big Lake, Molly could hear children shrieking as they splashed each other near the swan boat rentals. Every so often, a gentle breeze wafted the green smell of lake water their way.

"Of course I do, Moll. I wracked my brain for days trying to think of a special place you'd like. Didn't want to just ask you out for a drink or something lame like that." Dwayne brushed an ant off their blanket as it headed for Molly's bare foot. "Plus, I wanted somewhere we could talk, to get to know you better. I thought you'd love this big ol' tree with the chimes."

"You were right. I did and I do," she said, passing him a container of his favorite cold shrimp with peanut sauce. "I squeezed the lime over it already."

"Thank you, sweetheart." He leaned in and kissed her lightly. Dwayne knew her smaller container made it easier for Molly to eat without being able to see. He watched as she felt around with her chopsticks and popped a shrimp into her mouth. She amazed him every day with her ingenuity. And if she was a messy eater, well, it only made her more precious to him.

The sunlight cast shifting patterns onto her shiny dark hair through the leafy limbs of the moss-hung oak. "Why are you staring at me?" she smiled. "Do I have food on my face again?"

"No, baby, you're good. But how do you always know when I'm looking at you?"

"I can tell by your voice, but mostly I just feel it. I bet you could too, if you didn't have so many visual distractions." She wiped her mouth with the napkin anyway. "How's the shrimp?"

"Delicious, as usual, MooMoo. Thanks for making it."

Molly felt the blanket under them shift as he moved. She could tell he was directly in front of her now, possibly kneeling. She got a whiff of his scent, that blend of soap, deodorant and his unique smell that intoxicated her so.

"I've got another question for you," Dwayne said.

"Let me guess. 'What's for dessert?' There are Doberge squares in the picnic basket." She pointed in that direction with her chopsticks.

"My favorite, great! But no, baby, guess again."

"Hmmm, lemme think."

Mimi crossed the blanket at Dwayne's silent hand signal and climbed into Molly's lap. She pet the soft fur absentmindedly as she considered, her face tilted towards the sunlight. "Hey, what's this, Meems...?" Attached to Mimi's ever-present pearl necklace was a small, hard circlet. "Dwayne? Can you see what she's got here?" Molly's fingers explored the item gently. "Wait. Is this a...? Oh my God!"

"Molly, will you marry us?"

A strong gust of wind set all the chimes in the limbs of the great oak to pealing at once, almost, but not quite, drowning out the laughing, crying and barking from the plaid blanket below.

CHAPTER FIFTY EIGHT

"Dearest, are you familiar with the old Lindy Boggs Hospital at the corner of Jeff Davis and Bienville? I feel as if that would be a good place."

Jeanne took another sip of the lovely French burgundy as they sat on the veranda at The Columns. Inside, a small happy hour crowd congregated at the bar. A giant fan revolved overhead, hanging from the haint blue porch ceiling. She remembered when that insufferable family first erected the mansion in the late 1800s. That ridiculous sea captain and his two horrid sons...

"Of course I know it, it's one huge goddamn eyesore. The city just flat out abandoned it after Katrina. Left it to rot, which it's doing perfectly, I can tell you. Nothing but broken windows and graffiti now. Who the hell is Cronald Muck anyway, and how the hell did he get all the way up there to spray paint his tag?" Richard held his glass up to the light. "This wine is pretty good, Jeanne. You know how to pick them."

She smiled, remembering the fourteen hundred acres of Loire Valley prime terroir she had acquired so many, many moons ago. A lifetime ago, as some would say. *More like seven human lifetimes*, she thought. But who's counting? It had been a simple matter to move into the chateau of that winery and delete its occupants. She found herself reminiscing more and more these days. "It's not an exact science, my dear. Anyone can learn about wine." *If you live long enough. But you won't.* The pleasure of sampling eternally varied new wines alongside her old favorites was one of the benefits of existing as long as she had. Jeanne always enjoyed the sight of something red in her glass.

She knew the downside of such a long existence for one of her kind was an eventual descent into insanity, uncontrollable savagery and bloodlust. Sometime in the future, another of her community would be plotting her end for the good of the rest, but she couldn't worry about that now. Now it was her responsibility to remove the latest rogue fiend.

"I believe Lindy Boggs is perfectly suitable for our purposes. Have you ever been in that building, dear?"

"Yep, I was in there once to the ER and a couple times to visit some cop buddies who got hurt."

She sighed. She was going to have to walk him through this. "Do you think you could you find your way to the morgue? I believe that room on the lower level might serve our purposes best."

"Probably, but Mother of God, you know what hospitals are like. You could get lost going from one patient room to the one next to it."

"Well, I hope you're exaggerating, darling, because I'll need you to be in that morgue if we're going to remove this...person."

"So you still want to do that, huh?"

"It's not a question of me wanting to, my sweet. I have a responsibility." A sudden gust of wind blew Jeanne's cocktail napkin across the veranda and into a gardenia bush. "Plus I promised a...an old friend that I would take care of the matter and I must keep my word.

Unfortunately, I have a rather severe aversion to flames. I'll do it if I must, but I'd rather not. If you're having second thoughts though, I can find someone else to assist me."

"Holy Family on a houseboat, I told you I'm all in if it means cleaning the trash out of this city. Just tell me what you need me to do."

The term "useful idiot" crossed her mind and she bit her tongue trying not to smile.

"I knew I could count on you, dearest," she clinked her wine glass against his as a vintage green streetcar trundled by on St. Charles Avenue.

CHAPTER FIFTY NINE

"They coming! They coming! Get down, y'all!"

Candi popped her head up over the martial arts studio's counter to peer out the front window. "They look happy. She musta said yes."

"Keep your damn voice down. Of course she said yes," Parker stage-whispered. "She's not stupid. Anyone with eyes can see Rambo loves her to death."

Beuletta pulled on Candi's arm. "Get down here, girl, or they be seeing you. You gone ruin the surprise."

"I wanna see him open the door for her and whatever. I do love to see him do them nice things."

"All of you shut up and get your asses down if you insist on this stupid charade," Richard ordered from his spot against the wall. His knees wouldn't allow him to crouch under the front counter. *If I get down there I might not get back up,* he thought.

The bell over the door tinkled. Parker, Candi and Beuletta jumped up, yelling, "Congratulations!"

"Wow! News travels fast around here," Molly laughed. "Thank you!" She and Dwayne were beaming from ear to ear. Miss Mimi danced in circles at their feet.

"Let's see it." Parker grabbed Molly's hand. A square-cut emerald of an uncommon hue with diamonds on each side gleamed in a filagree setting.

Beuletta crowded in. "Hoowee! Lookit that! You done good, Dwayne!"

"That's a good looking ring," Richard added grudgingly.

"Wow!" Candi exclaimed. "That's real pretty! Hold up now, did I see that in the window of Miss Jeanne's shop?"

Molly turned towards Dwayne. "I'm afraid it's lost on me, baby. I hope you didn't spend too much for a ring I'll never see."

Candi cut in, "Miss Molly, that might be as it is in May, but you deserve the best iffen you can see it or not."

Richard rolled his eyes.

"It ain't May," Beuletta looked confused.

"Right on both counts, Candi," Dwayne smiled. "Molly does deserve the best I can give her, and it did come from Miss Jeanne's shop. I know Molly likes things with history, so Jeanne found me a ring with loads of it."

Parker pulled a bottle of champagne and a Chantilly cake from under the counter. The cake had a swipe of whipped cream missing off one side. Richard glared at Candi as she surreptitiously wiped her forefinger on her shorts.

Parker lit the sparklers on top with her lighter. They made an impressive display as they flared and sizzled all over the cake, the day's mail, and the computer keyboard.

Candi and Beuletta crowded around Molly.

"Where did he ask you at?"

"On a picnic blanket under the Chiming Tree in City Park."

"Did he get down on his knees?"

"Yes, he did! I think so, anyway."

"I bet you cried. Didja cry?"

"I sure did," Molly said. "I think I'm still in shock."

Molly did her best to answer their rapid-fire questions while they admired her unusual ring.

"Aw, Dwayne, you did so good! You deserve a standing ovulation."

Dwayne didn't even blink. "Thanks, Candi." He twisted open the bottle's wire muselet, popped the cork and filled five flutes.

Parker cut the cake and passed slices around. Richard held Miss Mimi on his lap and shared his cake with her when he thought no one was looking.

Dwayne looked over at Molly, who was trying to balance her plate, fork, napkin and glass of champagne with her white cane. He noticed she already had a smudge of whipped cream on her chin, and his heart overflowed. "Come here, sweetheart." He took Molly's cane and glass from her hands. "Do you really like the ring, MooMoo?" He asked, running his thumb over her chin. "We could get you a different one if you'd rather have something new, or a different shape stone or..."

"Not on your life," Molly smiled at him sheepishly, feeling the small sticky spot on her face. "It's perfect and I'm never taking it off."

***

From across town, Jeanne pinpointed the small celebration being held at the dojo. She smirked. Now she'd always know where Molly was.

Chapter Sixty

Just before midnight, Jeanne summoned her ghouls to the darkened gift shop in the Old Ursulines Convent Museum. There, they relieved the good Sisters of every rosary they had in stock, which was a considerable number.

The flock of ghouls then escaped her supervision into the adjacent St. Mary's chapel where they capered over the pews, the altar, and up and down the marble nave. They ascended the tiny spiral staircase in the rear to flick long talons against the tall pipes of the organ before being corralled once more. At Jeanne's command, they flew away through a broken window in the attic.

Outside on the Convent steps, a man curled around his empty bottle squinted into the humid night air above the one-thousand block of Chartres Street. What appeared to be a cloud of bats poured from the upper window in the oldest building in the Mississippi River Valley and flew off to the west. The man's graying dog leaped to its feet barking riotously, the frayed rope around its neck dragging on the ground. The uproar ended with a yelp when the mongrel was hit on the head by a string of rosary beads dropped from the sky.

***

At the abandoned Lindy Boggs Hospital a short time later, dozens of rosaries hung like Mardi Gras beads festooning every doorway, crack and crevice in the windowless basement morgue. Jeanne was quite familiar with this fiend's particular aversion to crosses and had no qualms about using it against him.

The long, empty hallways echoed with the sounds of cackling, hissing and claws being dragged across the concrete floor. A sulfurous stench wafted from the folds of the ghouls' leathery wings, competing with the odor of mold, mildew and unnameable biological fluids that had seeped into the cement over the years.

A splattered steel table with built-in gutters for sluicing away liquids stood in the middle of the room exactly as it had in the hours before Hurricane Katrina struck in 2005. What looked like a rusty grocer's scale sat on a chipped Formica countertop against one wall. Trash lay randomly strewn across the floor and piled in one corner. A greenish puddle spawning new microscopic life forms pooled around the backed-up floor drain.

"Out! Now!" Jeanne pointed to the one remaining exit without a rosary draped across it. As one, the ghouls leaped into the air and vanished in a dark, swirling vortex of fangs and wings.

On the outside of the building, a lopsided sign read, " ergency."

Chapter Sixty One

She heard Richard coming well before he reached the morgue, a large flashlight guiding his hesitant steps in the darkness.

"Jesus, this place is spooky as all get out!"

Jeanne studied the gas can in his hand. "Will that be sufficient, dear? It's quite damp down here."

"Should be plenty enough. You basically just want to do this one room, right?"

"Yes, I think that should do it."

"No problem, then. Where's our friend?"

"Oh, he'll be here, darling."

"So what's the plan?" He looked around at all the rosaries. "And what's with all the religious stuff? You gonna perform an exorcism?" he chuckled awkwardly.

"If only it were that easy, my dear," Jeanne sighed. She'd witnessed many exorcisms over the centuries, participated in a few, even officiated at one or two. So entertaining. The question the holy men, and they were invariably men, never anticipated was, what does one do with the cast-out demon? It amused Jeanne to have priests recruit her minions for her.

"I'll be back shortly, dear. You can get started. We've got about fifteen minutes." Jeanne exited the labyrinth of moldy, trash-lined hospital corridors, her night vision superb in the gloom. She ascended into the oppressive humidity of a New Orleans full moon. The cicadas whirred in the limbs of the live oaks standing like sentinels around the periphery of the deserted property.

She retrieved the bait from where she had stashed it in the trunk of Richard's car, unbeknownst to him. The sedated, rosy-cheeked newborn slept soundly in the basket, one pudgy fist curled under her dimpled chin, the peach fuzz on her round head glinting gold in the moonlight.

When Jeanne slammed the trunk closed, the anesthetized baby startled but didn't awaken. She draped a light blanket over the basket, obscuring its contents, and carried it back to the morgue where Richard was finishing up splashing gasoline around the room, down the hallway, up the staircase and out the side door.

"Christ doing cartwheels, I got gas all over my shoes and pants, dammit."

Jeanne frowned. This changed everything.

Richard continued. "Hey, be careful you don't strike a spark in here before we get out. This place is gonna go up faster than a whore's skirt during Fleet Week." He put the empty gas can down. "I'm dizzy just from the fumes. What's in the basket?"

"Just a little enticement for our friend, dear."

"Is he here? You never told me what his major malfunction is, but if this goes sideways, I can finish him for you another way." Richard patted the bulge at his hip. "These thugs are like roaches, there's always a dozen more waiting to take their place."

"That's sweet, darling, but entirely useless against a fiend."

"What is he, the Hulk? I promise you, this'll take care of him."

Jeanne cocked her head. "It's almost time, darling." Richard had thwarted her entire plan by stupidly sloshing gasoline on his clothes, now she'd have to light the fire herself. "Thank you for your help, but I imagine it's best if I do the rest, dear. We can't have you incinerating yourself by accident. Why don't you go start the car, I'll be with you momentarily."

Twist my arm, Richard thought, but didn't say out loud. He was only too happy to exit the gruesome morgue with its unidentifiable stains and stench of mold, not to mention the gas on his shoes and pants was making him nervous. *That's not how I want to die,* he thought, his hand with the flashlight trembling a little, casting dancing shadows on the walls of the long, dark corridor.

Richard wondered if he was about to run smack into the guy Jeanne needed to get gone. He unholstered his Glock. *I am getting too old for this crap. Maybe this should be my last one. Maybe I should let the chips fall where they will from now on, let NOPD deal with these goddam losers.*

He stumbled, put out a hand to right himself, felt something slimy under his palm. *Mother Mary and her marionettes, how did I get talked into this one?* He wiped his hand on his pants leg. *This isn't even my fight, but if Jeanne says this scumbag needs to go, I'm in. Christ Almighty with almonds on top though, I can't wait to get out of this creepy joint.*

Richard made it back to the Crown Vic without running into anyone. He opened the trunk, slipped off his wet shoes and placed them inside. *No point in stinking up the Vic with gas fumes, although I can't do anything about the pants until I get home but keep the windows open.* He was about to slam the trunk when he spotted something.

What in the name of Jehovah is that? With difficulty he stretched into the trunk and snagged... *a baby's pacifier? How the hell did that get in there?* he mused before tossing it aside. It rolled into the gravel by the curb.

Richard dropped into the front seat with a sigh. He turned the key in the ignition to start the a/c and put on Pavarotti singing "Una Furtiva Lagrima" while he waited for Jeanne to wrap things up.

CHAPTER SIXTY TWO

Jeanne placed the basket on the cement floor and removed the yellow daisy-printed blanket. The drugged child's cupid's bow lips moved in a sucking motion. She heard the heavy outer door close behind Richard as he left the building.

It was time.

Jeanne reached into the basket and slashed the femoral artery in one chubby pink thigh with her razor-sharp thumbnail.

The round blue eyes flew open, spilling over with tears. A surprisingly loud wail echoed around the morgue. Jeanne licked the exquisite ambrosia from her thumb, using all her centuries of experience to summon the willpower required to refrain from enjoying this rare delicacy herself.

The crying slowed, then stopped, as did the spurting blood which was now leaking from the wicker basket.

The fetid puddle in the middle of the floor began to bubble and hiss. The rusted metal grate covering the drain flew into the air, hit the wall and clattered to the floor, taking one of the rosaries with it.

Something rustled in the drain.

Jeanne retreated down the hallway and up the stairs, careful not to get gasoline on her sensible shoes.

Echoing down the mold-blotched corridor, a raspy voice croaked, "Come 'ere, cher, you."

Before exiting through the heavy emergency door, Jeanne pulled a pack of matches from her skirt pocket.

It had been many years since she was this close to anything that could start a fire. She much preferred to keep a healthy distance. It would have fit her plan so much better to have Richard drop the match, but since he had been idiotic enough to slosh gasoline on his clothes, she'd have to start the fire.

Jeanne gingerly lit one match - fire was not her friend - and dropped it in the liquid on the floor. She quickly stepped outside. The heavy door swung shut on the *whoosh* behind her.

Her promise had been kept. Now the Voodoo Priestess of New Orleans owed Jeanne a favor.

CHAPTER SIXTY THREE

Detective Dan stood on the sidewalk under a mossy live oak and tried to stay out of the way. Lights from the fire trucks, cop cars, and ambulances flickered rhythmically over the walls of the abandoned hospital complex and the houses across the street. Spray painted graffiti proclaimed "Cronald Muck" near an overhang at the top of the main building. The words seemed to pulse with the red and blue flashes.

A small crowd of people, many in their pajamas, gathered on the other side of the yellow tape under a streetlight. The smell of smoke and an odd sulfurous odor Dan couldn't identify hung in the humid air. Ash floated through the tree branches, landing on his head and shoulders like dandruff.

Just one night. He wanted just one goddamn night of uninterrupted sleep. The NOPD was so short staffed they were routing all kinds of calls to him. To tell the truth, he wouldn't be sorry if the whole place went up in flames. The complex was a known hangout for druggies, hookers and lowlifes of every kind. Each time a new and higher chain link fence was erected around the complex, within hours unauthorized access holes were cut in strategic places. Apparently bolt cutter sales were helping to keep the city's struggling economy afloat.

"What we got here, Joe?"

A fireman dragging a hose paused briefly. "You ask me, Imma say the hospital left a full oxygen tank or two in there when they moved out and some crackhead lit his pipe a little too close, you know?"

"Yeah, I figured it was something like that." Dan decided he'd fill out the paperwork tomorrow. He needed some shut eye. He yawned widely.

Joe nodded, "I feel ya, bro," and kept moving.

"Be safe in there, you hear?" Dan called after him.

Ten minutes later, Joe returned minus the hose. "Hey, just heard we found a body while the boys were clearing the east wing. Looks like a hooker that must'a given birth in there. It's a real shit show. No baby, though. The Chief'll let you know when you can get in to look around."

"Great. That's just freaking great." Dan ran a hand through his hair. A fire, a dead hooker and a missing baby in the same shift. He'd never get to bed now.

***

Early the next morning, Dan slumped at his cluttered desk and sipped his third cup of coffee. Bobby was working on the unreliable printer again, the only other detective in so far, and he was a tea drinker with no idea how to brew the java. Dan would have to make another pot when he finished this one, and this time he'd make it strong, the way he liked it. *Tastes like cricket piss.* The others should start trickling in soon. He didn't want to hear them bitch about the empty pot today. He wasn't in the mood.

The few hours of sleep he'd been able to grab had been restless and unrestorative. Something about the scene at the abandoned hospital kept whispering to him, but he hadn't had enough caffeine to be able to hear it yet. A huge fire, a dead body, a missing baby, all of it was disturbing, but there was something he felt he had missed. He read his preliminary report through again. The coroner would examine the body they'd recovered from the east wing and report back. The Fire Marshall still had to turn in his findings, but he was pretty sure the three alarm blaze had started in the basement in the west wing. *Where was the link?*

Dan leaned back in his chair and stretched before picking up his coffee again. In his mind, he reviewed the morgue scene once more. The dim, echoing hallway. The smell, a mixture of smoke from burnt paint and ceiling tiles, gasoline, mold and a faint, curious sulphorous odor. The blackened cinderblock walls of the morgue. The puddles left over from the fire hoses. A twisted hunk of metal that had probably once been a gurney attesting to the ferocity of the fire. The grate from the floor drain lying off to one side. A few other unidentifiably incinerated things scattered about the room. A plastic cup on the floor in one corner.

Dan slammed his mug on the desk, sloshing coffee onto his white shirt and his keyboard. "Damn it! Hey, Bobby throw me that roll of paper towels, will you?" He tore off a few and blotted gingerly at the mess before shuffling through the hardcopy photos on his desk.

There it was. In the last photo, in a barely illuminated corner of the ravaged morgue, a white plastic Port of Call go cup lay on its side, unscathed amidst the wreckage of the fire.

Chapter Sixty Four

Miriam was cleaning Aida's cage when the vision came.

Tuesday mornings were usually slow at the Voodoo Temple. She had no consultations, readings, or blessings scheduled, so it was a day to dust the altars and replace the offerings in the Sacred Room while chatting with Aida and listening to music. Dr. John was singing about being in the right place, but at the wrong time.

"How we doin' today, my beauty? You lookin' good like always. You wanna soak in your tub for a bit, baby doll?"

The iridescent boa slithered to the open door of the large cage, her tongue tasting the air, her unblinking black eyes taking in the priestess in the flowered porch dress she always wore while cleaning.

The cage door was never locked. Miss Aida was always free to come and go as she pleased. And she did. Like many of the older homes in New Orleans, the Voodoo Spiritual Temple had a shocking number of gaps in the floorboards and openings where it was generally expected that there should be none in order to maintain a building's stability. Large hollows, crannies and unexpected voids were everywhere and Aida utilized them all.

Roaming the neighborhood at will, the big snake more than earned her keep by eating the French Quarter's rats. If a noisy, trouble-making tomcat happened to go missing once in a while, no one complained.

"Come on, my love. Let's get you in some nice warm water out in the courtyard, then you can lay up in them tree branches like you like." Miriam stuck the handle of the feather duster in her side pocket and reached out both hands for the heavy snake. The instant her gnarled brown fingers touched the dry smoothness of Aida's scales, the vision came over her.

A dead woman splayed out on a cement floor, a pool of red-black liquid congealing under her legs. Rosary beads strung across mold-stained cinderblock walls. A red-faced newborn mewling in a basket. The overpowering smell of gasoline and blood. A horned head emerging from a gurgling floor drain.

Miriam yanked her hands back as if the snake had been electrified. The feather duster clattered to the floor. "No! No! Oh Lawd, what you done now, Miss Jeanne?" Aida slithered out into the courtyard and wound herself up the crepe myrtle tree, forgoing her bath, as Miriam stood frozen in the Sacred Room, the vision playing out in her eyes. *What kinda horror I done unleashed by asking for Miss Jeanne's help with that there fiend? She couldn't a just made it go away?* Her knees creaked and popped as she knelt to pray for forgiveness for inadvertently breaking the primary credo of her faith, "First, Do No Harm."

CHAPTER SIXTY FIVE

"I have to admit, this one's got me shakin' my head." Dr. Hebert took a huge bite of the fried oyster po' boy. He leaned against the stainless steel table and closed his eyes in ecstasy. "Dang, that's good! Nobody makes 'em like Parkway."

He looked over at Dan. "To answer your question, I'm gonna say the abdominal wound looks like it was made by something curved. Like a carpet knife but longer, you know? Kinda hooked?"

Both hands full, the doctor pointed his chin at a nearby table with a white sheet draped over it. "But here's the kicker. There was more'n one. Looks like a whole bunch of curved knives, some from the left and some from the right. I gotta study on it some more. I never did see anything like it."

He nodded at the brown paper bag in Dan's hands. "You not eatin' your'n?"

Detective Dan could never get used to eating in the company of dead people, but he knew the quickest way to get any info he needed from the Orleans Parish coroner was to bring him lunch from Parkway Bakery & Tavern. Doc Hebert was notorious for both his lateness in filing paperwork and his love of a fully dressed oyster po' boy sandwich.

Dan rolled the bag closed tightly against the horrific odors in the white tiled room. "Nah, I'll eat later. You enjoy." He tried breathing through his mouth. "So, Doc, the baby...?"

Dr. Hebert attempted to speak around another big mouthful as a clump of lettuce and mayo plopped onto his lab coat. "Probably close to full term, live birth. Can't tell too much more'n that considerin' you ain't found it yet. That placenta was just ripped out the mother. Quite a mess. Speakin' of which, you got napkins in there?" Dr. Hebert licked his fingers.

Dan's stomach lurched at the thought of where those hands had been. He dug some napkins out of the bag. "Here you go." He started to take a deep breath, thought better of it. "What else you got on the mother?"

"White girl. About 5'5". Malnourished. Heroin addict, right handed, tracks up n' down her left arm." He swiped at the front of his white coat with the napkins. "Meth too, her teeth are all shot to hell. Still waitin' on the toxicology. I'll bet you another one of these here," he waved the remains of his sandwich in the air, "she had no pre-natal care a'tall. Not that it matters now."

"Yeah, you're probably right," Dan sighed. "I don't have a good feeling about finding that baby alive." His job was never easy to stomach, but when there were kids involved it always felt so much worse.

"I'd have to agree. Your time might be better spent lookin' for the maniac who clawed open a pregnant woman's belly, ripped out that poor baby child, then tore the mama's head off." Dr Hebert looked at the ceiling. "Say now, come to think of it, the head being removed was just like those two tourists y'all found in St. Louis Cemetery No. 1 a while ago. Ain't that somethin'?"

"Hold up. How could you tell about her teeth if her head was missing?"

"I didn't say it was missing, I said it was torn off." Hebert smacked his lips on the last of his po' boy. "I examined it separately, same as those tourists."

Dan shook off that visual. "Forensics got nothing so far. No weapon, no fingerprints neither. Couldn't even find a footprint. And with all that blood in there too, what the hell?" He sighed. "I don't know, Doc. I'm telling you, it's like this perp just up and flew away out a window."

"Back to work." Dr. Hebert snapped on a new pair of latex gloves and pulled the sheet off the stainless steel table with a flourish. "You thinking this girl being dead in another wing of that old hospital is related to the morgue fire?

Dan looked quickly away. "Wasn't hardly anything left in there to say. The cinder block walls and the fire door contained it pretty well, but the boys will let me know if they come up with something."

Hebert stared down at the headless torso. "Maybe I'll have more for you in a day or two, but don't hold your breath," he said. "I'm thinking what I already told you is pretty much all I'll be getting out of this." He gestured to the body. "Thanks for lunch, Dan. I surely do appreciate it." He poked at something in the chest cavity with one finger. "I hope you find this guy soon, though. You know, I got two daughters in college right here at Tulane... Hell, I don't feel safe walking around myself knowing there's a weirdo out there with this level of crazy. Good luck catching him. I have a feeling you're gonna need it."

Exiting the coroner's office on Earhart Boulevard, Dan tossed his untouched po' boy in the trashcan just outside the door.

CHAPTER SIXTY SIX

J eanne forked a fat Louisiana oyster from the pearlescent shell resting on crushed ice, dipped it carefully in mignonette sauce and placed it on her tongue. "Sublime! I am very much enjoying it here, Richard. These oysters are every bit as good as those I was served in Honke Owariya."

She neglected to mention that sumptuous meal took place in Kyoto when she had dined with a certain debauched member of the imperial family and his newest geisha in 1493. The things they had done to that girl...

"Excuse me. Miss Jeanne, isn't it?" A 40-ish man in a beautifully tailored suit stood at their table holding out his hand. The silver at his temples glinted in the candlelight of the dining room. "I thought it was you. You sold me a little something for my wife's birthday." He inclined his head to Richard. "Good evening, sir. I am Bazile LeClerge."

Richard sat up straighter. He reached to smooth his tie before remembering he wasn't wearing one. "How you doing?"

"Of course," Jeanne said, reluctantly placing her hand in his for a brief moment. "Did Mrs. LeClerge enjoy your little gift?"

He stared into her eyes. "She won't take it off upon pain of death," he laughed mirthlessly, flashing perfectly straight, white teeth. "She's at that table over there." He pointed across the room to a much younger woman awkwardly waving at them. Her wrist sported an elaborate gold bracelet with diamonds of a size that could be seen from space.

"I do hope it brings her pleasure for a very...*very*... long time. So good to see you again," Jeanne said, cooly, dismissing him.

The man inclined his head to her, holding her eyes for a moment longer before nodding to Richard and returning to his table.

"Christ in chaps, what a pompous ass," Richard said. "Those teeth can't be real. Hey, isn't that the bracelet you were telling me about, the one that's supposed to be cursed or something?"

Jeanne sighed. Richard sometimes remembered the most inconvenient things. She'd have to be more careful about how much she shared with him when she was bored. She scanned the spacious, high-ceilinged dining room, every table full. Luckily he was easy to distract. "How were you able to get us into Arnaud's on a Saturday night, dear?"

"You gotta know people," he winked. "I called in a favor from Beau, that lawyer who sends me work sometimes? His firm has standing reservations at a few places."

"Speaking of legal matters, what are your police friends saying about the fire at Lindy Boggs?"

"We're good. Dan says they've got nothing." Richard waved away the hovering waiter and refilled their glasses himself with the crisp sauvignon blanc. He returned the dripping bottle to the ice bucket and lowered his voice. "But did you hear they found a dead hooker in a different wing of the hospital that same night?" He straightened the cutlery on either side of his plate, then looked over the flame of the candle between them. "You didn't have anything to do with that, right?"

"Of course not, darling." She waved her wine glass. A few drops of condensation fell, darkening the white tablecloth. "Ours was a unique situation. One and done is my motto." She took a delicate sip. "Unlike you."

Richard stared at her, his glass halfway to his lips. He stammered, "Jeanne, do we have a problem?"

"Of course not, dearest. You know I'm very much in favor of your little clean-up efforts around town."

He looked at her carefully before downing his wine. She let the heavy silence hang over their table. It was amusing to flex her muscles occasionally.

Jeanne regarded this human across from her. Sparse gray hair atop a freckled scalp. Average height. A slight paunch under his best button-down shirt. Watery blue eyes. Always talking about those damn cats he feeds. A slight shake to the hand that refilled her glass. He had cut his fingernails today, she could tell. The small, pink portion of newly exposed nail beds contrasted with the bevel of his thick yellowish fingernails. *He must have cut them for this evening.* It almost made her feel tender towards him. *Humans are so fragile,* she thought. *I'm surprised they live as long as they do.* "Sorry, darling, what did you say?"

"I said, speaking of that kind of thing, I think I'm finished with all that. Christ on horseback, I'm getting sick of doing the cops' job for them."

"We'll see, darling." She patted his hand, "Don't be hasty." Jeanne finished her wine, touched her napkin to her lips and placed it alongside her plate. "It's still early, dear." She smiled invitingly. "Would you like to come back to my place?"

Richard froze. *Bingo!* he thought triumphantly, before reality trumped the wine in his system. *Wait, can I actually pull this off?* he asked himself. In his younger days he never would have hesitated. Every date with a new woman, and there had been many, was an opportunity to prove himself. These days he worried it was an opportunity to embarrass himself, a concerning and concrete example of the spirit being willing but the flesh being weak. Usually he felt comfortable, relaxed, companionable with Jeanne and he'd been fine with that, never attributing his lack of urgency to go farther in their relationship to the physical limitations of his age. No awkward introspection had been required. Now she was changing things up between them, making him confront some uncomfortable possibilities.

On Richard's face Jeanne could see the war being fought inside his head. She decided to take a different tactic to accomplish her goal of ensuring his obedience. Lowering her voice and her lashes, she said, "A little cuddling would be a wonderful way to end this lovely evening, wouldn't it, dear?" She sighed convincingly. "Though, just between us, it's been quite a while for me. I'm far too nervous for more than that, I fear," she said, patting her pearls.

Richard realized that fear was exactly what he was feeling. And anxiety. Performance anxiety, to be exact. He felt uneasy with Jeanne tonight, her interaction with that LeClerge guy had felt off somehow, unsettling. *This is ridiculous*, he told himself, *Get it together, man! This sophisticated gal, who is very much out of your league by the way, is offering you on a silver platter what you've been chasing your entire life. Jesus and Geronimo, you've still got it!*

He pushed his chair back. "Sure, the cats can wait a while for their dinner." He stood up just as the massive chandelier in the middle of the room crashed to the floor, crushing a pretty young woman with a diamond and gold bracelet on her right wrist.

CHAPTER SIXTY SEVEN

That white plastic cup didn't get there by magic. Someone had to have dropped it after the fire and the guys sure as hell wouldn't contaminate a scene like that.

It wasn't much to go on, but it was definitely something. Dan made a mental note to ask Richard if he'd heard of any active arsonists in the area recently.

It was late Saturday morning and Dan was finally going through Sherree's things. What to keep, what to donate, what to save for her sister. His late wife's life was in three piles on the floor of what he still thought of as their bedroom.

To preserve his sanity while performing the task, in his head he reviewed the list of people who had entered the crime scene at the morgue fire.

This was her favorite blouse. Mine too. He'd always liked the way the light fabric clung to her and showed just the right amount of cleavage. He brought it to his face and inhaled, but after a year and a half, he couldn't catch a whiff of her scent. *Yeah, Sherree would never have hung a blouse in the closet without washing it first.* It made sense but it still hurt like hell to lose another piece of her.

He forced his thoughts back to the case. In his mind he compared the list of personnel who had entered the morgue to the list of those who had been at the scene of the tourist couple killed in St. Louis No. 1. He pulled a pair of brown suede boots from the back of the closet. *I don't remember these,* he thought. *Looks like they've never been worn. I'll give these to Tricia. She and Sher were always trading shoes.*

Dan and Sherree's sister had leaned heavily on each other in the weeks following her death, but in the normal course of life moving on, the phone calls became fewer and the drop-in visits had pretty much stopped as the months passed. *I should call Trish. Time gets away from me when I'm on a case and this one's the case from hell. I really should make more of an effort to stay in touch, though. Sher would want that.*

He folded all her jeans and placed them in the donation pile while mentally comparing both personnel lists to the one of those at the scene of the church ladies' murders in Lakelawn Metairie cemetery. *Hell, I'm pretty much the only overlap on all three sites and I know I didn't drop that damn cup.*

He'd cleared much of her closet and two drawers. *Enough of this, I've got to get out of here, clear my head. Might as well check out Port of Call, seeing as it's lunchtime.*

Dan found a parking spot just off Esplanade. He put his Police placard on the dash in a quaintly optimistic gesture designed to dissuade the local car thieves, and pushed through the swinging doors into the cool dimness of the crowded bar. Luck was with him and he snagged a barstool at one end.

The big guy behind the bar with the too small black teeshirt and ripped pants greeted him ahead of a clot of waiting tourists. Dan was used to that happening. Try as he might to blend in, the air of eau de law enforcement wafting around him outed him to all but the most casual observer as effectively as a blinking neon arrow.

"Hey, how you doin', cher? What you want, you?" The guy's bright red eyes looked Dan over.

"Hi, how you doing. I'll have a medium cheeseburger, a baked potato and an Abita Light when you get a minute."

"You want dat patate dressed?"

"Sure, load it up."

"Mais, no monsoon for you, cher? We make dem plenty plenty good here, we do."

"Nah, I've got things to do this afternoon," Dan said, thinking about the rest of Sherree's clothes he still needed to sort. He'd promised himself to finish up this week. "But since you brought it up, what can you tell me about those cups you serve the monsoons in?"

"What you need to know?" The man leaned his belly into the bar, taking all the time in the world while the tourists shuffled in exasperation. "We make da monsoons. We pour dem in da cups. Dey drink 'em up quick quick, dey do."

Dan looked around at the dark interior with the low beamed ceiling and the illuminated, though sparsely populated, fish tank among the bottles behind the bar. A strangely serene large pink grouper swam to the right until its head bumped the glass, then it turned and swam the other way for the same four strokes before repeating the process, ad infinitum. Dan felt he could relate to that.

The tables in the small sunken dining area off to the left were filled with tourists eating large hamburgers, while each seat at the bar was occupied with a local eating the same. Almost every person in the dive had a tall white plastic cup in front of them with a potent red liquid on the inside and "Port of Call" on the outside.

"Yeah, never mind, I guess."

"You want dat Abita in one o' dem big big cups? We got plenty cups, you know." He winked. "A little lagniappe for you, cher, no problem."

"Yeah, sure, thanks." Sometimes it was easier to go with the flow. A small beer buzz might numb him enough to make the afternoon task ahead of him less painful.

Dan sat back and sipped his beer in its go cup. He watched the bartender as he mixed drinks, presented checks, made change and served food delivered from the busy kitchen in the back. For a big guy, he moved quickly, his thin gray ponytail swinging back and forth as he bent and stood and reached and poured. *The rope holding up the torn pants is an interesting touch,* Dan thought. *Guy looks homeless but he seems to know what he's doing. And the flip-flops aren't surprising, but those toenails! Come on, man, get yourself some clippers already. Those long, yellow nails are almost enough to put a man off his feed!*

But when his order came out, Dan found his appetite was still intact. He dove in, savoring the fat, juicy burger and the cheesy baked potato with sour cream and chives in between swigs of his Abita and swipes of his napkin.

"Sure you don't want no monsoon, cher? Me, I do love me dem monsoons."

Something about this guy is off, Dan thought, *even for a dive bartender.* He studied him more closely after waving the offer away, his mouth full of the last bite of broiled ground beef. *Those red eyes. High as a kite, but you can't be a bartender around here without being baked 24/7, it's practically a requirement of the job. That hairy belly's going to split his teeshirt if he sneezes. Probably eating burgers and loaded potatoes every day he's at work, not to mention the beer.*

Dan signaled for the check and handed the guy cash. "Keep the change. By the way, I'm Dan. What's your name?"

The man leaned across the bar and held out a long-nailed hand. The skin on his arm was red and puckered. "Dey calls me 'Nefid,' dey do. Ol' cajun name, for true."

Dan shook the offered hand reluctantly. Something was definitely off but he couldn't quite pinpoint whether the guy was messing with him in some way or maybe was just garden-variety odd. "Nice to meet you, Nefid. That's a nasty burn you got there. It hurt much?"

"It don't bother me none," the bartender said, making no effort to conceal it.

"How long you been working here?"

The man flashed crooked brown and yellow teeth. "Feels like to be long long time, you know? Like to be stirring de roux, for true."

"Well, good burger. I'll be back." Dan slid off the barstool and patted his pockets for his car keys and phone.

The bartender cackled, "I be right here awaiting on you, me I will, yessiree, cher!"

Chapter Sixty Eight

Molly sank into the cushioned chair and folded her cane. She breathed in musky aromas of incense mixed with the distinctive smells of the tobacco and whiskey offerings on the spirits' altars. "I can't thank you enough, Miss Miriam. Whatever you said to Dwayne, it made all the difference." Molly fanned herself. "It's hotter than I thought today. The walk from the dojo to the Temple exhausted me."

Miriam was torn. What to do about Jeanne was weighing heavily on her mind, but she decided to embrace the distraction of Molly's impromptu visit for now. The spirits would tell her what to do when they were ready. "Just relax yourself now, baby." She peered closely at Molly's face. "Lemme get you some cold water. I'll be back directly."

When Miriam returned, Molly asked, "Did you hear about the horrible accident at Arnaud's?"

The acoustics in the Sacred Room told her that although the ceiling was high, the walls were covered in thick tapestries and though the room dimensions were generous, it was a crowded space.

"Terrible, terrible things happenin' round here," Miriam declared. "Here's some cold water for you, baby. Make you feel better right quick."

Miriam sat on her throne chair across from Molly. "Now, your man, Dwayne." She smoothed the skirt of her porch dress and clasped her hands together. "Change is a fruitful element that keep us rising in ourselves. That boy done been wholly traumatized at his crossroads. He was needin' a whole heap a' help bigger than what I can work, so the loas done spoke at him through me. They pointed him the way. May he be a pure rise in our consciousness and services through his life and our friends."

"Yes, he's such a good man." Molly paused. "I'm so glad he's happy again."

"Well, he gonna be real happy when you tell him your news!"

Molly's hand went to her belly. "How…?" She laughed. "Well, if anyone could tell so early on, I guess it would be you."

They chatted about when the baby was due and caught up on the mutual people they knew before Alain came from the shop to ask if Miriam could perform a walk-in consult. "Tell them they need to come on back in one hour," she said.

"I won't take any more of your time, I just came to say thank you for bringing Dwayne back to me." Molly hugged Miss Miriam, said goodbye to Alain, and walked home feeling newly energized.

In the Sacred Room, Miriam got down on her arthritic knees on the oriental carpet that had been worn thin by countless petitioners over the years. She stretched out her arms to either side and lowered her forehead to the floor while the inspiration washed over and through her. When the visions stopped coming, she struggled to her feet, her back aching, and slumped into the throne chair.

Aida slithered in from the courtyard, warm from the sun, and curled up on Damballah's altar around the main offering of a chicken's egg sitting on a mound of white flour.

Miriam leaned forward, her voice urgent. "Aida, you listen up hard now. Something powerful strong coming. Miss Molly's gonna have a baby and it needing protection. Big trouble heading here, for sure. Imma need your help."

On the altar, the big snake easily unhinged her lower jaw and gripped the egg with multiple rows of needle-sharp, recurved teeth. A chicken's egg was nothing for a serpent of her size to ingest. Slowly, carefully, she swallowed it whole. Miriam studied the process intently, as she had many times before, searching for a sign. A series of muscular constrictions moved the egg-shaped lump down the length of the snake. Miriam raised her arms and began to pray aloud.

Suddenly, a powerful contraction rippled like a wave along the boa's iridescent body. The egg crushed, the bulge disappeared. The Voodoo Priestess of New Orleans fell silent, her worst fears confirmed.

Aida slipped through the mound of white flour on the dais. Her sinuous body flowed like a stream to the floor, then into the sanctuary of her cage.

Miriam pushed herself out of the chair and approached the altar with trepidation. She stared at the pattern left in the flour.

It was unmistakably the letter V.

Chapter Sixty Nine

"Hello, sir. Did you find everything you were looking for?" The skinny teenager couldn't have been more disinterested. Above the embroidered "Waltham's" on his black polo shirt, a crookedly pinned name tag read, "Bill."

"No, actually, Bill, I did not. What aisle is the meaning of life in, huh?"

But the kid was obviously tuned out already. Richard had woken up in a foul mood. His back hurt with the change in weather and this waste of life was making him feel mean.

He shook an insulated tote bag in the boy's face. "I want the dairy, that's the cold stuff, in this bag, understand? Do what you want with the rest of the groceries." He pushed his shopping cart to the end of the checkout lane while the boy began loading the canned goods into a plastic bag.

"Double that bag, those cans are heavy," he snapped. "And feel free to move at a glacial pace." Richard had places to go and people to see and he had to bring all this back to his house before the milk curdled and the ice cream melted.

"Holy Mother of God, anytime before the continents drift back together, okay, Bill?" Richard snapped his fingers in the kid's face. The teenager paused and blinked at him. *Goddamn kid's either stoned on the job or retarded,* he thought. He sighed and looked out the front window of the supermarket where the sky over New Orleans was quickly darkening with storm clouds. *That's just great. Why the hell does it always rain when I gotta hump groceries in from the car?* His back spasmed again. It always let him know when the weather was changing.

The kid was now trying to figure out what to do with the bottle of cabernet Richard had purchased. "Wrap it in a brown paper bag and put it in with the rest. Come on, man, step it up. As much as I'm enjoying your scintillating company, I don't have all day to hang out here. "

As the kid fumbled with the bottle, Richard considered adding him to his List. *Goddamn potheads don't contribute anything to this city.* Richard watched him finish bagging the groceries. *They just take up space and steal from honest people. We'd all be better off without the likes of this one.*

He considered how best to do it, thinking of several satisfying options immediately. *But, aww hell, what if he's not stoned, just a retard?* Suddenly, Richard felt old and tired. He remembered deciding the one at the morgue would be his last. *Might have to reconsider that decision.* He placed the bags in his shopping cart. His back screamed when he hefted the bag with the cans.

"Thank you for shopping at Waltham's. Have a nice day," the teenager mumbled, pushing his lank hair off his pimply forehead.

"Yeah, yeah, you have a nice life, Bill," muttered Richard, pushing his cart through the automatic doors and into the parking lot just as the storm broke overhead.

Chapter Seventy

hree drummers in white pounded out their hypnotic rhythms as the wedding guests sweated into their finery in the flower-be-decked courtyard of the Voodoo Temple. Molly and Dwayne held hands in front of Miss Miriam under the arching branches of two glorious live oaks.

Almost nine o'clock at night and it's still hotter than Satan's ass crack out here. Richard loosened the tie that was threatening to choke him. Crows cawed loudly overhead as they flocked to their nightly roost uptown, adding to his unease. *God, I hate those filthy birds!* He'd need ice in his Jameson's after this. Holding Miss Mimi's hot, squirmy little body wasn't helping matters either. "Jesus, Joseph and George Harrison, will you hold still? It's got to be over soon, please God," he muttered. Mimi licked his chin and continued her efforts to get to Molly and Dwayne.

"Here, lemme take her," Candi said from the row of chairs behind him. She secured the little dog under one arm and turned to Beuletta. "This here feels just like we in church or whatever, don't it?"

"Uh huh. When the last time you was in church?"

"I been stopping in at St. Louis real regular-like whenever I pass by." She fingered her crucifix before changing the subject. "What you think they fixing to serve up after? I'm real hungry."

Richard turned around and glared at them. It sounded as if Miss Miriam might finally be wrapping things up.

Candi stuck her tongue out at him. She continued her musings. "Steak would be real nice." Mimi's ears perked up. "Just once I'd like to try some of that flaming young," she told Beuletta wistfully.

"Huh? You mean fee-lay min-yon?"

"Shut it, you two," Richard warned. "For the love of God, let her finish so we can get out of this heat."

Jeanne stood next to him, cool and composed in her black dress. She let the drums carry her thoughts away into the steamy night air, as she half-listened to Miss Miriam's voice intoning the wedding service.

When was the last time I heard drumming like this? Was it in Port-au-Prince during that revolution? 1791, I think. Quite an interesting time to be in Haiti. There was much opportunity there for those of her kind due to the political instability and the natural disasters that always seem to plague the island. *So many orphans to choose from!* And things hadn't changed much since then. But chaos has always been the vampire's friend. The memory of all that butchery was enticing. *I'll have to visit again soon.*

As the ceremony progressed, Parker slid out of her chair to stand at the back. She desperately needed a cigarette. Lighting up, she scanned the guests from behind and exhaled a cloud of smoke into the humid night air blanketing the gathering. Up front, she saw Richard standing next to Miss Jeanne in her black dress. *What the hell kind of woman wears black to a wedding?* Parker thought. *Maybe it's some kind of custom where she's from. Where the hell is she from anyway? France? Transylvania?* Parker couldn't remember. She was just glad her father had someone in his life to keep him busy so he'd have less time to hassle her about Lucy and her "lifestyle" and...just being alive, it felt like sometimes.

Parker leaned against the courtyard wall and watched as Candi and Beuletta took turns holding the squirmy little dog that was trying to get to the bride and groom. Parker had to admit her co-workers kept things interesting at the dojo. It seemed like every night she had another story to tell Lucy about their screwball antics.

As if sensing the weight of Parker's stare, Lucy turned around, fanning herself as she lifted her heavy braid off her neck. She smiled, causing Parker's heart to skip a beat. *God, she looks pretty in that new dress,* she thought. *She's good for me. She just might be the one.*

"And now Imma call down the blessing." Miss Miriam looked around at the wedding guests, some of whom appeared ready to pass out in the heat. Her eyes locked onto Jeanne's. *I don't trust that Miss Jeanne 'round Molly a'tall now. If she say water be wet, Imma hafta check.* She steadied herself. She needed the right frame of mind for this occasion. Miriam let her eyes continue roaming over the people in front of her.

Of course the courtyard of the Voodoo Temple had been ritually sanctified since that poor boy had gone crazy and killed his girlfriend in the apartment overlooking the bricks they now stood upon. Everyone knew Detective Dan had been the one to open that refrigerator and find her head on the second shelf. *And he ain't been wholly right since. Something like that's hard to shake off.* Miriam didn't know what kind of demon had possessed that boy, but she heard he had gone to Electric Ladyland after the dismemberment and gotten a tattoo that read, "No Regrets." Then he proceeded to jump off the roof of a nearby hotel. *For sure, that musta been one powerful demon. I hope it done moved on, but I can't 'zackly tell yet, everything being all kinds of unsettled.*

She took a deep, cleansing breath, raised her eyes and arms to the arching live oak trees and the night sky above, and focused on joining her two dear friends in matrimony.

"Molly and Dwayne, and whoever," she gestured to Molly's baby bump, causing the assembled guests to laugh. "We are here this night with all the ancestors who love us and we love them. And 'specially Erzuli to protect the new soul y'all created that gonna be joining us." She chanced a quick glance at Jeanne, who appeared to be smirkng up at a crow on a limb of the live oak. "May Ogun clear all obstacles out your path and renewed values in every aspect of your lives and joy be ever lifted each one. I now pronounce you husband and wife."

At that moment, Mimi succeeded in wriggling free from Candi's arms. She raced to the front of the gathering in her little white dress and pearl necklace. Dwayne picked her up amidst the clapping of the wedding guests, held her under one arm and thoroughly kissed his glowing bride as the music started.

"Amen and hallelujah," said Richard. "Which way's the bar?"

Chapter Seventy One

Jeanne still couldn't get the taste off her mind. Even with centuries of experience in restraint under her belt, she felt herself slipping when she thought about the bait, which was every day now. As a mother herself, she'd never had any trouble leaving the babies to others. Sure, she'd feed on the occasional screaming toddler and never think twice, but any available infants she'd always left to others. Things had changed.

Better than the most urgent sex she had ever had, more compelling than anything she had experienced yet in her long existence, the taste of that newborn in the morgue had been almost perfect. *If only it had been redheaded... Oh my!* A shiver rippled under her skin.

And she had had to waste that baby on the fiend.

She realized she was drooling and wiped the back of her hand across her mouth, smearing her lipstick. She wrenched her mind back to the mundane task at hand, paying the monthly Sewerage and Water Board bill. *Dark, sweet arterial blood spurting.* Drool dripped onto the check she was writing with her antique Murano fountain pen, splotching her perfect copperplate script. She tried to distract herself by admiring the craftsmanship of the exquisite Venetian millefiore, but it wasn't sufficient to hold her attention. Frustrated, she tore the check into tiny pieces. Jeanne knew that bait was gone, squandered, yet…. A dark river of compulsion surged deep inside her.

David felt her need through their connection. He appeared in front of her as if he had been summoned, which he had. "Go to Fritzel's," she barked. "Bring one back as soon as it's full dark. You know what I'll accept." He left the antique shop immediately. He liked this part.

He strode through the Quarter in the twilight, his legs still sturdy and strong after 400 years. He entered the jazz club bar and edged past the tourists in the front and a trio playing in the cramped middle room. Pushing through the exit that led towards the courtyard and the bathrooms, he turned left at an unmarked door. The man guarding the entry did not ask him for the password but quickly produced a key, unlocked the door and moved aside.

David climbed the dark narrow staircase, ascending steeply to a landing illuminated by an antique wall sconce with one red bulb. In the sitting room beyond, silver candelabras flickered on the ornately carved mantel of a wide fireplace. Opulent tufted settees and brocade armchairs rested on an ancient oriental carpet. More red bulbs under the fringed silk shades of gilded floor lamps painted the room in a rosy hue. A mural of a mesmerizingly intricate black and gold design graced the ceiling. David's footsteps were muffled by the thick carpet as he crossed the floor.

The smaller room beyond held a bar, the man behind it dressed in Victorian garb. Oval portraits of pale, tubercular men and women hung on the crimson and gold striped wallpaper.

A pair of teenaged twins dressed alike, in black from their knee socks and Mary Janes to the headbands holding back their long black hair, sat closely together on a settee in front of the fireplace, their posture mirroring each other. They stared into each other's dark eyes without speaking. They gave no indication of noticing David walk past them to the bar.

A tourist couple sat in one corner, the too-thin woman tittering anxiously to her silent husband about nothing as she peered around the room and sipped her expensive drink. The man pushed his Stetson back on his forehead, clutched his glass of bourbon and stared into the melting ice cubes, counting down the minutes until the Cowboys' game. This place gave him the creeps but it was on Carol's list of Spooky Places to Visit in New Orleans, so they'd had to come. He needed to pacify her if he wanted to watch the game without her bitching at him. He'd be damned if they'd stay for more than one drink, though. He'd pick where they went on vacation in the future.

A blond boy of about eighteen leaned languidly on the bar. He looked David over, his jeans hanging low on his bony hips, a flash of smooth, flat stomach showing beneath his tight tee shirt. David bared his teeth in a smile. The boy sauntered over, wound his skinny tattooed arms around David's neck and kissed him tenderly on the lips.

The tourist husband in the corner grimaced and threw back his drink. "Finish up, Carol. Time to go," he said through clenched teeth. The wife looked around the room one last time, soaking in every detail. *This place is so eerie!* She couldn't wait to tell the bookclub ladies about it when they got home. *And the people are so strange!* She'd suggest they read "Interview With a Vampire" next.

The twins on the couch continued drowning in each other's eyes.

David caught the bartender's attention, pointed to the boy's glass and held up two fingers. Two cosmos quickly appeared in front of them. They leaned on the scarred mahogany bar close together. David downed his drink. The boy sipped his while explaining at length how his latest favorite heavy metal band was better than his previous favorite. Cosmos weren't David's style. Mead, or lacking that, ale, was. Old habits die hard. But it didn't matter. This part didn't matter at all.

When the boy was almost done with his drink, David threw some bills on the bar and took him by the hand. He led him down the creaky stairs, through the bar and across the now-dark Quarter to Royal Street.

"You really live here? I love this old shit!" the kid raved as David escorted him through Miss Jeanne's shop and up the stairs in the rear of the building. The boy stumbled in his green Converse high tops, gawking up at the masterpieces hung at intervals in the narrow stairwell. David urged him onward in the dim light.

"Awesome digs, dude! Are you rich?"

David ignored him. He knew she could hear them coming.

When they reached the top landing, Jeanne flung open the door, her body vibrating with a palpable energy. Dressed in her ever-present long skirt, sweater set, pearls and sensible shoes, her eyes blazed with an unholy lust.

"Who the fuck is this?" The boy tried to pull away but David gripped his wrist, yanking him into the apartment. "Hey, I'm not into thi...".

Jeanne kicked the door shut behind them.

Chapter Seventy Two

David was at his wit's end. He'd acquired the blond boy over a week ago, but Jeanne still hadn't let him clean away the mess. The stench in their apartment was overpowering, not to mention the flies and maggots that had become a serious nuisance. David much preferred Jeanne's previous fastidiousness to this new aspect of her personality. He was wondering what to do when the phone rang.

Jeanne sat in the kitchen at their marble-topped table, a detached leg clenched in both hands, her face buried in the torn muscles of the thigh. A blood-soaked green high top Converse sneaker was still laced tightly to the foot. She wiped her bloody hands on her skirt and picked up the phone, bits of tendon hung off one crimson-smeared cheek.

"Hello?"

"Hey, it's me. What are you doing?" asked Richard.

"Just having a little snack, dear."

"I've got to get some lunch, I'm starving. What are you eating? "

"A little something David picked up for me here in the Quarter. I'm not sure what you'd call it, but it's delicious."

"That sounds pretty damn good to me right now. Save me some, will you? Hey, I was calling to see if you wanted to go to the Prytania with me tonight. They're showing that movie, what the hell is it called? Questions For a Vampire? No, something like that, though. Anyway, it's supposed to be decent."

Jeanne's mind immediately flashed back to the 1931 Dracula movie based on that fine Romanian, Vlad Tepes. She paused with the gnawed femur halfway to her mouth as she remembered. *Now there was a true prince!* Anyone who would impale 80,000 of his enemies on spikes in his own front yard was a man after her own heart.

She'd been traveling to their assignation when he died of some ridiculous war injury. Transportation being what it was in 1476, she had been delayed and wasn't able to arrive in time to turn him. *Such a waste!* She only got to pay her respects at his final resting place near the Lake Snagov Monastery. Jeanne deeply regretted being deprived of his most interesting company throughout the centuries. A good number of those monks, though, had provided her a delectable opportunity to vent her frustration before returning to Bucharest. The monastery never recovered from her short visit.

Richard's voice on the phone pulled her back to the present time in her own kitchen. "Whatever the hell it's called, it's got that pretty boy in it you like so much, Brad Pitt."

David couldn't help overhearing their conversation. His hearing was that superb. He snickered.

Jeanne shot him a reproving glance. She snugged the phone between her ear and her shoulder, using both hands to tear off a long strip of decaying soleus muscle. She plucked off a squirming maggot and popped it in her mouth before saying, "Thank you, darling, I'd love to, but not tonight. I've got some unfinished business I need to attend to here, but I promise I'll see you soon." She let the phone fall onto the table where it landed in a small puddle of yellowish green fluid.

David reached over and grabbed up the phone. He wiped off the blood and grease. No one ever talked about how greasy humans are, especially after a week of decomposition. He stood patiently next to the kitchen table with a roll of paper towels and a plastic bottle of cleaning spray.

"David, David, David," Jeanne sang. "You don't approve, do you?" She smirked up at him, bits of rotting tissue in her teeth and hair. "Why should I let all of this go to waste just because I drained the last delicious ounce six days ago?"

She scooped a chunk of yellow fat from between two tendons and licked it off her fingers. "I know we don't usually do...this," she gestured with a gore-slathered hand at the body parts littering the table. "I'm not sure why I never considered eating the leftovers before, but I seem to have developed a real appreciation for them lately."

She waved the tibia at him. "Wouldn't you like to try some?"

He placed the roll of paper towels and spray bottle on the table and walked away.

"Not even a little taste?" she called after him, laughing.

David would dispose of the remains later, after she'd finally been satisfied, but he had to think of something. This couldn't go on.

Chapter Seventy Three

Miss Mimi sat on Molly's lap every chance she got. As the months passed and Molly's belly grew bigger, her lap grew smaller and smaller, but still Mimi would wriggle in, close to Molly and as close to the baby as she could get.

Dwayne had wept tears of joy when Molly told him she was pregnant. The ultrasound appointments were occasions for more tears of wonder and amazement, to the point where the technicians automatically handed the big guy a box of tissues whenever the couple appeared in the obstetrician's office.

As difficult as it was for her to get around in her ninth month, Molly refused to stay home. The martial arts classes were all full and there was too much to be done there. Dwayne didn't argue the point. He'd much rather have her in the dojo where he spent so much time teaching than have her home alone. He bought a comfortable recliner for the office, some room-darkening shades and urged her to take a nap every afternoon.

"We gone be aunties soon, Beuletta!" Candi stage-whispered, carefully closing the door to the office where Molly rested in the recliner with Mimi tucked in next to her. "Imma teach the baby how to swim and whatever. Derla's a real pretty name, you think?"

"Nah, that there baby gone be a boy. I'm partial to the name Wylie."

"Hell no! That sounds like a cartoon coyote," Parker said, dragging on her cigarette as they lounged near the propped open back door. "I like the name Avery. It can be for a boy or a girl." She blew smoke in the direction of the exit.

When Dwayne dismissed the karate class of boisterous twelve and thirteen-year olds, he joined the ladies by the back door, a towel slung over his wide shoulders. "Those kids gave me a workout today," he said, mopping his face. "They're getting really good. Where's Molly?"

"She nappin'," said Beuletta.

"Hey, Rambo, pick one - Derla, Wylie or Avery," said Parker.

"Oh boy, that's tough," Dwayne laughed. "I think I'll let Molly decide. We did talk about naming the baby after my brother, though. His name was Oliver."

"May he rest in the deep," said Candi.

"I didn't know he drowneded." Beuletta looked puzzled.

"God give me strength," said Parker as she ground out her cigarette.

CHAPTER SEVENTY FOUR

Bazile and his latest wife held hands as they strolled the gravel path in City Park. The pergola above was heavy with heirloom roses, delicately perfumed wisteria and hanging specimen plants. This wife was American, a master gardener who enjoyed visiting the botanical gardens a little too often for Bazile's taste.

At least she hadn't wanted to go to the cinema again. *Fast and Furious! Really? Where are the geniuses of this era? Where are the Michelangelos? The Newtons? The DaVincis? Now they have Kanye West and Britney Spears.* He was bored, but that was usually the case, an unfortunate side effect of having lived for so very long.

He cast his thoughts back to another time, another garden, long ago. He remembered strolling the grounds at the palace of Versailles with the great landscape designer himself, Andre Le Notre. *Now, there was a worthy partner!* Andre had held Bazile's interest for much longer than most. He had been a brilliant conversationalist and raconteur in four languages, and a fabulous piece of ass.

The latest wife was taking notes again, bent over a yellow flower in the Solanaceae family. She possessed the artificially sun-streaked blonde hair and flawlessly adjusted smile of all New Orleans former debutantes, but her ass was a disappointment. Her connections in New Orleans society were impeccable however, and almost made up for the fact that in the bedroom she wasn't fit to touch the hem of Andre's cloak. Bazile smiled, remembering the time Andre had arranged to meet him on the Pont Saint-Michel and arrived wearing nothing under that cloak. He felt a surge of arousal.

Bazile brought his focus back to the present. What number wife was this one? He couldn't remember and it didn't matter. He'd invariably need another before long, thanks to Maman. He had always hated being alone and luckily women were, without fail, attracted to him like moths to a flame. It was easier to acquiesce when they insisted upon marriage, since the ceremony held no significance for him. The women all thought they'd snagged him forever with a piece of paper and some words spoken in front of a priest. A priest! He chuckled inwardly. *Forever is such an odd concept. Time just...is.*

He remembered being human, of course, although he had only been so for forty-something years. He wondered how much time the woman next to him had left before Jeanne threw another of her revenge tantrums. The night he'd turned her, Bazile had thought his mother would rejoice in the opportunity to be with him for eternity, but he'd neglected to consider that she might object to being stuck in an eighty-three year old body forever. *That word again. Forever. It came up so often, yet meant so little.*

Much to his surprise, Maman had actually taken it quite badly.

Luckily, there was an inexhaustible supply of women to keep him from being alone and to validate his place in human society. *To hide in plain sight, if you will.* He enjoyed his wealth and the social status that came with it, the occasional alleviation of his boredom. The women all wanted to share their short, dull, human lives with what they believed to be a sophisticated, handsome man of substantial means. *Humans are stupefyingly easy to deceive.*

"You're very deep in thought, Baz." Wife Number Whatever took his hand again. "What are you thinking?" She adjusted the shoulder strap of the Louis Vuitton bag he had given her for her twenty-eighth birthday last month.

These Americans and their nicknames. This was the most tiresome part, always having to keep up a front, always having to remember their names and other unnecessary details. Sometimes it was a relief when Jeanne exacted her retribution.

"I was just thinking how I hope we're still holding hands when we're old and gray, my love."

"Baz! You're such a romantic!" She gave him a vivacious smile right before an enormous stag horn fern in a wrought iron basket fell from the pergola above and smashed her skull open like an overripe melon dropped from a highway overpass. A few cracked, bloody teeth rolled across the path, coming to rest under the striped leaves of a variegated hosta.

He stepped back from the grisly mess already seeping into the gravel, his fawn Brunello Cucinelli's irredeemably splattered.

Bazile rolled his eyes, *Really, Maman, this is getting quite tiresome.*

CHAPTER SEVENTY FIVE

That night, Molly stood by their bed in the only dress that still fit her. "Dwayne, wake up. I think it's time to go."

"Huh, what?" Dwayne blinked awake. "Now? Are you sure?"

"Yeah, pretty sure. My water just broke all over the kitchen floor."

"Baby, what were you doing in the kitchen?" He was wide awake now. "You know I'll get you anything you need."

"I just wanted a snack, but why don't we talk about it in the car," Molly suggested.

She found her pre-packed bag where she had left it as he slid into his jeans and a tee shirt. Then he took the bag from her and put it aside. He gently pulled her to him. "Are you scared, Moo Moo? I'm a little scared."

"I'm more scared about what comes afterwards. Taking care of a baby without being able to see is going to be hard."

"Please don't worry, sweetie. Blind people raise children all the time. We can do this." Dwayne picked up her bag and took her arm. "We've got each other plus a whole herd of people who can't wait to get their hands on this baby."

CHAPTER SEVENTY SIX

David was distressed. He was very aware that Jeanne was the oldest vampire he knew. Over their many long years together, he had even pieced together some of her story, how she had come to be turned as an old woman, a particularly cruel destiny. But he had never realized she was old enough to succumb to the fate he knew awaited them all eventually. Madness. Nor had she told him what came after that.

The blond boy had slaked Jeanne's immediate need, but was obviously not enough to erase her memory of the blood of the baby used to trap the fiend. It was all she talked about now. David couldn't be sure she hadn't talked to others about it as well, which would be unfortunate. Taking prostitutes, vagrants, runaways or willing donors was one thing, but Jeanne rambled on, uncharacteristically loquacious, about how it had been such a long time since she'd had a newborn.

"So succulent. So pure and sweet. So mouthwateringly delectable." She went on and on.

Saliva dripped from her lower lip when she told him that she could still taste the blood she'd licked off her thumb after slashing the baby's femoral artery. Lately her hair was unkempt and her clothes were stained. She certainly didn't look like the fastidious Jeanne he had known for centuries.

David packed up their valuables, closed the shop, and hung a "Closed Due to Illness" sign on the door, as he had had to do numerous times over the years whenever a move became necessary. People eventually noticed how long he and Jeanne had been around without aging. When the rumors and gossip reached a conspicuous level, Jeanne would decide where they'd go next. This time would be different. This time Jeanne wasn't able to make the decision to move along. For the first time in his existence, that responsibility fell to David.

Jeanne ranted about how, if she had to do it over again, she'd have used some other bait and saved the last one for herself. That uncharacteristic miscalculation unnerved him more than anything else she had done so far. He could see the bloodlust, the dark thirst overtaking her mind. They had been together so long, he could tell. If she went rogue, if she succumbed to this infant-slaughtering delirium, it would surely bring unwanted attention on them all. The others would stop her then, she'd be ended as surely as she had ended that fiend in the Lindy Boggs Hospital morgue. *Who will I be without her?* he wondered.

Jeanne took that moment to speak up. "Another. I need another baby. And I know where to find one."

***

Richard heard Jeanne cough weakly. "I'm so very happy to hear Molly has delivered her baby safely, dear, but you must visit them in the hospital without me. I wouldn't want to get anyone sick if I'm coming down with a cold." Jeanne aimed another cough into the phone as evidence before reaching for the sticky goblet with one slick hand, the other holding the phone to her ear. She took a gulp of the still-warm red liquid as the drained girl on the floor breathed her last.

David pulled on the girl's bare feet. *A substitute prostitute,* he thought, playing his usual word game as he dragged the body out of the room. He knew this one wouldn't satisfy Jeanne for long. *Not while she's still obsessing over that baby.* He dropped the girl's legs unceremoniously when he reached the tiled kitchen floor. Pulling open the closet door, he rummaged around for a tarp. *Execute the dissolute, destitute, substitute prostitute.* He chuckled. *That was good.*

Richard heard a muffled thunk when the phone slipped from Jeanne's wet hand. "Jeanne? What's going on over there?"

She righted the phone and pulled herself together. "Sorry, dear. I'm all thumbs today." He heard slurping noises as she licked her hands clean. "Must be the medication for my cold. But please call me after your visit to the hospital, I do so want to hear all about that delicious baby."

CHAPTER SEVENTY SEVEN

"Lookit them tiny fingernails!"

"You would notice those first, Beuletta," said Parker.

"Hey, watch out you don't scratch her with one of those spears you call nails." Richard adjusted his glasses and peered at the tiny bundle.

"She so pretty, lookit that red hair!" Beuletta gently touched the baby's downy fuzz with one of her own blue and silver striped fingernails. "Oh, she done smiled at me!"

"Did not. Babies get gas or whatever, that's all," said Candi.

"Oh, you the expert, huh?"

At the center of the crowd in the hospital room, Olivia started to fuss. Molly held her to her shoulder and patted her back until she settled.

"You a natural, Miss Molly."

"Yeah, you got this."

"I appreciate the support, but I really don't feel confident," Molly said. "For example, I know where all Olivia's stuff is in her room right now, but what if something gets moved and I can't find it when she needs it?"

"Baby, we'll be okay," Dwayne said. "We've got plenty of help if we need it. Olivia's going to be just fine." Dwayne carefully took his daughter from Molly and gazed into her now-sleeping face. "I know I'm prejudiced, but she really is beautiful, isn't she?"

"Yeah, she really is," Richard, who hadn't seen a baby in many years, had to admit. "But Christ in flames, where'd that hair come from?"

"My brother, Oliver, was a redhead. Mom and I used to call him 'Punkin.'" At the mention of his family, Dwayne's smile slipped. "I sure do wish they could have met her." He'd received the news last year that his mother was involved in a fatal car crash after a night of heavy drinking. "Mom never did get over Punk's death," he said.

Candi stood on tiptoes and slung her arm around his neck. "Dwayne, this right here is the end of a error. You a daddy now. You enjoy that baby girl."

"The end of a... Jesus, give me strength," said Richard. "It's 'end of an era.' Candace."

"Whatever."

Richard sighed. "But she's right, Dwayne. Look at me and Parker, for Christ's sake. Just be there for her. Don't do what I did."

Parker's mouth fell open. "Wait, what? What have you done with Richard?"

Richard kept his eyes on the tiny baby in Dwayne's arms. "I'm just saying...maybe there were some things I could have done differently."

The deafening silence in the room was only broken when the baby let out a loud fart.

"Okay! I believe it's time for Miss Olivia to be changed." Molly held out her arms to take the baby. "Thank you all so much for coming to meet her. Hey, Richard, where's Miss Jeanne?"

"She said she didn't feel too good today." Richard slipped his glasses into his shirt pocket. "But she said to tell you she'll be by first thing when you get out of the hospital."

"Of course! In all the excitement of Livvy's arrival, I forgot that life goes on as usual for everyone else. Please tell her we hope she feels better and let her know we should be home tomorrow afternoon."

Richard saluted as he left. Candi and Beuletta followed him out reluctantly. Parker trailed behind, her eyes still wide at Richard's uncharacteristic admission.

"Looks like there's hope for Richard and Parker yet." Molly smiled up at Dwayne.

He sat on the edge of the hospital bed and put his arms around her and the baby. "I couldn't be happier right now," he whispered in her ear. "Thank you, sweetheart."

"Me too! I'm happy and exhausted and excited all at the same time. Can you believe what we made?"

"She's perfect." Dwayne wiped his eyes. "We're going to give her a wonderful life. Let's try to enjoy every second of it."

Across town, on Royal Street, Jeanne's scalp prickled with anticipation.

CHAPTER SEVENTY EIGHT

It had been a gorgeous day, one of the rare ones when those New Orleanians whose windows weren't painted shut turned off the air conditioning and wrestled them open to let in the unexpectedly mild breeze.

That night, when her phone app indicated the full moon was high, Molly wheeled the baby's bassinet onto the back deck. She stretched out on a lounge chair, Mimi tucked in close beside her. The wind chimes tinkled faintly overhead. In the distance, an ambulance raced towards the river, it's siren blaring. Molly had been worried that Mimi would be jealous of Livvy, but the chihuahua easily incorporated the baby into her circle of approved family and friends.

Molly was glad she'd encouraged Dwayne to celebrate Livvy's birth with his buddies. She needed some alone time to center herself and meditate. She felt so fortunate. Their baby was healthy and happy. And beautiful, according to everyone who saw her. Molly could hear the difference between polite comments and heart-felt compliments.

She reached over to make sure Livvy was covered by the light cotton blanket. The baby's soft breathing told her all was well with her daughter, but Molly still placed her hand on the tiny back just for the pleasure of feeling her breathe.

Two and a half years ago, Molly couldn't have imagined this much serenity and joy in her life. She had been injured physically in the attack behind Tierney's and her peace of mind had been shattered for a time. But after she healed, opened the martial arts studio, and met Dwayne, she felt as if all her stars had aligned, bringing her to this moment in time, this peaceful night.

In the bassinet, Livvy twitched. Molly felt Mimi's ears prick up. The baby gave a little grunt and fell back asleep. Mimi relaxed again.

Molly breathed in the scent of the night-blooming jasmine that covered the wooden fence between her yard and Richard's. When Livvy was older, she would teach her about the healing properties of moonlight and the beauty of flowers and the importance of being kind and, well, everything! Molly felt positively swollen with love.

She felt a tingling, then a wetness on her shirt. *Ugh, swollen with milk, too.*

She rose from the lounge and paused at the bassinet. Mimi jumped down to follow her. Livvy snored on. "Be right back, my love," she whispered.

Molly had done laundry earlier and knew exactly where her freshly folded tee shirts were. She jiggled the wonky latch on the sliding glass door and stepped inside with Mimi following closely. She pulled the door shut behind them to keep the mosquitos out while making a mental note to ask Dwayne to look at the unreliable latch tomorrow.

***

Jeanne arose from where she crouched in the darkest corner of Molly's yard. All semblance of composure had deserted her upon hearing the details of the newborn.

From David's reaction to her, she was aware her appearance had…changed. On some level she knew that if she wanted to accomplish her goal, she couldn't appear in Molly's hospital room. She had had to wait. She could wait no longer. The engagement ring from Jeanne's shop was doing its job as a beacon. She knew Molly never took it off. Molly was at home, and where she went, that baby went.

A plump, pink-skinned redhead, according to Richard! A ginger, the preferred prey of vampires for millennia. She felt the dark seething of a powerful need again, the strongest she had felt in centuries. She felt intoxicated, unmoored. The wait had been maddening.

Jeanne brushed the leaves off her skirt, the drool off her chin, and patted her pearls into place.

She strode towards the deck.

CHAPTER SEVENTY NINE

*T*onight would be a helluva good night for cleaning house. Long overdue, in fact. Richard had been waiting for the right time to have a little fire in the backyard burn barrel, maybe get rid of some trash and some mementos. Some evidence, if he was going to be honest. He'd been second-guessing himself ever since the screw-ups with Tutu Guy and then Dwayne's "relocation."

The birth of Molly's baby also had him thinking about his own missed opportunities with Parker. He did have a few regrets there. *That ship has sailed, though. You can't raise a kid twice. You only get one shot at that,* he thought.

Richard didn't like to think about things he could have done better. *A man's got to look forward. Make changes, if necessary, and move on.* He thought a minute. *Or maybe just set things straight if he can,* he said, staring into the burn barrel, one hand rubbing the ache in his back, *before a man runs out of time.* He quickly banished that uncomfortable thought.

In the deepening twilight of the humid evening, a cawing murder of crows winged their way overhead to their uptown roost.

Yup, it's time to cash in. No more. That thing at the old hospital with Jeanne was my last one, whatever the hell that was. He made a mental note to ask her again about that last guy, the one she called, "the fiend." *Sometimes she can be so secretive. That woman's got a dark side,* he mused. *Well, this city's gonna have to get by without my help. Let the police do their goddamn jobs and get rid of the scum. I'm hanging up my vigilante hat.*

He smirked, enjoying that very Charles Bronson-ish visual. *I did some good work over the years. Necessary work. Down and dirty work, for sure. Required work, even. Hell, I guess I did okay for a guy raised by crazies in a survivalist compound.*

Standing over the burn barrel in the rapidly darkening yard, he flashed back to his first kill, his mother's second husband. He still refused to think of that piece of shit as "stepfather," or any other word that would relate the guy to him. In his mind's eye, once again he saw his dog through the rear window of Dirtbag's old clunker, howling, tied to the porch railing of their ramshackle rental as they drove away. Buzzards circled overhead. He hadn't known life could get more painful than that. But he had learned quick enough that was only the beginning. *Yeah, I righted a few wrongs. I can live with that.*

Night had fallen completely while Richard stood there, ruminating. The light of the full moon shone down on his achy, arthritic fingers as they balled up pages of the Times Picayune he'd saved over the years and dropped them in the metal barrel next to the shed. Crumpled articles about missing persons and unidentifiable bodies bounced off some old rope and a couple of tarps on the bottom. *No point in burning a perfectly good roll of duct tape and a bag of zip ties. Those things have legitimate uses too, I hear,* he chuckled.

The box of latex gloves in his car could be explained away and his guns were all legally permitted. The knives had all been returned one at a time to his favorite steakhouse. *No worries there,* he thought. *The right tool for the right job.*

His tribe of cats slipped away under the raised house and dispersed into the neighborhood. *Sure, anytime there's work to be done, you guys disappear. Thanks a lot.* He was just grumbling though, he loved every one of them.

Richard poured gasoline over the items in the burn barrel. His stiff fingers slipped trying to hold the wet gas can, the same one he had used at the old Lindy Boggs hospital. It fell into the barrel with a thunk. *Oh well, might as well get rid of that too,* he thought. *It's got my fingerprints all over it.*

The cicadas in the trees shrilled their electric song.

He fumbled with the small matches, struck one with difficulty and dropped it in. He lurched back as the flames whooshed up. *Okay, the whole gas can might've been a little too much. Jesus's jewelry! Almost forgot my 'mementos,' the point of this whole shebang.*

He pulled the shed door open. Shuffling to the rear of the small building, he stretched up for his mother's old Uneeda biscuit tin behind the cardboard box of screws. He pried the top off and looked down at the items he had saved.

A gold tooth from that pimp of Candi's.

A red feather he'd plucked from the Mardi Gras headdress of that fool who'd followed Miss Dina home that time.

One black lens from the sunglasses off that pedophile. Richard regretted not cutting that guy's dick off, but he hadn't wanted to touch it.

Links from a silver chain from that piece of scum who'd been selling crack on the corner.

A long, disgusting pinky fingernail rattled around in the bottom of the tin. He'd peeled it off slowly with pliers. He'd been in a very bad mood that day and the guy had definitely deserved it.

Richard remembered the ripped square of paper printed with "406" came from Tutu Guy. He didn't want to think about that mistake right now.

It was a night for new beginnings.

When he reemerged from the shed a moment later, it was into the searing light of his backyard engulfed in flames.

CHAPTER EIGHTY

In the yard next door, Jeanne hiked up her mid-calf length skirt and took the stairs to Molly's deck two at a time, strong and sure and silent. The thrall of bloodlust glittered in her eyes. The entirety of her being focused on the white bassinet. Her iron-gray hair hung in tangles around her face, her usual sleek chignon a distant memory. She hadn't changed her clothes since the madness overtook her and her signature sweater set was ripped and filthy. Dirt smeared her face, settling deep into the grooves running down either side of her mouth. Six of her fingernails were broken off below the quick, the elegant pale pink polish on the remaining four an inelegant counterpoint.

She strode across the deck to the bassinet and ripped the blanket off.

CHAPTER EIGHTY ONE

The amount of leakage surprised Molly, but then she was new to every aspect of motherhood. In the bedroom, she felt around in the armoire until she touched the pile of shirts she had folded earlier. *I leaked right through everything and Livvy's not due to wake up for her feeding for another hour. I'm going to need a clean bra, too, or I'll smell like sour milk when Dwayne gets home. Being a new mother is a messy business.* She pulled a clean tee shirt from the pile. *Now where did I put those bras?*

In the kitchen, Mimi began to bark at the glass door to the deck.

CHAPTER EIGHTY TWO

Victor stood unsteadily and held his beer glass high. "To your new baby girl! Again!"

"Guys! Guys! Thanks, but this really has to be my last one," Dwayne burped. "I gotta get home."

Stephen stumbled out from behind the bar with a tray of shots in one hand. He slammed it down on their long table in the center of the room, spilling a few, as the friends at Finn McCool's Irish Pub crowded around. The guys whooped and clapped him on the back.

"You ain't goin' nowheres anytime soon, bruh," Richie shouted in Dwayne's ear.

"Yeah, D, we celebratin' yo baby girl tonight!"

"And the Saints' win!"

"WHO DAT!" the entire bar shouted in unison. Dwayne's friends made sure his money was no good and his car keys had disappeared. The evening sped by in a haze of slurred toasts, intense conversations quickly forgotten, and off-key singing best forgotten quickly.

At midnight, the mournful tolling of the cathedral bells rolled over the city like a fog, unheard by the new father and his buddies.

CHAPTER EIGHTY THREE

"Christ on a stretcher!" Richard was thunderstruck by the enormity of the blaze that had so quickly escaped the burn barrel. The giant bamboo stalks between the two properties flared like tiki torches against the night sky, embers riding the updraft, only to alight and start more fires. The flames leaped into the landscaping around Molly and Dwayne's deck next door. Greedy tongues of fire raced up their wooden steps.

Backlit by the flames, a hunched silhouette loomed over the bassinet on Molly's deck. Richard could see it wasn't Molly and it definitely wasn't big enough to be Dwayne. The figure tore off the blanket and cast it aside. It reached inside the bassinet.

The fence collapsed into Molly's yard with a roar, the noise jolting Richard into action. Molly's baby was in danger.

Not taking his eyes off the sinister form, he reached into the shed and yanked his taser from the hook just inside the door.

Richard charged over the piles of flaming foliage and downed fencing between the yards. He had just reached the bottom of the stairs when he heard Livvy shriek.

***

In the bedroom, Molly froze, a stack of tee shirts in her hand. Mimi was barking hysterically in the kitchen. A dull roaring sound increased in intensity as she listened.

Livvy's scream pierced her heart. The pile of carefully-folded laundry hit the floor as she raced through the house, bouncing off the TV stand and crashing into a kitchen chair on her way to the door to the deck.

CHAPTER EIGHTY FOUR

Oblivious to the flames that she'd normally shrink back from, Jeanne snatched up the baby and admired her prey. Not even a week old! She held her up high, admiring the strawberry hair in the light from the conflagration as Livvy squirmed awake and bawled indignantly.

Just as Richard described her, plump and pink! Jeanne couldn't wait another second. She brought the wailing infant close to her face and inhaled deeply. Layered just under the acrid tang of smoke, the whiff of milk on the newborn's breath made her shiver in an agony of anticipation. Jeanne's saliva dripped onto the baby's yellow onesie. She had waited so long for this. She forced herself to think clearly. *Where to begin? That succulent, waving arm? A chubby thigh? One of those rosy, round cheeks?* She leaned in.

CHAPTER EIGHTY FIVE

Molly's outstretched hands slammed against the sliding glass door. She fumbled with the latch, screaming, "Ohgodohgodohgod!" as she pounded. The dull roar was louder now. Mimi barked frantically. The wonky latch stuck fast. Molly beat on the hot glass with her fists and screamed, "Livvy!"

***

Something gave in Richard's knee as he stumbled up the burning stairs. He ignored it and pulled himself along the railing with his free hand, his other gripping the taser. Halfway up the steps, his chest tightened, squeezing his lungs, making it hard to draw a breath.

Thick smoke filled the air. An unholy glow lit both yards, enhancing the dancing shadows in the far corners. Richard forced his leaden legs to the top of the stairs, where he leaned heavily on the railing, gasping for air and clutching at the searing pain in his chest.

Through the flames, a hunched silhouette loomed over the screaming baby. It turned towards him.

Richard saw Jeanne's pearls at its throat. He recognized Jeanne's ubiquitous sweater set and calf-length skirt, filthy and torn, on its body. He made out Jeanne's features on its face, but there the recognition ended. This creature that so resembled Jeanne otherwise, had dripping fangs in a slavering mouth, the lips pulled back in a rictus of ecstasy. The blue eyes he'd recently seen looking back at him over the gentle glow of a candle in the elegant dining room at Arnaud's, were now black, dead doll's eyes.

Richard finally understood.

Fighting pain and weakness, he lifted his arm and fired. The figure recoiled, dropping the child into the bassinet before bursting into a shower of sparks worthy of a New York City fireworks display.

Richard barely registered the astonishing sight as he fought for breath while the flames around him flared and danced. He tried to approach the crib, but his legs wouldn't obey him. It seemed to recede in front of his eyes. His heart clenched as he fell to his knees on the smoldering deck. His last thought was, *Aww, crap, I didn't get to burn my mementos.*

CHAPTER EIGHTY SIX

David leaped up over the burning deck railing from the yard below. The old man lay face down with a taser in his hand. David picked it up and slid it into his pocket. He wondered what Jeanne would want him to do with Richard. They hadn't discussed him, but this was an important decision that would have ramifications for centuries. *Should I turn him? Leave him? Disappear him?*

Inside the house, Molly pounded on the glass doors and shrieked for her baby.

She's blind, ignore her, he told himself. He thought briefly about taking the child fussing in the crib, but then he prioritized his thoughts. *Jeanne. Save Jeanne.*

A blackened lump about the size of a barbecued chicken lay on the smoldering deck near the bassinet. He knew he'd find her here.

David pried the lump off the deck, where the heat had combined with the bodily fluids to make that an ugly task. He tucked it under one arm and sailed over the deck railing to the ground.

Stepping around the smoking piles of fence and shrubbery, he strolled down Palmyra Street in the direction of the Voodoo Temple.

That Priestess Miriam owed Jeanne a favor and no one would think to look for her there. A place to stay for a while with time to recover, to renew, to decide what to do next. That would even the score between the two queens nicely. It might take a while, but he would wait for Jeanne. They had nothing but time.

CHAPTER EIGHTY SEVEN

Candi turned the corner onto Palmyra Street. She'd been free-lancing to make the rent and she was exhausted. She needed a shower and eight hours of sleep, maybe some mac and cheese and a glass of milk, if that quart left in the fridge hadn't turned, then she'd be good as new.

Walking the two blocks from the streetcar in the ninety degree heat felt like two miles. *I'm so hot I might just burst into flames,* she thought.

Dragging up the steps to her house, she sagged in front of the door and said, "Open scissor me," aloud just to see if it would work.

The door remained firmly shut. *Whatever.* She dug through her purse for her key. As she slotted it into the lock, she felt the wind shift. She raised her head and sniffed the air.

Smoke!

First, she checked herself to make sure she hadn't actually burst into flames, then she whipped around. She noticed for the first time all the cats lined up on her side of the street, staring across at…flames shooting into the sky behind Richard's and Molly's homes.

Oh Lawd, Oh Lawd, please let everyone be okay! Her exhaustion forgotten, Candi dropped her purse and sprinted across the street, past Richard's Crown Vic at the curb. She wondered if Molly was home with the baby as she ran along the alley between the two houses.

"Dickie! Molly!" she yelled as she ran. "Fire! Help!"

Most of Richard's backyard was in flames, as was the bamboo between the homes and part of Molly's deck. The dividing fence had fallen over and was burning in places. Through the smoke, Candi saw Richard facedown on Molly's deck.

"Hey! Dickie, are you okay?" She shouted up over the crackling and whooshing noises from the fire as she picked her way over downed pieces of burning fence towards the stairs. "Where's Molly and the baby?"

Richard didn't move.

Candi raced up the stairs and turned him over onto his back. His eyes slitted against the smoke, he murmured, "You...were right," before grimacing and lapsing into unconsciousness.

She shook him. "Don't you go transmissioning to glory on me, Dickie, you hear?"

Candi pulled her phone out of her bra and dialed 911. Then she heard the frantic banging on the sliding glass doors.

The latch finally jarred loose with the pounding from Molly's fists. She heaved the glass sliding door open and was confronted with the heat and sounds of a nearby fire. Molly ran to where she had left the baby's crib.

Smoke infiltrated her lungs, making her cough. Her arms and face stung from flying embers. The deck was warm under her sneakers. Her hands found the bassinet and clasped the crying Livvy to her chest. "Thank God!" she recited over and over as she comforted the unharmed child.

"Hey, Miss Molly, I got Dickie over here!" Candi called out to her. "He's hurt bad!"

"Candi? Is that you?" Livvy coughed in Molly's arms.

They heard the sound of sirens growing louder as a firetruck turned onto Palmyra Street.

Chapter Eighty Eight

The Fire Marshall determined the blaze had started in Richard's burn barrel next door, so Molly and Dwayne could only assume Richard had been coming to warn them about it when he collapsed.

"I should have been here with you and Livvy. I'm never leaving you two again," Dwayne swore the next day, his voice catching as they surveyed the damage. The deck would need repair and both adjacent yards were blackened, sodden, and trampled by the firefighters, but neither house had been badly damaged.

Mimi growled at an oily-looking splotch in front of where the bassinet had stood.

"Baby, please stop beating yourself up. You didn't do anything wrong. Celebrating the birth of your daughter with your buddies is what new fathers do all the time." Still trembling 24 hours later, Molly pulled him close. "No one could have predicted there'd be a fire. Besides, I told you to go out, remember? Please don't blame yourself."

He gazed down at her. "I could have lost you and Livvy and Mimi, all for having a few beers with the guys. I'd never forgive myself."

Dwayne looked as if he had to do something proactive, anything, or he'd burst into flames himself. He took a screwdriver from his back pocket and knelt to fix the sliding door latch with shaky hands.

"That should do it." He stood and took Molly in his arms. "You know you're my world, right, Molly Moo?"

"I know, baby, me too." She rested her head on his chest. "Poor Richard! I feel awful about what happened." She wiped a tear on Dwayne's shirt. "If I had been able to see he was there, I could have helped him. It's lucky Candi wasn't hurt as well."

They were both quiet for a moment. "I better start on repairing the deck before it gets too hot out," Dwayne said. "Why don't you call the hospital and find out when visiting hours are?"

CHAPTER EIGHTY NINE

Detective Dan rubbed his burning eyes and downed his scotch and soda. His thoughts kept going around and around and around in his mind like the Carousel Bar at the Hotel Monteleone . *What other explanation could there be? Nah, couldn't be that. But what else could it be?*

Matt and Dan had walked the property after the ambulance and the fire trucks left. The Fire Marshall had alerted Dan to the blaze as a courtesy, aware that he and Richard knew each other well. It was clear to see the fire started in the burn barrel, then spread quickly to the wooden fence and the bamboo between the two homes, then the deck next door.

In the dirt beside the singed but still-standing tool shed, Dan had found a Uneeda Biscuit tin with some items inside that disturbed him greatly. On a momentary hunch, he'd decided to keep his find to himself.

After a cursory inspection of the site, Matt pronounced the fire accidental, with minimal property damage and no loss of life. He filed his report and closed the investigation.

Now Dan sat at his kitchen table with his second scotch of the evening and poked at the items on the stained placemat with his pen.

He'd kept everything in the small ranch the same since Sherree passed on, but it might be time for new placemats. *Hell, do I even need placemats?* "Yeah, you do," he heard her voice in his head. "Don't live like an animal." He'd already turned over the ones she'd bought and rotated them too. Now both sides of all four were covered in coffee and food stains. She'd always kept a tidy house. *Can you put placemats in the washing machine?* Sherree would have known. Damn, he missed her. Nighttime was the worst. He had always bitched about working long hours when she was alive, but in truth, now he welcomed the distraction of his job.

Maybe I should get a dog. He dismissed the thought immediately. He wasn't ever home long enough to take care of a dog. *Maybe a cat? Yeah, maybe I'll adopt one of those strays Dick's always feeding. At least there'd be something to greet me when I do make it home.*

He refocused his attention on the items on the table in front of him. A gold tooth, a couple of links from a silver chain, a red feather, something that could be a small piece of hard plastic or it could be a fingernail, a ripped square of paper with the number 406 printed on it, and one lens from a pair of sunglasses.

He pushed them all around some more with the end of his pen, hoping an explanation would jump out at him. None of the items screamed anything obvious to Dan, but the red feather niggled at the back of his brain. In a town where sequins, glitter and feathers were an everyday part of life, the feather shouldn't have tripped his internal alarm, but somehow this one did.

Dan briefly considered making himself a third scotch and soda but decided against it. He had to get up early for work tomorrow. *If I don't get called out again tonight,* he thought.

Suddenly it clicked.

The red feather from Richard's tin. The huge red feathered head-dress on that dead guy on Bourbon Street who was costumed like an Indian. The same guy who, when they finally ID'd him, turned out to have a restraining order against him to stay away from Miss Dina, who happened to work at Richard's favorite watering hole.

Coincidence? Maybe, maybe not. Ah, shit. I gotta pay ol' Dick a little visit, get some answers before I decide what to do with this tin of highly suspicious items.

He'd have to tread lightly, though. He and Richard had history together, some dealings that might not look too kosher to others in the bright light of day. That Dwayne thing, for example. *That one sure did go sideways quick.* He shook his head, regretfully. *Around here, there are times you just have to do things a little differently to get the right results.* He wouldn't submit this stuff to Forensics yet. He'd wait, just in case. He swept the items off the table and back into the Uneeda biscuit tin. Then he locked it in his home office safe. Just in case.

Dan pulled out his phone and dialed a number. "Hey, how you doing? Can you tell me your visiting hours, please, darlin'?"

Chapter Ninety

"Just a few things I found interesting." Richard looked Dan in the eye, daring him to continue his line of questioning.

Propped up in the hospital bed, a cannula jammed up his nostrils and an IV in the one age-spotted arm that wasn't wrapped in a special burn dressing, Richard looked every one of his eighty-something years. Under the sheet, one knee was wrapped securely for support. He smoothed the sheet over his legs with trembling hands. "You could get rid of them for me, though. If you're so inclined."

Dan ran his hand over his face, looked away and sighed, his shoulders slumping. This was always the problem with these things. The control eventually got away from you and endangered the whole shebang, just like that situation with Dwayne.

But he could fix this. He would fix this. *One hand washes the other and all that. We've had plenty of our other little collaborations go off like clockwork. Yeah, it's too late in the game not to stick together. I'm too close to retirement to let this screw me up now.*

"Yeah, okay. I can do that for you. Sure, I will." He returned Richard's stare. "Anything else you need me to do, pal?"

"Nope. That should do it." Richard looked away first. "Unless you got any pull with Doc Leo to break me out of here. The food's pretty good but they've got me so tied down with all this crap," he gestured to the IV, "I can't even get up to take a leak."

"Yeah, everyone knows the hospital cafeteria has the best hot boudin this side of heaven. I eat lunch here once a week. But you're supposed to go home tomorrow, Dick. I think you can stand one more night, can't you?"

"No, I cannot. Jesus in a jalopy, I'm bored out of my skull."

Suddenly, Richard remembered something. For the first time since his heart attack on Molly's deck, he remembered...*Jeanne.*

"Hey, Dick, you okay? You just went white as a ghost." Dan reached for the call button. "Should I call the nurse?"

"No, no. I...uh," Images flashed across his mind as it all came back to him at once. Fangs dripping strings of saliva, pearls and a filthy sweater set, a pair of dead, black, doll's eyes, Livvy screaming in her yellow onesie. *I'll be damned, Candace was right all along!*

He sat up and gripped Dan's arm. "Where is Jeanne?"

"Oh yeah, they didn't tell you? Sorry, buddy, I know you two had kind of a thing going. I went by her shop to let her know about the fire and that you were going to be okay, but the shop was closed. Still closed, as far as I know, but I'll ask around about her, if you want."

"No, don't!" Richard gripped Dan's arm, then quickly collected himself and let go. "I mean, thanks, but I'll be out of here tomorrow and I'll look her up."

Dan frowned. "I'm sure she's okay, Dick. Settle down now or I'm gonna call that nurse in here and not the pretty one, neither."

Richard didn't hear him. *I gotta talk to Candace.*

CHAPTER NINETY ONE

Hospitals always made Candi anxious.

What's Dickie needing to talk to me about all secret-like? She and Beuletta had planned to visit him soon but Richard was emphatic that she come tonight and come alone. *Maybe he done lost his mind, getting all paranormal and such, what with the fire and his heart attack and whatever. Maybe he even done got that Old Timers disease now.*

The streetcar was only half full as she boarded and paid her $1.25. "Hey, Miss Brinda, how you today?" she asked the conductor, taking a seat before greeting the other passengers with a polite wave and a "Hello, hello! How y'all doing?"

The locals all mumbled some variation of, "Uh huh, hey baby, good, good, how you?" while the tourists looked away, unaccustomed to greetings from a stranger.

"Hello there, my love!" Under Brinda's neon yellow safety vest, she wore a skin-tight pink tank top that showed a hella lotta cleavage for the streetcar. Her inch-long false eyelashes weighted her lids at half-mast. Her rhinestone-bedazzled gold fingernails rested lightly on the controls. A six-inch tall plastic Jesus swayed precariously under the speckled windshield as she scanned Canal Street for traffic.

Brinda adjusted her generously proportioned bottom on the padded seat, crossed herself, kissed it up to God, and set the streetcar in motion towards the next stop.

"I'm going to visit Mr. Dickie in the hospital. He done had a heart attack," Candi babbled. "I can't abide hospitals, make me all nervous and such." She twisted her fingers together as she spoke. "You like hospitals, Brinda?"

"They don't bother me none, baby," Brinda said, slowing the streetcar to avoid t-boning a Hyundai that had turned onto the tracks. She clanged the warning bell twice and the car lurched out of the way. "You tell him I be praying for him, okay, my love?"

"Ain't that nice! I know he'll appreciate that." Candi beamed at the nearby passengers, pleased her friend would soon be receiving healing prayers from a god-fearing woman like Miss Brinda.

At Canal and Broad, Brinda deployed the lift to receive an elderly woman in a wheelchair and her even more elderly aide in green scrubs. Having secured the wheelchair and patted the old woman on the knee, she waddled leisurely back to the front of the streetcar, performed the necessary blessing ritual and continued on riverside to the next stop.

"Which hospital you want, my love? University, Tulane or Vet'ran's?"

Candi fidgeted on the bench, her anxiety ramped up again at the mention of her imminent destination. "Imma get off this stop, Miss Brinda, and thank you kindly for talking with me. You done helped settle my nerves some."

"Okay, baby. You be safe now, you hear?"

Candi stood in front of the imposing hospital complex, the various square and rectangular edifices with their many entrances strewn over several acres of flat, empty land like a child's abandoned building blocks on a play mat. She fingered her crucifix, "Oh Lawd, where I'm supposed to find him at?"

One half hour and many wrong turns later, a bedraggled, sweaty Candi tripped on an electrical cord and fell onto Richard's hospital bed, waking him from a deep sleep.

"Mary Magdalene in mourning, Candace! Watch what you're doing!"

"I see you feeling perkier already." she said. "You doing okay, Dickie?" She wrung her hands together without waiting for his reply. "I don't like it here none. They got all kinds of sick people and whatever. People dying, even!"

"Yeah, speaking of that, we gotta talk." Richard pushed himself to a sitting position with difficulty. "I, ah...I saw something...something that changed my mind about what you told me."

"Huh?"

"About Jeanne. The day of the fire? You remember the fire, Candace?" He lowered his voice. "I saw her with my own eyes on Molly's deck. You were right. She may not be hu...I mean, she's definitely not..." He glanced at the doorway. "I...hell, you were right, she's a...a vampire."

"I done told you so!" Candi stage-whispered. "I try every day not to think much on what I seen behind Tierney's that night with her and David and that Wardell guy." She looked furtively around the hospital room as if she expected Jeanne to materialize at any moment.

"Now Candace, pay attention, this is important. No one has seen Jeanne since the fire. Where did she go that day? Holy Host in flames, I can't remember anything after climbing the steps of Molly's deck and seeing her with Livvy."

"I don't know, Dickie. There weren't nobody around when I got there 'cept you lying on your face and Miss Molly banging to get out the house to her baby."

"What about her guy, David? Have you seen him?"

"No, I ain't seen him neither." She thought a moment. "Maybe Beuletta knows where he's at. She been sweet on him a while now."

"What?! Christ on crack, he's probably one of them, too! Didn't you warn her?"

"I tried, Dickie! Really I did!" Candi wailed. "But she's head over feet for him, she wouldn't listen none!" She twisted a hank of lank blonde hair around and around. "Wouldn't nobody listen, not you neither 'til now!"

"Okay, okay, calm down! Let me think a minute." Richard ran his hand over his forehead and found his glasses where he'd propped them before falling asleep.

"I'm getting outta this goddamn place tomorrow one way or another. I'll try to find Jeanne. If she's not around, then I guess Livvy is probably safe for now, but you've gotta talk to Beuletta before she gets herself into real trouble with that David."

He placed his glasses on the small table next to the bed so he could read the paper later. *Goddamn things are always disappearing on me.* "But don't say anything to anyone else. No one will believe you and I don't need people thinking my mind's going in addition to my ticker."

Candi shuffled from foot to foot. "Can I go home now?" she asked, looking longingly at the door.

"Yeah. And Candace?"

She turned.

"I, ah," he cleared his throat. "Thanks for coming to see me."

"Sure thing, Di-"

"And don't call me Dickie, dammit!"

CHAPTER NINETY TWO

The front door of the small rental swung open just as Candi reached for the doorknob. "There you are! Where you going all fancied-up, Beauletta? I been trying to get ahold of you!"

Beuletta patted her braids. "You called me? I musta been in the shower." She giggled, "I got me another date with my big, quiet man, that David what works for Miss Jeanne."

"No, nope and hell no!" Candi said.

"What's that you saying?"

"Where's he at? He got Miss Jeanne with him?"

"Why you asking me all these questions, huh? What's going on?"

"Come on back inside, Beuletta. You gonna need to sit down for this."

***

"What do you mean, 'you already know?'" Candi asked from her perch on the rickety barstool she had salvaged one garbage pickup day.

"I mean, jus' like I said, I know 'bout all that." Beuletta sat carefully on their lone, more stable armchair so as not to wrinkle her dress. She always got the chair as a concession to her greater bulk. "He done showed me what he like. It ain't so bad. Heck, I done worse with lotsa guys. He just nick me on my shoulder blade somewheres here." She gestured towards her back with one long purple fingernail. "Then he suck on it and lick it up." She giggled. "Hand to God, girl, it's kinda hot!"

"It don't hurt none?" Candi asked, staring at the cracked linoleum floor.

"Nah, after the first time, it feel good." Beuletta smiled contentedly. "We together now."

Candi sat back, flummoxed. "I never did picture you getting mixed up with them kinda people."

"Girl, don't go getting all judgy now. You know people like what they like. I gotta go. He takin' me somewheres special tonight." Beuletta heaved herself up out of the chair. "So don't you worry none, okay? He treat me real good. Ain't that most important?" She checked herself in the mirror before heading for the door. "I'll be back when I'm back."

"Whatever," Candi whispered to her back. She knew people gonna do what people gonna do, but Dickie wasn't going to like this one little bit.

CHAPTER NINETY THREE

Two weeks later, Candi and Beuletta strolled arm in arm down Royal Street, window shopping and sipping daiquiris on their day off. Passing Miss Jeanne's antique shop, they noticed a sign in the empty window, "Closed until further notice due to illness."

Beuletta sighed, "I hope Miss Jeanne's okay. She a nice lady."

Candi shivered and kept her mouth shut. She'd never forget what she saw that terrifying night behind Tierney's Oyster Bar, but she remembered Dickie said no one would ever believe her, not even her best friend.

A street punk stepped into their path. "Hey, ladies! Can you help me out with this?" He grabbed his crotch. "How about a freebee?"

"Outta our way, motherfucker," Beuletta said without breaking stride, "or Imma kick my foot so far up your ass you can kiss my toes from the inside out."

The guy slunk away back to his spot holding up a wall.

"Good one, Beuletta. We gotta nip that kinda stuff in the butt now we working at Miss Molly's."

"When you right, you right, girl." Beuletta continued her line of thought. "So, talk is, Miss Jeanne's shop is gonna be David's now. He big man in charge 'cuz Miss Jeanne be having health issues." She sucked on her straw. "I might be in love."

"Girl, if it was me, I'd look somewheres else for a man."

"Uh huh. Anyway, it's nice Parker and Lucy be taking care of all of Mr. Richard's cats for him."

"Just until he gets back on his grumpy old feet. I do like having Parker and Lucy staying on the block. It's like family around or whatever." Candi scratched at a mosquito bite on her ankle. "Hey, you feel like a movie? Maybe we can catch the manatee."

Beauletta squinted at her. "Catch the what?"

"You know, the early movie. It's cheaper."

"Oh yeah, I wanna see Denzel's new one. Or his old one. Hell, I'll watch that man pick his teeth with a piece of hay for two hours. Let's go."

CHAPTER NINETY FOUR

David had no idea how this was supposed to work. It was excruciating *and more than a little gruesome, to be honest,* to watch Jeanne become...well, herself again. And he wasn't even sure what the end result would be. *Would she be herself? Would she be strengthened or weakened by the slow, horrifying process? Could she even survive this ordeal?* There hadn't been much of her left. He was doubtful if even Jeanne could come back from that blackened lump to the Jeanne he had known.

He'd never seen the process before, but it seemed to be quite a transition. *A transmogrification,* he thought. *No, more like a transubstantiation.* He smiled at his own word play. *Yeah, that's it.* Like a priest transforming bread into the body of Christ, Jeanne was transubstantiating herself from whatever Richard's taser had done to her, into a higher form.

Hopefully.

But it was taking so long. It had been twelve weeks since the incident and she was...well, definitely not there yet.

David heard a knock at the door. *Merde!* He checked himself. Profanity was for those with a limited vocabulary and his was extensive. *Who has found us here? It can't be that damn Bazile LeClerge already,* he thought. Bazile had seized control of their little group in New Orleans shortly after Jeanne became incapacitated. He had been reveling in his authority ever since.

David would have to brazen it out. He stalked to the door and flung it open. Bazile stood on the side steps of the Voodoo Temple, a banded straw hat in his hand, the silver strands in his dark hair glittering in the morning sun. He sported a bespoke linen suit in the softest shade of blue. *Who wears a three-piece suit in New Orleans in July?* David sneered to himself. But it was a beautiful suit.

"David," Bazile said. "How is Maman today?"

David stepped aside as Bazile swanned past him, handing David his hat as he entered. He knew better than to deny Bazile access.

He who fights and runs away, lives to fight another day. David enjoyed little remembrances of the important people he had ended. In a random twist of fate, the novelist Oliver Goldsmith had been one of his first. *A shame no one really remembers him now.* David had no idea who Goldsmith was when he'd surprised him at his cluttered writing desk in London on the fourth of April, 1774. Afterwards though, he had picked up the blood-splattered paper with the famous aphorism about fighting versus running away drafted upon it. He had folded it carefully and kept it all these years. *Probably worth a small fortune,* David thought, *especially with so much of his DNA on it.*

Goldsmith's penned words had served David well over the years. David's formal education was non-existent, but he was sharp and perceptive and he had an excellent memory. He never regretted not attending the secret lessons held behind his mama's shack at the rear of the big house on the bend of the river, even though he got whupped plenty of times for his absence.

Later, David had met Jeanne through their mutual interest in old things, as many of their kind did. For vampires, antique shops often share a purpose similar to coffee shops for humans. In general, the great cities of Europe, and New Orleans in America, were favored haunts for those with long memories, a taste for a refined lifestyle and all the time in the world. New Orleans' cult of willing S & M donors, its sizable homeless population, and especially its culture of genteel lawlessness, combined to present some of the best opportunities for those living even the most extreme alternative lifestyles to thrive.

They met in such an antique shop near the Grote Markt in Brussels during the heyday of the guilds. David had been shaking his head, chuckling at a collection of silver, leather and ivory implements being sold as something loosely translated from the Dutch as a "vampire slaying toolkit."

When Jeanne ducked in from the square during a sudden downpour and caught sight of the smirk on his face, she knew. No human would look at those items in that way. And he recognized something in her immediately. He had been searching the world for another like himself. The loneliness had been crushing. In that small, dusty shop, David was overcome with an immense, visceral relief. Ever since then, he had voluntarily bound himself to her.

Reentering the room where David stood reminiscing, Bazile murmured, "Looks like Maman's still got some way to go," more to himself than to David. He retrieved his hat from David's hand and smoothed the brim. "Thank you kindly. I'll inform the others of her progress. Please give Miss Miriam my regards." Bazile strode out the door, the shine on his handmade shoes the last part of him to disappear into the morning haze, an oppressive humidity already blanketing the air of the French Quarter.

David resisted the urge to slam the door. He closed it softly and engaged the lock for the sake of appearances. Any nosy humans who might be watching would expect him to lock the door in a city where crime was always a problem. He knew a mere door lock wouldn't keep out their kind, though. Turning back, he took a deep breath and forced himself to cross the floor to the room where Jeanne lay...metamorphosing. *Another good word,* he thought. David still collected words, although he never spoke them aloud.

To keep his mind off the horror on the floor, he began to make a list. He'd need to pick up more "supplies." He couldn't be gone long though. Someone had to keep on eye on Jeanne, and Miriam and Alain had already been very generous in offering the empty storerooms for Jeanne's "recuperative period," although they had no idea what that would entail. It was best to keep it that way. Unfortunately, David had no idea either.

He didn't want to make her condition public to those in their community more than it already was by asking what to do for her. Lately she had started making groaning and keening noises. Her condition changed every day and not always for the better. So, for now, he sprinkled her with water occasionally and kept her in the dark.

I am surprised they found us so soon. He knew they'd search the Royal Street shop first, but he'd thought they'd be safe here. He considered moving her again, but what would be the point? Bazile would simply find them again.

Also, the Voodoo priestess owed Jeanne a favor. Ridding New Orleans of that rogue fiend had been no simple task. Utilizing the Temple's storerooms for Jeanne's recuperation would even the score between them. For now.

Chapter Ninety Five

Miriam hadn't visited the Temple's storerooms since David and Jeanne moved in some months ago. David was always quiet and respectful, he had even helped her weed the courtyard a few times and brought in her groceries if Alain wasn't around. But she hadn't seen Jeanne, and frankly, Miriam didn't want to ask why.

She was very aware that the use of those rooms was in repayment of the debt she'd incurred for the benefit of the good people of New Orleans. There had been no more killings that couldn't be classified, sadly, as every day, inner-city murders relating to carjackings, robberies or gangs. She was happy to have the debt repaid, but still....

The noises coming from back there were getting difficult to conceal from visitors to the Temple. Tourists who wandered in off Rampart Street looking for some "Voodoo Black Magic" trinket to take home as proof of how dangerously wild they were on vacation thought the infrequent shrieks were part of the Temple's ambiance. Her regular clients though, would know differently.

Alain didn't raise any questions when the howls and moaning began, but he was going to have to speak up soon. Generally, he took care of the business of the Temple. He rang up sales in the small shop up front where they sold incense, statues of the loas, blessed bracelets and rings, gris-gris bags, oils, books, and such. He made sure their rent was paid on time in addition to the electric, water, and cable bills. He scheduled the weddings, baptisms, house blessings and psychic consultations and collected the donations for those rituals. He kept the books and paid their taxes. Miriam shared her gifts with the world.

And extensive gifts Alain knew them to be. She had an intuitive, deep, loving understanding of people and a spiritual connection to the divine that he didn't understand, but he deeply appreciated, having seen the results many times over. After so many years, Alain had respect for, and a deep faith in his wife. She was unlike anyone else he had ever met.

So when the screams and howls from the storerooms became more frequent, he smiled and told the neighbors he and Miriam had gotten a new puppy. "I do apologize for the disturbance," he told them. "The poor little guy should settle down into a routine soon, then I'll bring him around to meet you."

Chapter Ninety Six

"She gone! Miss Aida, she gone!" Miriam burst through the curtain, startling the people browsing in the Temple's shop.

Alain looked up from the register where he was in the process of making change for a deeply tanned blonde from California who'd been extolling the virtues of her new life coach while she purchased incense. "Oh no, my love! I'm so sorry!" he moaned. "I just saw her about an hour ago. She appeared the picture of health!"

He stepped around the blonde to embrace Miriam. "She was a wonderful friend to us for many, many years," he said sadly.

The blonde stepped between them and placed a beringed hand on each of their arms. "I am so very sorry for your loss," she proclaimed. "I know we've just met, but my shaman always says..."

Miriam craned around her to see Alain. "No, no, she ain't passed on! She done left. She ain't in none of her reg'lar places and I can't feel our connection none!"

Confused and unaccustomed to being ignored, the blonde woman turned to her daughter, who was texting furiously on her phone and her son, who was testing the sharpness of the various daggers for sale on his wrist. "River, stop that! Sage, do you not see what your brother is doing?" she barked. To Alain, she called, "You can keep the change." She herded the pre-teens out the door. "Come on, kids, it's almost time for our ghost tour and Mommy needs a cocktail first."

Alain locked the front door. "Let me help you look for her, darling. Maybe she's simply found a new place to sunbathe."

"I can't feel her none, though. She done broke our connection." Miriam wrung her hands.

Alain walked slowly with Miriam through the shop, the Temple and even their upstairs private rooms where Aida had never gone. They looked in unpacked cardboard boxes. They looked behind the couch and Miriam's sacred throne chair. They looked under their bed, in their bed and in the closet. They checked the kitchen and Aida's favorite places in the courtyard, including the massive intertwined limbs of the two live oaks.

"My love, I know this is a long shot," Alain was exhausted from moving furniture and getting down on his knees. He was no longer a young man. "Could she have gotten into the storerooms where our guests are staying? Come to think of it, I haven't heard any...noises...from over there today."

As soon as he said it, Miriam knew that's where Aida had gone. Their connection reasserted itself with a jolt and she knew that Aida was alive. "You right, praise be! That's where she's at!"

Watching his wife's face relax, Alain felt relief wash over him. All would be well. They would have an explanation for the snake's sudden disappearance soon. Or not. Alain could live with that as long as Miriam was happy again.

"Imma go 'round and git her. Thank you, baby!" Miriam hastened around to the side entrance of the Temple and knocked on the door.

CHAPTER NINETY SEVEN

The quiet had alerted him.

The moans, grunts, and shrieks from the back room had become a constant background noise to David's days, not unlike the low hum of traffic passing the Temple on Rampart Street with the occasional unmuffled motorcycle roaring by.

David was headed to the back room to check on Jeanne when the knock came. He couldn't afford to ignore it. Miriam and Alain had not bothered them yet and David knew their time here was almost up. He'd been scouting alternative places for Jeanne to continue her recuperation. There was an abandoned warehouse on Tchoupitulous, a boarded up house in Gentilly, and a shop off Canal Street that had been vacant for over a year, but each had its drawbacks. If only Jeanne could hurry the process...

David felt an inexplicable sense of urgency to check on her. *Why the sudden silence?* He played his internal word game to calm himself as he walked to the door. *Silence. Pretense. Decadence. Grievance. Vengeance.*

The Voodoo Priestess of New Orleans stood on the steps in her colorful caftan. "Hey, David. Baby, how you doing?"

He nodded.

"I don't want to bother you none, but Miss Aida done gone missing and I jus' have a powerful feeling she's in that there back room you and Miss Jeanne been usin'. Could you go on and take a look for me?"

David nodded again. He didn't exactly shut the front door in Miriam's face, but he did let it swing gently closed while he walked back towards the storeroom. What he saw there froze him in his tracks.

The big boa constrictor was in the middle of the wooden floor, wrapped around the malformed, now-goat-sized lump of scorched flesh that was Jeanne in her current state. Aida had unhinged her lower jaw and was swallowing David's mistress whole.

"No, baby! Stop!" Miriam shouted. She shoved David aside as she stumbled around him to get to Aida. She knelt with difficulty, and placed her hands on the thick, iridescent coils of the snake. "Aida! No, no, no! We can't be interferin' in this, baby. We got to let only them what's made us take us back to glory, and the same with these here kind."

The boa's undulations halted, the lidless black eyes stared.

David stood immobile as his mind raced. *Should I tear the snake apart? Would that harm Jeanne further? Can the Priestess make that creature let Jeanne go?* His black eyes bored into Aida's, his fists clenched at his sides.

"It ain't up to us, baby! Ain't none of it up to us!" Miriam pleaded.

The jaws with the rows of curved, needle-sharp teeth that held Jeanne's transitioning body in place repositioned slightly.

"Please, Aida, please let go. You'll see, this here will all sort itself out without you doing none of this, baby. It ain't nothing to do with us. You don't need to be taking this on."

Aida seemed to be considering Miriam's words.

David made a decision and lunged.

Aida was quicker. Two powerful movements in quick succession and Jeanne became nothing more than a lump in the thick body of the snake. Aida took her time slithering across the room and out the front door as Miriam and David stared in shock.

Miriam recovered first. "Oh Lawd, Lawd! Don't hurt Aida none, David! She just doin' what snakes do. Help me up, will you? My knees ain't what they was." Miriam struggled to stand, leaning on his arm. Breathing heavily, she motioned to the oily spot on the floor. "That there was Miss Jeanne, right?"

He nodded from where he stood impotently in the middle of the room, still disbelieving what had just happened.

Miriam scrubbed her hand over her face. "Gimme a minute here, I need to put this together," she said. "I'm just an old woman and I'm real slow, but I ain't stupid. Lemme sit down while I think on it."

David helped her to the lone wooden chair.

"Miss Jeanne ain't been seen nowheres around since that fire at Molly's. She get hurt there?"

David looked at her.

"And she couldn't help herself none to heal up?"

David, still stunned, waggled one hand in a side-to-side motion.

Miriam exhaled hard, stood, and brushed the dust from her dress. "I'm real sorry about what Miss Aida done." She patted his arm as she shuffled past, looking as if she had aged ten years in the last ten minutes. She had been unable to fulfill her "Do No Harm" credo again. "Lemme pray on it some, okay?"

Miriam knew one less vampire in the city would make no difference, but the disappearance of Jeanne in particular would disrupt the balance of power in their community, causing even more trouble.

"Lawd, what next?" she muttered. "Imma need some special kinda guidance on this."

CHAPTER NINETY EIGHT

Think, damn it, think! David admonished himself over and over as he paced the broken path. *This can't be the end of Jeanne.*

He had left the Temple and wandered aimlessly for miles in the heat, ending up at the old abandoned golf course off Wisner Boulevard near City Park.

Now a desolate urban wilderness sprawled over 150 acres in the heart of New Orleans, it was also a favorite haunt of his to prowl at night. The narrow golf cart paths were too overgrown for casual strollers and the course was too isolated for joggers and dog walkers to inhabit without safety concerns, especially after dusk.

In the humid darkness, coyotes hunted rabbits and sometimes David hunted coyotes. Willing, reusable donors like Beuletta were fine for a while, but occasionally he had a need to chase something down and tear it apart. The coyotes of City Park fit the bill nicely and there were fewer reports of missing pets in the surrounding neighborhoods. *Win/win.*

The fairways were now hip-high fields of weeds dotted with large trash trees draped in vines. *Should I kill that damn snake? Would it make any difference?* He ducked under a low hanging branch, glimpsing the moon through the trees. *Then I'd be incurring the wrath of the Voodoo Priestess. Should that make any difference to me? She's just a human.*

He tried playing his word game to calm himself as he tramped through the weeds to his preferred vantage spot under the lacy limbs of a forty-foot-tall cypress. *Wrath, path, bath...* He couldn't concentrate, couldn't come up with any good words.

What will happen to Jeanne now? He shuddered to think. *Will she become just a spludge of snake shit? No! Not possible for a Vampire Queen! There must be a way to bring her back, to resurrect her. Resurrect, inject, disrespect, dissect, reject, misdirect, neglect.*

Feeling more focused now, he leaned against the tree, thinking. Cicadas whirred their night songs in the heat. A few small brown bats chased winged insects over the tall grasses. He smelled a lone coyote lurking nearby. *Not now! Focus! Snakes are themselves symbols of renewal, aren't they? Maybe something could still be done....* He needed to talk to one of his kind who was more experienced, more knowledgeable in their ways.

It was time to contact Bazile.

Chapter Ninety Nine

"Merde!" Sparks flew from Bazile's fingertips as he raged. "What were you thinking to leave her alone? Why did you not call me *immediatement*? Where is she now?" Questions and spittle flew from his lips.

The uptown mansion on St. Charles Avenue was filthy. Dusty cobwebs hung from the crystal chandeliers. Bloody bones of suspicious origin lay strewn across the antique Persian carpet where Bazile had carelessly dropped them from his greasy fingers. Black and white feathers scattered in front of him as he paced.

David stood with his back against the living room wall. It had been painted in an au courant shade of designer white, marred only by an unidentifiable crimson smear at about human neck height. He watched impassively as Bazile stormed about, screaming.

"She was healing! *Bientot*, I would have had Maman *encore avec moi!*" He kicked over the freeform, transparent coffee table. It shattered against the marble of the massive hearth, scattering pieces of glass across the room. "*Espece d'idiot stupide!*" When agitated, Bazile unconsciously reverted to his native tongue.

The headless, dripping carcass of a brown rat leaked into the cushions of the elegantly upholstered couch. Bazile hated to clean up after a meal and he had yet to begin finding a replacement for Wife Number Whatever. The latest Vietnamese maid was lying drained and broken in the shed near the pool house under a fifty-pound bag of chlorine pellets. That was going to become a problem very soon with temperatures in the nineties. *What more? Maman consumed by a snake! Merde! It is simply too much to bear!*

CHAPTER ONE HUNDRED

"Miss Aida will return when she's ready, my dear. I'm sure there's no need to worry." Alain was washing the dishes after a dinner of Miriam's mouth-watering fried chicken, fresh snap beans, and flaky buttermilk biscuits. He glanced at his wife in her housecoat. Her gnarled brown hands dried a coffee cup, then absent-mindedly placed it in the refrigerator. Alain quietly retrieved it and put it with the others in the cupboard.

Miriam usually didn't share too much about her work with her husband, but this latest situation had obviously greatly disturbed her peace. She was unusually quiet ever since Aida apparently ate something in the storeroom she shouldn't have. His wife had only picked at her food lately and he knew she wasn't sleeping well either.

"I've been trying to remember," Alain rinsed a plate and placed it in the drain. "This is obviously not my area of expertise, my love, but didn't you tell me once that snake skin has great restorative properties?" As a long-time former English professor at Tulane University, he had a limitless capacity for facts and an excellent memory.

Miriam's dish towel halted mid-swipe. She dropped it on the kitchen counter along with the serving spoon she had been drying, and scuffled to the Sacred Room in her fuzzy pink slippers.

Alain found her standing precariously on a wooden chair, squinting at the spines of some very dusty books. "Darling, remember your bad hip! Please come down. Let me help you."

"That big one right there." She pointed to an ancient, leather-bound tome. "That's it, baby. Bring it down real gentle-like." She gestured for him to place it on the table.

Turning the pages carefully, her arthritic finger traced the spidery script until she found what she was looking for.

Chapter One Hundred One

Richard pulled himself up the front steps one at a time. He stumbled at the top as a crow swooped out from under the awning, cawing loudly. His 3.0 readers tumbled from his sweating forehead to the porch floor. Somewhere in the back of his mind, the lack of cats registered. "Holy Hosts in heaven, how I hate those goddamned birds," he muttered, scanning the floor for his glasses. That's when he saw the snake.

It lay quietly across the entire width of the porch right in front of his doorway, its variegated markings vibrant in the shade of the overhang. About halfway down its length, a large lump distended the thick body.

Richard straightened up so quickly he felt his back pop in protest. He lurched down a few steps, his hand over his heart, wild-eyed and staring.

"Serpents, saints, and sinners!" he exclaimed aloud, looking around to see if anyone could corroborate this unlikely apparition. The street was empty for once, everyone who could, getting out of the heat as quickly as possible. He shook his head. *This can't be what it looks like,* he thought, *Where the hell are those glasses?*

At that moment, the large snake lifted her head, tasted the air with her red, forked tongue a few times and nudged Richard's spectacles across the floor to him.

His mouth fell open. It was then he remembered hearing Molly talk about the beautiful boa constrictor that lived with Miss Miriam and Alain at the Voodoo Temple.

"If that's any of my cats in there," he looked pointedly at the lump in the boa's midsection from the safety of six feet away, "we're going to have a problem."

Never taking his eyes off the creature, he snatched his glasses up, backed down the steps with difficulty, and with one hand supporting his lower back, staggered across his small lawn to Molly's house.

A murder of crows studied his movements from the phone lines overhead.

Chapter One Hundred Two

"Hoowee! I wish I coulda saw your face!" Candi slapped her hand on Molly's long dining room table. "Walking up on that big ol' snake just a'lying there like that!"

Miss Mimi jumped off her lap, the dog's pearl necklace jingling against her tiny black and gold Saints tee shirt.

"I'da been a'scared for sure!" Beuletta passed the praline sweet potatoes, which were the same color as her orange Thanksgiving Day party fingernails.

Candi continued. "And Dickie, I know your Episcopal vision ain't no good neither, so I bet you didn't see it 'til you got right up on it, huh?"

"Can you see this?" Richard made a rude gesture with the hand not holding his fork.

Molly laughed, "Yeah, if you don't know her, you wouldn't know how sweet Aida is." She cocked her head, listening for the baby, then went back to eating her turkey.

"I am happy happy to have her back where she belong!" Miss Miriam said, while Dwayne poured her more wine. "Thank you, my baby.

We can't figure out how she made her way 'cross o' town, but the loas done guided her somewheres people knew her and could get her to home."

"Aida's a real big girl," Beuletta giggled, patting her lips with a napkin. "Kinda like me."

"Girl! You don't look nothing like no snake!" Candi squealed.

Beuletta made her eyes big and round. "Both o' us got black eyes." She stuck her tongue out at the others around the table. "Both o' us got red tongues. And if I run outta lotion, I even got me some scaly skin!"

Their laughter startled Livvy awake. Mimi danced in circles near the playpen and barked.

Candi, Beuletta, and Parker all pushed back their chairs, but Candi was fastest and swooped the baby up. "Ooooo, li'l redheaded girl! I got you, baby. Don't you cry, Auntie Candi is here."

Livvy gave her a big wet smile, showing off a single ridged tooth in the middle of her bottom gum.

Candi settled back at the table, the baby on her lap. "You getting so big! Before we know it, you'll be going off to kidney garden with them other kids."

Richard rolled his eyes. "Give me strength," he said around a mouthful of food.

Parker handed the baby a spoon which she waved around gaily before throwing it to the floor.

"Is there any more of that pecan pumpkin pie left?" Richard asked.

Parker moved the pie next to her dad's free arm. His other arm was still bandaged. The burns hadn't been healing as quickly as Doc Leo would have liked. "You want whipped cream on it, too?"

"I wouldn't say no to some of that."

"Wait a minute. Should you be eating that with your heart condition?" Parker asked.

"You gotta die of something. Death by whipped cream wouldn't be a bad way to go. Besides, you're still smoking those cancer sticks, so enough with the sermons."

Lucy's gentle touch on her knee reminded Parker to take a deep breath and let it go.

Dwayne tapped on his wine glass. "Hey, everyone! I'd like to say something."

The room quieted except for the baby who continued to babble to herself, bang on the table and pinch crumbs off a nearby plate with two fingers and some very intense concentration.

"I guess I should have done this before we ate, but it seems as if things happen a little differently around here. I just want to say thanks for coming over and sharing our meal. It's been a crazy year..."

Everyone started talking at once.

"It sure was! Lord, so much done happened!" said Beuletta.

"Sure am glad that's behind us, except the part where Livvy got borned!" said Candi.

"Praise be. The spirits of those who done gone before us helped us through to better days," said Miss Miriam.

"Amen!" Parker and Richard said at the same time.

"So grateful," said Lucy, bowing her head.

"There certainly were quite a few exceptional occurrences this year," said Alain.

"I'm so thankful everyone is safe," Molly said. "Well, we're still hoping for news of Miss Jeanne, obviously."

"Yes, let's hope to hear that Miss Jeanne is okay soon," Dwayne continued, raising his glass.

Richard, Candi and Miss Miriam all looked away simultaneously.

Livvy's pale blue eyes, so like her mother's, filled with tears. Her lower lip quivered and a piteous howl filled the dining room.

"Dwayne, could you find her Baby Snake, please?" Molly asked.

"Got it right here. There you go, sweet baby." He waved it in front of Livvy, who reached out a chubby hand and grabbed it. She immediately stuffed it in her mouth, content once more. Dwayne took the baby from Candi. "Okay, let's do a diaper change, then its bedtime for you, Livvy, my girl. Say 'night night,' and give Mama a kiss."

CHAPTER ONE HUNDRED THREE

Aida lay limp on the straw of her cage, her clouded black eyes staring off into space.

"What you need, baby, huh? Maybe you wanna nice warm bath?" Miriam wrung her hands when there was no reaction. "How about your tree? You wanna set up in them branches an' get some sun on you? I'll help you iffen you want to go outside."

The boa gave no indication that she knew the Priestess was there.

"You got you stomach troubles, my love?" Miriam leaned in. "I bet that Miss Jeanne done gave you a bad bellyache, huh?" she whispered.

The large lump that was Jeanne had disappeared, but Aida's condition had deteriorated rapidly. The previously shiny, iridescent scales of her long body were now dull and dusty-looking. Her normally glittering black eyes had clouded over, becoming an opaque blue-ish white. Her crimson forked tongue no longer flicked out, tasting the air and gathering information. Aida lay immobile.

Alain came from the kitchen. "Come now, darling. Staring at poor Miss Aida won't help her. You've got to keep your strength up." Alain urged a bowl and spoon into Miriam's hands. "My gumbo isn't as good as yours, but maybe you can tell me what it needs. Come now, my love, see if you can eat a little for me."

"I jus' don't know what's wrong. I think she might be fixing to pass on," Miriam moaned.

"I've always heard you say, 'When a body is being called to their maker, it's best to let them go.' Isn't that correct, my dear? Maybe it's her time?"

The big boa lifted her head a fraction of an inch and hissed.

Alain and Miriam jumped back.

"Lawd, she ain't never fussed at nobody in her life!" Miriam exclaimed.

"That was decidedly out of character for her, I agree," said Alain, swiping at the spilled gumbo with a napkin.

"Iffen she ain't better by morning, Imma need your help to get her to the vet doctor, okay baby? And maybe I should close up her cage door for now."

"Really, my love? You've always given her carte blanche to come and go as she pleases. But whatever you think best, darling.."

***

That night, in the silence of the Temple's Sacred Room, with moonlight streaming in the window, Aida rubbed her snout on the side of her cage. She was tired with an exhaustion that permeated every one of the 1638 bones in her long body, but the urge to do this compelled her.

She rubbed and rubbed her nose on a small patch of rough-sawn wood in the corner until the skin split. She had been blind for days, but she didn't need to see to do what was necessary. She rubbed her mouth and lidless eyes on the wood, skinning back the thickened, scaly covering in one piece, like peeling a sock off inside out, an inch at a time.

Her head freed, her ear holes uncovered, she could see again and hear the insect orchestra in the bushes outside the window. From where she lay, completely spent, she saw with crystal clarity the dust motes dancing in the moonlit air of the Sacred Room. She flicked out her tongue. It would probably not rain in the morning, but the night jasmine was blooming next door and the mouse that lived under the washing machine had finally given birth.

Bone-weary, Aida set herself to the tedious job of stripping off the rest of her old skin. As she labored, she thought about where to hide it once she was done. If the skin didn't come off, the evil of what she had consumed would poison her. But if the shed skin fell into the wrong hands, even if they were unsuspecting and well-intentioned hands, the result could prove disastrous.

She struggled for hours through the night, wriggling and writhing, squirming and thrashing within her wood and wire cage with the locked door that had always been open to her before. Her rest breaks got longer and longer as the hours crawled by.

The night felt endless, her labors fruitless, yet she persevered.

Chapter One Hundred Four

After his screaming fit wound down, Bazile, much to David's horror, began to sob. Great gulping howls of anguish echoed through the mansion as Bazile stood in the living room clutching at where his heart should be, while making no move to retie his gaping silk dressing gown.

He threw himself upon the sofa in hysterics. The decapitated and leaking rat slipped down between the cushions unnoticed.

This inconsolable mama's boy will be of no help for the foreseeable future. David took advantage of Bazile's distress to slip away. He slid through the beveled-glass front door of the mansion, down the wide painted steps of the veranda, and through the lush garden to the tall wrought iron gate tipped with fleurs de lis. He crossed St. Charles Avenue to the neutral ground in the middle.

Fishing $1.25 from his pocket, he boarded the next streetcar with the tipsy Garden District tourists and tired locals running their errands. David enjoyed riding the streetcar. The packed closeness of the sweaty bodies, the regularity of the boardings and exitings, the call of the familiar street names, it never got old for him. New Orleans was home and the streetcar, along with the river, was her lifeblood.

The conductor slowed, clanged the bell and rolled to a stop. A drunk lay across the tracks, an empty bottle by his head. The conductor stood up, peering down through the windshield. He rang the bell a few more times. The man didn't flinch. The conductor sat down and pulled out his phone. The vintage cars of the St. Charles line are cooled only by the breeze when they're in motion. The tourists began to grumble in the heat.

Fifteen minutes later, neither the man on the tracks, nor the streetcar had moved an inch. A scrawny old mawmaw in a front seat harrumphed and stood up. She climbed down the steps and out the folding doors. The other passengers crowded to the front to get a better view in anticipation. They were not disappointed.

The old woman bent down, grabbed the drunk by one leg and hauled him off the tracks, dumping him unceremoniously in the neutral ground grass. Then she kicked his empty bottle off to one side. She brushed her hands off and reboarded the streetcar. "I gots places I gots to be," she announced, dropping back into her seat.

The other passengers clapped and cheered. "Yasss, you ain't playing! Thank you! You fierce, mama!" The conductor pocketed his phone, clanged the bell and continued down the tracks towards the Quarter.

David stood swaying and thinking as he hung on the pole. It was up to him now to take control of Jeanne's situation. *Situation, deviation, multilation, violation, ruination.* His mind cleared.

He had one more option left to get help, but it was a long shot.

Chapter One Hundred Five

The Voodoo Priestess of New Orleans threw open the door to the Temple.

"Where you been at, David? I done looked everywheres for you!" Miriam was practically bursting with excitement. "Bring yourself inside, baby. I been feeling real bad about what Aida done to Miss Jeanne. I got my suspicions about that lady, but I ain't got no hard proof and I done swore to do no harm to other folks." She took a breath. "So I been praying on it, an' I read up on it some, and I done found something you gotta see!"

She pulled him into the Sacred Room and pointed a gnarled finger at the ancient text lying open on the table. "Read that there page!"

Five minutes later, David looked up, a questioning hope in his eyes. *Is it possible?* he wondered. *Could this work!*

"And lookit this! Aida done shed her skin just in time!" Miriam held up an eight-foot-long snakeskin. "She looking so much better today."

David didn't spare a glance for the creature in its cage with the door closed and locked for once. That snake was, after all, the cause of his current problems. Well, that and Jeanne becoming obsessed with that redheaded baby and getting tasered. But according to the dusty grimoire in front of him, that troublesome snake was the possible solution as well.

"When I took this here shed skin from her, she was trying to hide it or something, I don't 'zackly know, but I read in that there book you could maybe use it to bring back Miss Jeanne." Miriam looked away, "If you think that's best. Imma leave that up to you." She looked David in the eyes. "Ain't for me to say, but I'd pray on that some before deciding."

David tried to look as if he'd actually consider prayer.

Miriam's gaze landed on the snake's cage. "Aida didn't wanna let go of that shed skin none. She ain't 100% herself yet." She smoothed the folds of her house dress. "She still feeling a little bitey, so Imma let her rest up some more before I let her out."

David couldn't care less about the mental health of that thing. He now had a glimmer of a potential resolution to his problems. Maybe, just maybe, his mistress wasn't gone forever.

Chapter One Hundred Six

Driving riverside down Toulouse, Richard veered around another pothole, then inched by a double-parked Camaro, rap music blaring as the owner extracted several unwieldy boxes from the back seat. *Clowns and idiots. I'm surrounded by nothing but goddamn clowns and idiots.* The thumping bass beat assaulted his ears through the rolled up windows of his Crown Vic. *Who needs to blast their music that loud? Are these morons all deaf?* He reached over and turned up the volume of his own radio. Pavarotti was just beginning the cathedral scene of Faust that Richard liked.

He turned right onto Royal Street. *Jeanne's still not answering her phone,* he mused. *I'll just do another quick drive by to make sure nothing's changed at her shop.*

Richard had no idea what he'd say to Jeanne if he ever saw her again.

'Hey, why didn't you mention you were a vampire?' *Nope.*

'Eaten any babies lately?' *Definitely not.*

'Are you planning on coming back to finish Molly's baby off?' That one was a possibility, as it was his real concern, after all. *Maybe there's a more diplomatic way to put it. Christ on a cannonball, how did I get mixed up in this?*

He rolled past the corner art gallery displaying what appeared to be pastel rags stapled haphazardly to a ripped, torn canvas. *Miserable Mother of God, is that what passes for art these days?* He shook his head, returning his thoughts to Jeanne. *Apparently I'm not in any danger myself,* he mused. *She could have offed me any time we were alone together. But, Holy Ghost on horseback, I saw her with Livvy as plain as the nose on my face. And she saw me, so help me Jesus. Am I a target now?*

Absentmindedly, he reached to scratch his left arm before stopping himself. Bandaged from wrist to elbow, the burns itched terribly as they healed, but they didn't bother him as much as the knowledge that he was now officially a "heart patient."

He heard Doc Leo's voice in his head, 'Try not to get too over-excited, Richard. Take deep breaths and count to ten. Cut the booze and fat from your diet. Yeah, yeah, I know. Just try, okay? I don't want to see you back in my Emergency Room.' *He's telling me to calm down? Yeah, right! He doesn't have a clue that we've got real, live vampires loose in this city!*

He winced as the Crown Vic dropped into another pothole. *God dammit to hell! I'm gonna need new shocks again,* he thought, slowing to a crawl. *Guess I'll find out if Jeanne's after me if she ever turns up, but I'd really like to know her intentions for Molly's little girl.*

Exasperated, he pounded the steering wheel with his unbandaged arm. *Just wish I could remember more of what happened on Molly's deck! And where the hell is Jeanne now? Why doesn't she answer her phone?*

He braked to avoid hitting a gaggle of twenty-somethings wearing neon pink wigs as they teetered across the street in their heels and minidresses. Each one wore a white satin sash reading, "Bridesmaid," their go-cups sloshing in their unsteady hands. *It's not even ten a.m., for Christ's sake, girls!*

Jeanne's storefront was just ahead on the left.

Rolling slowly past the plate glass window, Richard scanned the shop's facade again, as he had at least once a week for the last six months. What he saw there this time made him slam on the brakes. A horn honked behind him. A shaft of morning sun penetrated the dark interior of the dusty antiques store, illuminating the "Closed" sign hanging on the door. Behind it David stood, still as a marble statue, the rubies in Jeanne's ram's headed cane glowing in his clenched fist.

Their eyes locked.

David held the eye contact as he slowly, impassively, reached down and with a single motion flipped the hanging sign to "Open."

A crow pecking at a cigarette butt in the gutter took wing. Flying low over the stopped Crown Vic, it shat in the middle of the windshield. Richard didn't notice, the whole of his attention lasered into the dim interior of the antiques shop.

The car behind him honked loudly again, startling him and breaking the deadlock. He reflexively took his foot off the brake and, his mind racing, slowly rolled on down Royal Street as Pavarotti's voice rang out from the car radio, building towards the high notes of an aria in a language Richard had never bothered to learn.

C'est l'enfer qui le suit!
(It is hell that follows you!)
C'est l'eternel remords.
(It is everlasting remorse.)

L'angloisse eternelle
(It is everlasting anguish)
Dans l'éternelle nuit!
(In everlasting night!)

* * *

ACKNOWLEDGEMENTS

Thank you, dear Reader, for your time and attention. I hope you enjoyed reading this novel as much as I enjoyed writing it.

Many, many people were involved in the process of getting this book out into the world. First among them is Mike Rands, publisher at Bayou Wolf Press and editor extraordinaire, plus all-around nice guy. Thanks for taking a chance on me and walking me through the process.

Thanks to my family, who heard about the story ad naseum and/or read innumerable drafts; specifically, my brother Ken, my sister Adrienne, and my son Kade, who is the strongest person I know. Ken gets an extra thank you for creating my website, www.SueBirdWrites.com, from the jumble of half-baked thoughts and images I threw at him.

Eternal gratitude goes to my Mom, who passed her love of reading on to all her children and my Dad for being our family's rock. With your quiet examples always in the back of my mind, you allow me to believe that anything is possible in the face of evidence to the contrary.

Many thanks and much gratitude to the earliest readers of my work, especially the hard-working and talented members of my critique groups. Even if you didn't help me with this particular story, rest assured that somewhere along the way, you helped me become a better writer with your detailed feedback and thoughtful suggestions: Kathleen Griffin, Kathleen Smyth, Connie DeDona, Leigh Ryan, Lance Bradley, Chris Smith, Jane Kahramanidis, Liz Lardaro, and Karen Miritello.

Thanks to my instructors in New Orleans, New York and Ireland who were so generous in sharing their knowledge and advice: Stephen Rea, James Nolan, Nancy Dafoe, Rachel Dickinson, Sheila Myers, and Irene Graham.

Elizabeth Gilliland Rands and David LaFaire deserve medals for their hard work and artistic vision for the cover art and for tolerating my input regarding the same. Thanks also to Juliette Miranda LaFaire for feeding me gourmet meals and encouragement while I endured the publishing process.

Danke to Johann Wolfgang von Goethe for the lines I plucked from his *Faust* for my last chapter and merci beaucoup to Patrick Van Hoorebeek for the translation of those lines.

Thanks to all the bartenders who supported me throughout this journey, especially Ulysses, Zoe, Bailey and Donna. Any omissions or errors within these pages are all your fault.

My friends at the Lighthouse of New Orleans deserve a big shout out here. Your kindness and patient instruction helped to boost my confidence in my abilities at a time when I really needed it, having broken my arm for the second time by tripping over invisible (to me) things in the street.

The ladies of the Krewe of Sue initiated my Southern experience and helped me stay sane through COVID. Thank you for hilariously translating the intricacies of New Orleans culture for this Yankee.

Special thanks to Mary Robin Williams for being a singular beacon of light and love.

Dwayne, you know who you are.

And finally, a very special thank you is owed to Jim Olsen, who sparked it all with a single offhand remark over Chinese food one evening before a storm.

ALSO BY SueBird Sparrow

Magnets and Ladders literary magazine of Behind Our Eyes,
Fall/Winter 2024-2025
"Free Flight," creative non-fiction short story *RENEWED*, 2024
print anthology, New Orleans Public Library
"The Cave of the Bats," creative non-fiction short story *Down in the
Dirt Magazine,* v.223, September, 2024
"Free Flight," creative non-fiction short story
Shattered Facades, print anthology, September, 2024
"Free Flight," creative non-fiction short story *Dark Speculations An-
thology, Tales of Various Shapes & Shadows, Vol. 3, Oct., 2025*
"Bride" horror short story *Spotlight Literary Journal,* Writers in the
Mountains, January, 2024
"La Corrida" creative non-fiction short story *New Bayou Books blog,
January 2023*
"Writing With Abandon" Guest Columnist *Please See Me Literary
Journal, March 2020*
"Dancing in the Dark" creative non-fiction story story *Hang Gliding
& Paragliding Magazine*

"*Earthquake Flattens Canoa, Ecuador" news article, July/August
2016
"*The Pilot's Partner" creative non-fiction short story, December
2013 *Chronogram Magazine*
*"Dusk" prose poem, February 2016
*"The BASE Jumper" haiku poem, April 2016

ABOUT THE AUTHOR

SueBird Sparrow is an award-winning, visually impaired author, dreamer and extroverted introvert living out her current incarnation in human form in New Orleans, Louisiana. Her horror, suspense, paranormal and speculative fiction short stories have appeared in various anthologies, magazine and journals. *The Devil Drinks Monsoons* is her debut novel.

SueBird is happily at work on her next two books; a 1727 historical revenge saga that traces the effects of a generational curse set in place by an outcast French nun and a supernatural thriller about an immortal and immoral cat. She's the author of the *Marcelle the Intrepid Iguana* children's book series about a blind, but adventurous, reptile. All her books are set in New Orleans, but you knew that.

When not telling tales, SueBird can be found dancing to blues music, memorizing drinking toasts in foreign languages, or transcribing the epic poems whispered by her companion tortoise, Gordon Ramsay.